RAVELSTEIN

VIKING

75 years
•

ALSO BY SAUL BELLOW

The Actual

It All Adds Up

Something to Remember Me By

The Bellarosa Connection

A Theft

More Die of Heartbreak

Him with His Foot in His Mouth and Other Stories

The Dean's December

To Jerusalem and Back: A Personal Account

Humboldt's Gift

Mr. Sammler's Planet

Mosby's Memoirs and Other Stories

Herzog

Henderson the Rain King

Seize the Day

The Adventures of Augie March

The Victim

Dangling Man

RAVELSTEIN

Saul Bellow

VIKING

I would like to thank my editor,
Beena Kamlani,
for her talent and her clairvoyance.

—S. B.

VIKING
Published by the Penguin Group
Penguin Putnam Inc., 375 Hudson Street,
New York, New York 10014, U.S.A.
Penguin Books Ltd, 27 Wrights Lane, London W8 5TZ, England
Penguin Books Australia Ltd, Ringwood, Victoria, Australia
Penguin Books Canada Ltd, 10 Alcorn Avenue,
Toronto, Ontario, Canada M4V 3B2
Penguin Books (N.Z.) Ltd, 182–190 Wairau Road,
Auckland 10, New Zealand

Penguin Books Ltd, Registered Offices:
Harmondsworth, Middlesex, England

First published in 2000 by Viking Penguin,
a member of Penguin Putnam Inc.

7   9   10   8   6

PUBLISHER'S NOTE
This is a work of fiction. Names, characters, places, and incidents
either are the product of the author's imagination or are used
fictitiously, and any resemblance to actual persons, living or dead,
business establishments, events, or locales is entirely coincidental.

LIBRARY OF CONGRESS CATALOGING-IN-PUBLICATION DATA
Bellow, Saul.
Ravelstein / Saul Bellow.
p.   cm.
ISBN 0-670-84134-X
I. Title.
PS3503.E4488 R38 2000   99-056336
813'.52—dc21

This book is printed on acid-free paper. ∞

Printed in the United States of America
Set in Granjon
Designed by Betty Lew

A la bella donna della mia mente.

To Janis,

The star without whom I could not navigate.

And to the real Rosie.

Odd that mankind's benefactors should be amusing people. In America at least this is often the case. Anyone who wants to govern the country has to entertain it. During the Civil War people complained about Lincoln's funny stories. Perhaps he sensed that strict seriousness was far more dangerous than any joke. But critics said that he was frivolous and his own Secretary of War referred to him as an ape.

Among the debunkers and spoofers who formed the tastes and minds of my generation H. L. Mencken was the most prominent. My high school friends, readers of the *American Mercury,* were up on the Scopes trial as Mencken reported it. Mencken was very hard on William Jennings Bryan and the Bible Belt and Boobus Americanus. Clarence Darrow, who defended Scopes, represented science, modernity, and progress. To Darrow and Mencken, Bryan the Special Creationist was a doomed Farm Belt absurdity. In the language of evolutionary theory Bryan was a dead branch of the life-tree. His Free Silver monetary standard was a joke. So was his old-style congressional oratory. So were the huge Nebraska farm dinners he devoured. His meals, Mencken said, were the death of him. His views on Special Creation were subjected to extreme ridicule at the trial, and Bryan went the way of the pterodactyl—the clumsy version of an idea which later succeeded—the gliding reptiles becoming warm-blooded birds that flew and sang.

I filled up a scribbler with quotes from Mencken and later added notes from spoofers or self-spoofers like W. C. Fields or Charlie Chaplin, Mae West, Huey Long, and Senator Dirksen. There was even a page on Machiavelli's sense of humor. But I'm not about to involve you in my speculations on wit and self-irony in democratic societies. Not to worry. I'm glad my old scribbler has disappeared. I have no wish to see it again. It surfaces briefly as a sort of extended footnote.

I have always had a weakness for footnotes. For me a clever or a wicked footnote has redeemed many a text. And I see that I am now using a long footnote to open a serious subject—shifting in a quick move to Paris, to a penthouse in the Hotel Crillon. Early June. Breakfast time. The host is my good friend Professor Ravelstein, Abe Ravelstein. My wife and I, also staying at the Crillon, have a room below, on the sixth floor. She is still asleep. The entire floor below ours (this is not absolutely relevant but somehow I can't avoid mentioning it) is occupied just now by Michael Jackson and his entourage. He performs nightly in some vast Parisian auditorium. Very soon his French fans will arrive and a crowd of faces will be turned upward, shouting in unison, *Miekell Jack-sown*. A police barrier holds the fans back. Inside, from the sixth floor, when you look down the marble stairwell you see Michael's bodyguards. One of them is doing the crossword puzzle in the *Paris Herald*.

"Terrific, isn't it, having this pop circus?" said Ravelstein. The

Professor was very happy this morning. He had leaned on the management to put him into this coveted suite. To be in Paris—at the Crillon. To be here for once with plenty of money. No more of the funky rooms at the Dragon Volant, or whatever they called it, on the rue du Dragon; or in the Hotel de l'Académie on the rue des Saints Pères facing the medical college. Hotels don't come any grander or more luxurious than the Crillon, where the top American brass had been quartered during the peace negotiations after the First World War.

"Great, isn't it?" said Ravelstein, with one of his rapid gestures.

I confirmed that it was. We had the center of Paris right below us—the place de la Concorde with the obelisk, the Orangerie, the Chambre des Députés, the Seine with its pompous bridges, palaces, gardens. Of course these were great things to see, but they were greater today for being shown from the penthouse by Ravelstein, who only last year had been a hundred thousand dollars in debt. Maybe more. He used to joke with me about his "sinking fund."

He would say, "I'm sinking with it—do you know what the term means in financial circles, Chick?"

"Sinking fund? I have a rough idea."

Nobody in the days before he struck it rich had ever questioned Ravelstein's need for Armani suits or Vuitton luggage, for Cuban cigars, unobtainable in the U.S., for the Dunhill accessories, for solid-gold Mont Blanc pens or Baccarat or Lalique crystal to serve wine in—or to have it served. Ravelstein was one of those large men—large, not stout—whose hands shake when there are small chores to perform. The cause was not weakness but a tremendous eager energy that shook him when it was discharged.

Well, his friends, colleagues, pupils, and admirers no longer had to ante up in support of his luxurious habits. Thank God, he could now do without the elaborate trades among his academic pals in Jensen silver, or Spode or Quimper. All of that was a thing of the past. He was now very rich. He had gone public with his ideas. He had written a book—difficult but popular—a spirited, intelligent, warlike book, and it had sold and was still selling in both hemispheres and on both sides of the equator. The thing had been done quickly but in real earnest: no cheap concessions, no popularizing, no mental monkey business, no *apologetics,* no patrician airs. He had every right to look as he looked now, while the waiter set up our breakfast. His intellect had made a millionaire of him. It's no small matter to become rich and famous by saying exactly what you think—to say it in your own words, without compromise.

This morning Ravelstein wore a blue-and-white kimono. It had been presented to him in Japan when he lectured there last year. He had been asked what would particularly please him and he said he would like a kimono. This one, fit for a shogun, must have been a special order. He was very tall. He was not particularly graceful. The great garment was loosely belted and more than half open. His legs were unusually long, not shapely. His underpants were not securely pulled up.

"The waiter tells me that Michael Jackson won't eat the Crillon's food," he said. "His cook flies everywhere with him in the private jet. Anyhow, the Crillon chef's nose is out of joint. His cookery was good enough for Richard Nixon and Henry Kissinger, he says, and also a whole slew of shahs, kings, generals, and prime ministers. But this little glamour monkey refuses it. Isn't there something in the Bible about crippled kings living under the table of their conqueror—feeding on what falls to the floor?"

"I think there is. I recall that their thumbs had been cut off. But what's that got to do with the Crillon or Michael Jackson?"

Abe laughed and said he wasn't sure. It was only something that went through his head. Up here, the treble voices of the fans, Parisian adolescents—boys and girls shouting in unison—were added to the noises of buses, trucks, and taxis.

This historic show was our background. We were having a good time over our coffee. Ravelstein was in high spirits. Nevertheless, we kept our voices low because Nikki, Abe's companion, was still sleeping. It was Nikki's habit, back in the U.S., to watch kung fu films from his native Singapore until four o'clock in the morning. Here too he was up most of the night. The waiter had rolled shut the sliding doors so that Nikki's silken sleep should not be disturbed. I glanced through the window from time to time at his round arms and the long shifting layers of black hair reaching his glossy shoulders. In his early thirties, handsome Nikki was boyish still.

The waiter had entered with wild strawberries, *brioches,* jam jars, and small pots of what I had been brought up to call hotel silver. Ravelstein scribbled his name wildly on the check while bringing a bun to his mouth. I was the neater eater. Ravelstein when he was feeding and speaking made you feel that something biological was going on, that he was stoking his system and nourishing his ideas.

This morning he was again urging me to go more public, to get away from the private life, to take an interest in "public life, in politics," to use his own words. He wanted me to try my hand at biography, and I had agreed to do it. At his request, I had written a short account of J. M. Keynes's description of the arguments over German reparations and the lifting of the Allied blockade in 1919. Ravelstein was pleased with what I had done but not quite satisfied as yet. He thought I had a rhetorical problem. I said that too much emphasis on the literal facts narrowed the wider interest of the enterprise.

I may as well come out with it: I had a high school English teacher named Morford ("Crazy Morford" we called him) who had us reading Macaulay's essay on Boswell's *Johnson.* Whether this was Morford's own idea or an item in the curriculum set by the Board of Education, I can't say. Macaulay's essay, commissioned in the nineteenth century by the *Encyclopedia Britannica,* was published in an American textbook edition by the Riverside Press. Reading it put me into a purple fever. Macaulay exhilarated me with *his* version of the *Life,* with the "anfractuosity" of Johnson's mind. I have since read many sober criticisms of Macaulay's Victorian excesses. But I have never been cured—I never wanted to be cured of my weakness for Macaulay. Thanks to him I still see poor convulsive Johnson touching every lamppost on the street and eating spoiled meat and rancid puddings.

What line to take in writing a biography became the problem. There was Johnson's own example in the memoir of his friend Richard Savage. There was Plutarch, of course. When I mentioned Plutarch to a Greek scholar, he put him down as "a mere litterateur." But without Plutarch could *Antony and Cleopatra* have been written?

Next I considered Aubrey's *Brief Lives.*

But I shan't go through the whole list.

I had tried to describe Mr. Morford to Ravelstein: Crazy Morford was never downright drunk in class, but he obviously was a lush—

he had a drunkard's red face. He wore the same fire-sale suit every day. He didn't want to know you, he didn't want to be known by you. His blue abstract alcoholic look was never directed at anyone. Under his disorderly brow he fixed his stare only at the walls, through the windows, into the book he was reading. Macaulay's *Johnson* and Shakespeare's *Hamlet* were the two works we studied with him that term. Johnson, despite his scrofula, his raggedness, his dropsy, had his friendships, wrote his books just as Morford met his classes, listened to us as we recited from memory the lines "How weary, stale, flat and unprofitable seem to me all the uses of this world." His grim cropped head, his fiery face, his hand clasped behind his back. Altogether flat and unprofitable.

Ravelstein wasn't much interested in my description of him. Why did I invite him to see the Morford I remembered? But Abe was right to put me onto the Keynes essay. Keynes, the powerful economist-statesman whom everybody knows for *The Economic Consequences of the Peace,* sent letters and memoranda to his Bloomsbury friends reporting on his postwar experiences, in particular the reparations debates between the defeated Germans and the Allied leaders—Clemenceau, Lloyd George, and the Americans. Ravelstein, a man not free with his praises, said that this time I had written a first-class account of Keynes's notes to his friends. Ravelstein rated Hayek higher than Keynes as an economist. Keynes, he said, had exaggerated the harshness of the Allies and played into the hands of the German generals and eventually of the Nazis. The Peace of Versailles was far less punitive than it ought to have been. The war aims of Hitler in 1939 were no different from those of the Kaiser in 1914. But setting this serious error aside, Keynes had a great many personal attractions. Educated at Eton and Cambridge, he was polished socially and culturally by the Bloomsbury group. The Great Politics of his day had developed and perfected him. I suppose in his personal life he considered himself a Uranian— a British euphemism for homosexual. Ravelstein mentioned that Keynes had married a Russian ballerina. He also explained to me that Uranus had fathered Aphrodite but that she had had no mother. She was conceived by the sea foam. He would say such things not because he thought I was ignorant of them but because he judged that I needed at a given moment to have my thoughts directed toward them. So he reminded me that when Uranus was killed by the Titan Cronus, his seed spilled into the sea. And this somehow had to do with reparations, or with the fact that the still blockaded Germans just then were starving.

Ravelstein, who for reasons of his own put me on to Keynes's paper, best remembered the passages describing the German bankers' inability to meet the demands of France and England. The French were after the Kaiser's gold reserves; they said the gold must be handed over at once. The English said they would settle for hard currencies. One of the German negotiators was a Jew. Lloyd George, losing his temper, turned on this man: he did an astonishing kike number on him, crouching, hunching, limping, spitting, zizzing his esses, sticking out his backside, doing a splayfoot parody of a Jew-walk. All this was described by Keynes to his Bloomsbury friends. Ravelstein didn't think well of the Bloomsbury intellectuals. He disliked their high camp, he disapproved of queer antics and of what he called "faggot behavior." He couldn't and didn't fault them for gossiping. He himself loved gossip too well to do that. But he said they were not thinkers but snobs, and their influence was pernicious. The spies later recruited in England by the GPU or the NKVD in the thirties were nurtured by Bloomsbury.

"But you did that well, Chick, about Lloyd George's nasty *youpin* parody."

Youpin is the French for "kike."

"Thank you," I said.

"I wouldn't dream of meddling," said Ravelstein. "But I think you'd agree that I'm trying to do you some good."

Of course I understood his motive. He wanted me to write his biography and at the same time he wanted to rescue me from my pernicious habits. He thought I was stuck in privacy and should be restored to community. "Too many years of inwardness!" he used to say. I badly needed to be in touch with politics—not local or machine politics, nor even national politics, but politics as Aristotle or Plato understood the term, rooted in our nature. You can't turn your back on your nature. I admitted to Ravelstein that reading those Keynes documents and writing the piece had been something like a holiday. Rejoining humankind, taking a humanity bath. There are times when I need to ride in the subway at rush hour or sit in a crowded movie house—that's what I mean by a humanity bath. As cattle must have salt to lick, I sometimes crave physical contact.

"I have some unclassified notions about Keynes and the World Bank, his Bretton Woods agreement, and also his attack on the Treaty of Versailles. I know just enough about Keynes to fit his name into a crossword puzzle," I said. "I'm glad you brought his private memoranda to my attention. His Bloomsbury friends must have been dying to have his impressions of the Peace Conference. Thanks to him they had world-historical ringside seats. And I suppose Lytton Strachey and Virginia Woolf absolutely had to have the inside dope. They represented the higher interests of British society. They had a duty to know—an artist's duty."

"And what about the Jewish side of the thing?" said Ravelstein.

"Keynes didn't like it much. You may remember that the only friendship he made at the Peace Conference was with a Jewish member of the German delegation."

"No, they wouldn't really have cared for a man as common as Lloyd George, those Bloomsburies."

But Ravelstein knew the value of a set. He had a set of his own. Its members were students he had trained in political philosophy and longtime friends. Most of them were trained as Ravelstein himself had been trained, under Professor Davarr and used his esoteric vocabulary. Some of Ravelstein's older pupils now held positions of importance on national newspapers. Quite a number served in the State Department. Some lectured in the War College or worked on the staff of the National Security Adviser. One was a protégé of Paul Nitze. Another, a maverick, published a column in the *Washington Times*. Some were influential, all were well informed; they were a close group, a community. From them Ravelstein had frequent reports, and when he was at home he spent hours on the telephone with his disciples. After a fashion, he kept their secrets. At least he didn't quote them by name. Even in the Crillon penthouse today the mobile telephone was held between his bare knees. The Japanese kimono fell away from legs paler than milk. He had the calves of a sedentary man—the shinbone long and the calf muscle abrupt, without roundness. Some years back, after his heart attack, the doctors told him he must exercise, so he bought an expensive sweat suit and elegant gym shoes. He shuffled around the track for several days and then gave it up. Fitness was not his cup of tea. He treated his body like a vehicle—a motorbike that he raced at top speed along the rim of the Grand Canyon.

"I'm not too surprised at Lloyd George," Ravelstein said. "He was a contentious little fucker. He visited Hitler in the thirties and came away with a high opinion of him. Hitler was a dream of political leaders. Whatever he wanted done was done, and quickly. No muss, no fuss. Very different from parliamentary government." It was enjoyable to hear Ravelstein on what he called Great Politics. He speculated often on Roosevelt and Churchill. He had a great respect for de Gaulle. From time to time he got carried away. Today, for instance, he spoke of Lloyd George's "pungency."

"Pungency is good," I said.

"In the matter of language the Brits had it all over us. Especially when their strength began to bleed away and language became one of their important resources."

"Like Hamlet's whore who must unpack her heart with words."

Ravelstein, with his bald powerful head, was at ease with large statements, big issues, and famous men, with decades, eras, centuries. He was, however, just as familiar with entertainers like Mel Brooks as with the classics and could go from Thucydides' huge tragedy to Moses as played by Brooks. "He comes down from Mount Sinai with the commandments. God had handed down twenty but ten fall from Mel Brooks's arms when he sees the children of Israel rioting around the Golden Calf." Ravelstein loved these Catskill entertainments; he had a natural gift for them.

He was very pleased with my Keynes sketch. He remembered that Churchill had called Keynes a man of clairvoyant intelligence—Abe loved Churchill. As an economist, Milton Friedman had it over most others, but Friedman was a free-market fanatic and had no use for culture, whereas Keynes had a cultivated intelligence. He was, however, wrong about the Versailles Treaty and deficient in politics, a subject of which Ravelstein had a very special understanding.

Abe's "people" in Washington kept his telephone line so busy that I said he must be masterminding a shadow government. He accepted this, smiling as though the oddity were not his but mine. He said, "All these students I've trained in the last thirty years still turn to me, and in a way the telephone makes possible an ongoing seminar in which the policy questions they deal with in day-to-day Washington are aligned with the Plato they studied two or three decades ago, or Locke, or Rousseau, or even Nietzsche."

It was very pleasant to win Ravelstein's approval, and his students kept coming back to him—men now in their forties, some of whom had figured significantly in running the Gulf War, spoke to him by the hour. "These special relationships are important to me—top priority." It was as natural that Ravelstein should need to know what went on in Downing Street or the Kremlin as it had been for Virginia Woolf to read Keynes's private report on German reparations. Possibly Ravelstein's views or opinions sometimes worked their way into policy decisions, but that wasn't what mattered. What mattered was that he should remain in charge somehow of the ongoing political education of his old boys. In Paris too he had a following. People who had taken his courses at the École des Hautes Études, just back from a mission to Moscow, also rang him up.

There were sexual friendships and intimate confidences as well. Beside the wide black leather sofa back home where he took the calls was an electronic panel of which he made expert use. I couldn't have operated it. I had no high-tech skills. But Ravelstein, though his hands were unsteady, controlled his instruments like a Prospero.

In any case he didn't have to worry now about the telephone bills.

But we are still atop the Hotel Crillon.

"You have good instincts, Chick," he said. "Too bad you didn't have more nihilism in your makeup. You should have been more like Céline with his nihilistic comedy, or farce. The scorned woman saying to her boyfriend, Robinson, 'Why can't you say "I love you"? What's so special about *you*? You get a hard-on like anybody else. *Quoi! Tu ne bandes pas?*' A hard-on to her is the same as love. But Robinson the nihilist is high-principled about one thing only, not to lie about the very, very few things that really matter. He'll try any kind of obscenity but he draws the line at last, and this tramp woman, deeply insulted, shoots him dead because he won't say 'I love you.'"

"Does Céline mean that this makes him authentic?"

"It means that writers are supposed to make you laugh and cry. That's what mankind is looking for. The situation of this Robinson is a replay of the drama of the Middle Ages in which the most vicious, abandoned criminals turn again to the Blessed Virgin. But there's no disagreement here. I want you to do me as you did Keynes, but on a bigger scale. And also you were too kind to him. I don't want that. Be as hard on me as you like. You aren't the darling doll you seem to be, and by describing me maybe you'll emancipate yourself."

"From what, exactly?"

"Whatever it is that controls you—some sword of Damocles hanging over you."

"No," I said. "It's the sword of Dimwitoclese."

The conversation, if it had taken place in a restaurant, would have made the other diners think that we were telling sexy jokes, having a rollicking time. "Dimwitoclese" was Ravelstein's kind of gag, and he laughed like Picasso's wounded horse in *Guernica,* rearing back.

Ravelstein's legacy to me was a subject—he thought he was giving me a subject, perhaps the best one I ever had, perhaps the only really important one. But what such a legacy signified was that he would die before me. If I were to predecease him he would certainly not write a memoir of me. Anything beyond a single page to be read at a memorial service would have been unthinkable. Yet we were close friends, none closer. What we were laughing about was death, and of course death does sharpen the comic sense. But the fact that we laughed together didn't mean that we were laughing for the same reasons. That Ravelstein's most serious ideas, put into his book, should have made him a millionaire certainly was funny. It took the genius of capitalism to make a valuable commodity out of thoughts, opinions, *teachings*. Bear in mind that Ravelstein was a teacher. He was not one of those conservatives who idolize the free market. He had views of his own on political and moral matters. But I am not interested in presenting his ideas. More than anything else, just now, I want to avoid them. I want to be brief, here. He was an educator. Put together in a book his ideas made him absurdly rich. He was spending the dollars almost as fast as they came in. Just now he was considering a new $5 million book contract. He could also command big fees on the lecture circuit. And he was a learned man after all. Nobody disputed that. You have to be learned to capture modernity in its full complexity and to assess its human cost. On social occasions he might be freaky, but on the platform you could see how well grounded his arguments were. It became only too clear what he was talking about. The public saw a higher education as a right. The White House affirmed it. Students were like "the mackerel-crowded seas." Thirty thousand dollars was the average annual college tuition. But what were students learning? The universities were permissive, lax. The Puritanism of an earlier time was gone. Relativism held that what was right in San Domingo was wrong in Pago Pago and that moral standards were therefore anything but absolute.

Now Ravelstein was no enemy of pleasure or opposed to love. On the contrary he saw love as possibly the highest blessing of mankind. A human soul devoid of longing was a soul deformed, deprived of its highest good, sick unto death. We were offered a biological model that dismissed the soul and stressed the importance of orgiastic relief from tension (biostatics and biodynamics). I don't intend to explain here the erotic teachings of Aristophanes and Socrates or of the Bible. For that you must go to Ravelstein himself. For him Jerusalem and Athens were the twin sources of civilization. Jerusalem and Athens are not my dish. I wish you well with them. But I was too old to become Ravelstein's disciple. All I need to say now is that he was taken very seriously even in the White House and on Downing Street. He was Mrs. Thatcher's weekend guest at Chequers. Nor did the President neglect him. Reagan invited him to dinner, and Ravelstein spent a fortune on formal attire, cummerbund, diamond studs, patent leather shoes. A columnist on the *Daily News* said that to Ravelstein money was something you threw from the rear platform of speeding trains. Ravelstein with shouts of laughter showed me the clipping. Through it all he was deeply amused. And of course I didn't have the same reasons for amusement. The vast hydraulic forces of the country had not picked me up, as they had him.

Although I was Ravelstein's senior by a good many years, we were close friends. There were sophomoric elements in my character as there were in his, and these leveled the ground and evened things up. A man who knew me well said that I was more innocent than any adult had the right to be. As if I had chosen to be naïve. Besides, the fact is that even extremely naïve people know their own interests. Very simple women understand when it's time to draw the line with a difficult husband—when to siphon the money out of their joint back account. I paid no particular attention to self-preservation. But luckily—or perhaps not too luckily—this is cornucopia-time, an era of abundance in all civilized nations. Never, on the material side, have huge populations been better protected from hunger and sickness. And this partial release from the struggle for survival makes people naïve. By this I mean their wishful fantasies are unchecked. You begin, in accordance with an unformulated agreement, to accept the terms, invariably falsified, on which others present themselves. You deaden your critical powers. You stifle your shrewdness. Before you know it you are paying a humongous divorce settlement to a woman who had more than once declared that she was an innocent who had no understanding of money matters.

In approaching a man like Ravelstein, a piecemeal method is perhaps best.

I had come up to his penthouse luxury suite on this June morning in Paris not so much to discuss the biographical essay I was going to do as to collect some facts about his parents and his early life. I didn't want more detail than I could use and I was by now familiar with the large outlines of his life story. The Ravelsteins were a Dayton, Ohio, family. His mother, a powerhouse, had put herself through Johns Hopkins. His father, not a successful man, was the local representative of a large national organization, banished to Dayton. A fat neurotic little man, a hysterical parent, a disciplinarian. Little Abe, when he was punished, was ordered to strip naked and then he was beaten with the strap that held up his father's pants. Abe admired his mother, hated his father, despised his sister. But Keynes, to glance at him once more, had little to say of Clemenceau's family history. Clemenceau was a seasoned cynic; he loathed and distrusted the Germans; he wore gray kid gloves at the negotiating table. But we'll ignore the gloves—what I mean is that we aren't doing psychobiography here.

This morning, moreover, Ravelstein was in no mood to go into the facts of his early life.

The place de la Concorde was losing its early freshness. The traffic below was thinner but the June heat was thickening, rising. In the sun, our pulse beats were somewhat slower. After the first surge of the feelings, the strong tickle at the heart of a life vindicated by an incomplete victory over many absurdities, everything had come together to place Abe Ravelstein, an academic, a lousy professor of political philosophy, at the very peak of Paris among the oil sheiks at the Crillon, or among CEOs at the Ritz, or playboys at the Hotel Meurice. Under the sun, our conversation pausing, he lapsed or slumped for a while; his hemispheric eyebrows were drawn upward. His lips, poised to say more, said nothing for the moment. On his bald head you felt that what you were looking at were the finger marks of its shaper. He himself was momentarily elsewhere; he was subject to these intermittences. Though his eyes were open, it was possible that he didn't see you. As he seldom had a night of uninterrupted sleep, it wasn't unusual, especially in warm weather, for him to lapse briefly, to doze, to drop out, two long arms hanging over the sides of his chair and the strange shapes of his mismatched feet. One was three sizes bigger than the other. And it wasn't only the broken sleep, it was the excitement, the wringing, the tension of his pleasures, of his mental life.

His fatigue this morning might have been due to the grand dinner he had given us last night, an extraordinary party on the place de la Madeleine chez Lucas-Carton. Digesting all those courses was bound to take it out of you. The main dish was chicken seasoned with honey and baked in clay. The ancient Greek recipe had recently been found by archaeologists in an Aegean dig. We dined on this delicious dish attended by no fewer than four waiters. The *sommelier,* wearing his badge of office on a chain of keys, supervised the filling of the glasses. For each course there was an appropriate wine, while other waiters working like acrobats reset the china and the silver. Ravelstein had a look of wild happiness, laughing and stammering, as he did when he was on a roll—beginning every clause in his long sentences with "Thee-ah, thee-ah, thee-ah this is the finest cuisine in Europe. Thee-ah, thee-ah Chick is a great skeptic when it comes to the French. He, thee-ah, thinks their cooking is all they have to show for themselves since the disgrace of the thee-ah-thee-ah 1940 when Hitler danced his victory jig. Chick sees *la France pourrie* in Sartre, in the loathing of the U.S.A. thee-ah and worship of Stalinism and in philosophy and linguistic theory. Thee-ah hermeneutics—he says *harmo*neutics are little sandwiches eaten by musicians during the intermission. But you have to admit that you can't get a meal like this anywhere else. Notice how Rosamund is glowing. Now there's a woman who relishes exquisite food and thee-ah thee-ah thee-ah restaurateur's presentation. Also Nikki, someone who can judge cookery—you wouldn't deny it, Chick."

No, I would not. Nikki was training in a Swiss hotel school. I can't say more than that because I'm not the ideal person to recall the minute particulars but Nikki was an accredited maître d'. He was ready to go into fits of laughter when he modeled the cutaway coat of his trade for Ravelstein and me, and put on his professional dignities.

Now tonight's dinner had been laid on for me. It was Ravelstein's way of thanking his friend Chick for the support he had given him in the writing of his bestseller. The idea of the entire project, he said, was mine from the first. It would never have been done if I hadn't urged him to do it. This was always and handsomely acknowledged by Abe—"It was Chick who put me up to it."

There is a parallel between inner-city phenomena and the mental disarray of the U.S., the winner of the Cold War, the only superpower remaining. That's one way of boiling it down. This is what Ravelstein's books and articles had to tell us. He took you from antiquity to the Enlightenment, and then—by way of Locke, Montesquieu, and Rousseau onward to Nietzsche, Heidegger—to the present moment, to corporate, high-tech America, its culture and its entertainments, its press, its educational system, its think tanks, its politics. He gave you a picture of this mass democracy and its characteristic—woeful—human product. In his classroom, and the lectures were always packed, he coughed, stammered, he smoked, bawled, laughed, he brought his students to their feet and debated, provoked them to single combat, examined, hammered them. He didn't ask, "Where will you spend eternity?" as religious the-end-is-near picketers did but rather, "With what, in this modern democracy, will you meet the demands of your soul?"

This tall pin- or chalk-striped dude with his bald head (you always felt there was something dangerous about its whiteness, its white force, its dents) did not step up to the platform to bore you silly with the correct order of the epochs (the Age of Faith, the Age of Reason, the Romantic Revolution), nor did he present himself as an academic, or as a campus rebel encouraging revolutionary behavior. The strikes and campus takeovers of the sixties had set the country back significantly, he said. He did not court students by putting on bull-session airs or try to scandalize them—entertain them actually, as histrionic lecturers do—by shouting "Shit!" or "Fuck!" There was nothing at all of the campus wildman about him. His frailties were visible. He obsessively knew what it was to be sunk by his faults or his errors. But before he went under he would describe Plato's Cave to you. He would tell you about your soul, already thin, and shrinking fast—faster and faster.

He attracted gifted students. His classes were always full up. So it presently occurred to me that he had only to put on the page what he was doing *viva voce*. It would be the easiest thing in the world for Ravelstein to write a popular book.

Furthermore, to be perfectly frank, I was tired of hearing about his unsatisfactory salary, his Byzantine borrowing habits, and the deals and arrangements he made putting his treasures in hock, his Jensen teapot or his Quimper antique plates. After following with more exasperation than interest the story of his beautiful Jensen teapot five years in the hands of Cecil Moers, one of his own Ph.D.'s, given as security for a $5,000 loan (and finally sold by this Ph.D. for ten thousand to some dealer), I said, "How long can you expect me to put up with this boring dispute, this boring teapot, and all your other boring luxury articles? Look, Abe, if you're living beyond your means, a struggling aristocrat victimized by his need for beautiful objects, why don't you increase those means?"

At this, I recall, Ravelstein brought both hands to both his ears.

The hands were finely made, the ears were gross. "What—should I register with an escort service?"

"Well, you're not much of a dancer. You might hire out as a dinner-table conversationalist. Like a thousand bucks a night... No, what I have in mind for you is a book. You could base a popular book on your actual class notes."

"Yah," he said. "Like Fielding's poor Parson Adams who goes to London to have his sermons printed. The parson needed money, and he had nothing to sell except his sermons. He had written them out. I don't even have notes. The advice you're giving me, Chick, is the advice of a much-published author. You remind me of Dwight Macdonald. He said to Venetsky, one of his friends, who was dead broke—absolutely at wit's end for money—'If you're in such a bind, Venetsky, why don't you sell one of your bonds. One can always do that.' It never would have occurred to him that Venetsky *had* no bonds. The Macdonalds had them. The Venetskys didn't."

"This is Macdonald as Marie Antoinette."

"Yes!" Ravelstein shouted, laughing. "Thee-ah old depression joke about the hobo who pitches a rich old lady and says, 'Ma'am, I haven't swallowed a bite of food in three days.' 'O you poor man, you must force yourself,' she says."

"I don't see how you can miss on this," I told Ravelstein. "All you have to do is prepare a proposal. At the very least you can get a small advance. It couldn't be less than twenty-five hundred dollars. My guess would be nearer to five thousand. Even if you never write a word of this proposed book, you'll pay off some of the debts and revive your borrowing power. How can you lose?"

He jumped at this. To bilk a publisher out of a few thousand bucks and at the same time free himself to wheel and deal was tremendously appealing. In outlook, he was anything but petty. But he did not expect my Utopian brainstorm to come to anything. He had gotten used to the theater of small-time intrigue where he could ironically, satirically dramatize and assert his exceptional stature and scope. So the outline was prepared and sent, a contract was signed, the advance was paid. The priceless Jensen silver teapot was gone for good, but Ravelstein's credit line was reopened. He wired money to Nikki in Geneva, who bought a new outfit from Gianfranco Ferre. Nikki had the instincts of a prince, he dressed like one—in Nikki, Ravelstein saw a brilliant young man who had every right to assert himself. This was not a matter of style or self-presentation. We are speaking here of a young man's nature and not of his strategies.

To his own surprise, Abe Ravelstein then found himself writing the book he had signed up to do. The surprise was general among his friends and the three or four generations of students he had trained. Some of these disapproved. They opposed what they saw as the popularization, or cheapening, of his ideas. But teaching, even if you are teaching Plato or Lucretius or Machiavelli or Bacon or Hobbes, is a kind of popularization. The products of their great minds have been in print for centuries and accessible to a general public blind to their esoteric significance. For all the great texts had esoteric significance, he believed and taught. This, I think, has to be mentioned, but no more than mentioned. The simplest of human beings is, for that matter, esoteric and radically mysterious.

One more odd bit from that evening at Lucas-Carton. It ended with an after-dinner wine. We had come to the estuary of the feast and were once more facing the gulf of common fare. Ravelstein pulled out his French checkbook. He had never before had a Paris account. For long years he had been a tourist or midlevel worshipper of French civilization—but under a budgetary cloud—wanting to be a high-stepper, but broke. On our own side of the Atlantic there was a shadow parallel to this. As a Jew you are also an American, but somehow you are also not. Imagine, however, reaching into your pocket to leave a grand seigneur tip and finding little more than lint along the seam. But Ravelstein, with his shaking hand, wrote tonight's check in an ecstasy. Now the waiter had brought a dish of chocolate truffles with the bill and it broke Ravelstein up to see Rosamund opening her purse and wrapping up the small peaked chocolates covered with cocoa dust. "Take 'em! Take every last one," said Ravelstein the Jewish comedian. He raised his cracked nightclub voice. "Those are edible souvenirs. Every one you eat will bring this feast back to you. You can write it down in your diary and remember how bold and forward you were, dumping these truffles into your bag."

Ravelstein thought all the better of you for stepping out of line. Later, he would occasionally say to Rosamund, "Don't give me that well-bred-young-lady, lace-paper-doily routine. I saw you swiping those chocolates at Lucas-Carton." The fact is that he liked minor crimes and misdemeanors. Just under the surfaces of his preferences there were always ideas to be found. In this instance the idea was that uniform good conduct was a very bad sign. Ravelstein himself, moreover, had a weakness for goodies—what he called *friandise*. On his way home from the office he often stopped at the grocery store to buy a bag of kid candy. He'd stuff himself with sugared fruit-jellies, preferably lime-flavored half-moons.

What made Rosamund's scooping up of the truffles particularly appealing was that she was a very pretty, well-brought-up, mannerly, intelligent young woman. It pleased him that she had fallen in love with an old guy like me. "There's a class of women who naturally go for old men," he said. As I've already indicated, he was drawn to irregular behavior. Especially where love was the motive. He rated longing very highly. Looking for love, falling in love, you were pining for the other half you had lost, as Aristophanes had said. Only it wasn't Aristophanes at all, but Plato in a speech attributed to Aristophanes. In the beginning men and women were round like the sun and the moon, they were both male and female and had two sets of sexual organs. In some cases both the organs were male. So the myth went. These were proud, self-sufficient beings. They defied the Olympian Gods who punished them by splitting them in half. This is the mutilation that mankind suffered. So that generation after generation we seek the missing half, longing to be whole again.

I was no sort of scholar. Like all, or most, of the students of my generation I had read Plato's *Symposium*. Wonderful entertainment, I thought. But I was sent back to it by Ravelstein. Not literally *sent*. But if you were continually in his company you had to go back to the *Symposium* repeatedly. To be human was to be severed, mutilated. Man is incomplete. Zeus is a tyrant. Mount Olympus is a tyranny. The work of humankind in its severed state is to seek the missing half. And after so many generations your true counterpart is simply not to be found. Eros is a compensation granted by Zeus— for possibly political reasons of his own. And the quest for your lost half is hopeless. The sexual embrace gives temporary self-forgetting but the painful knowledge of mutilation is permanent.

Anyway, it was just after midnight when we got up to go. Across the way there was a brilliant display of orchids. We were drawn by the lights and colors of the flower shop and we crossed the empty street. There was a vertical opening in the plate glass—two lines of brass edging—to let the flower odors into the carbon monoxide of the place de la Madeleine. More French seduction. The hookers used to congregate in front of the great church, where all state funerals are held. Ravelstein reminded me of this.

There was Ravelstein for you. If you didn't know this about him, you couldn't know him at all. Without its longings your soul was a used inner tube maybe good for one summer at the beach, nothing more. Spirited men and women, the young above all, were devoted to the pursuit of love. By contrast the bourgeois was dominated by fears of violent death. There, in the briefest form possible, you have a sketch of Ravelstein's most important preoccupations.

I feel that I do him an injustice by speaking so simplistically. He was a very complex man. Did he really share the view (attributed by Socrates to Aristophanes) that we were seeking the other that is a part of oneself? Nothing could move him more than a genuine instance of this quest. Moreover, he was forever looking for signs of it in everyone he knew. Naturally his students were included. Odd, for a professor to be thinking of the kids in his seminars as actors in this staggering eternal drama. His first move when they arrived was to order them to forget about their families. Their fathers were shopkeepers in Crawfordsville, Indiana, or Pontiac, Illinois. The sons thought long and hard about *The Peloponnesian Wars,* about the *Symposium,* and the *Phaedrus* and didn't consider it at all singular that they were soon more familiar with Nicias and Alcibiades than with the milk train or the ten-cent store. Bit by bit, Ravelstein also got them to confide in him. They told him their stories. They held nothing back. It was amazing how much Ravelstein learned

about them. It was partly his passion for gossip that brought in the
information he wanted. He not only trained them, he formed them,
he distributed them into groups and subgroups and placed them in
sexual categories, as he thought appropriate. Some were going to be
husbands and fathers, some would be queer—the regular, the irregular, the deep, the entertaining, the gamblers, plungers; the born
scholars, those with a gift for philosophy; lovers, plodders, bureaucrats, narcissists, chasers. He gave a good deal of thought to all of
this. He had hated and shaken off his own family. He told students
that they had come to the university to learn something, and this
meant that they must rid themselves of the opinions of their parents. He was going to direct them to a higher life, full of variety and
diversity, governed by rationality—anything but the arid kind. If
they were lucky, if they were bright and willing, Ravelstein would
give them the greatest gift they could hope to receive and lead them
through Plato, introduce them to the esoteric secrets of Mai-
monides, teach them the correct interpretation of Machiavelli,
acquaint them with the higher humanity of Shakespeare—up to
and beyond Nietzsche. It wasn't an academic program that he offered—it was more freewheeling than that. And on the whole his
program was effective. Not one of his students became a Ravelstein
in scope. But most of them were highly intelligent and very satis-
factorily singular. He wanted them to be singular. He loved the
kinkier students—they could never be kinky enough to suit
him. But of course they had to know the fundamentals and know
them diabolically well. "Isn't *he* the twisted one?" he'd say about
one or another of them. "Were you sent an offprint of his latest article—'Historicism and Philosophy'? I told him to put it in your
box."

I had looked at it. It left me feeling like an ant who sets out to cross the Andes.

Ravelstein urged his young men to rid themselves of their parents. But in the community that formed around him his role became, bit by bit, that of a father. Of course, if they weren't going to make it he didn't hesitate to throw them out. But once they became his intimates he planned their futures. He'd say to me, "Ali is as smart as they come. Do you approve of the Irish girl he's living with?"

"Well, I haven't seen much of her. She does seem bright."

"Bright is only part one. She gave up a career in law to study with me. She's got a very superior set of knockers, also. She and Ali have lived together about five years."

"Then she has a legitimate investment in him."

"I see what you mean. Though you make him sound like a piece of property. And remember he's a Muslim. He's got a regular human pyramid of an Egyptian family . . . I mean." He wondered whether it was uncommon for Muslims to fall in love. Passionate love was his perennial interest. But in the Middle East, arranged marriages remained the custom. "Still, Edna, in her own right, beats any pyramid." He had studied Edna, too. He gave much thought to student matches. "She's a deep one, obviously, and quite a beauty, too."

As I have said, we had planned today to discuss the memoir I was going to write, but this wasn't a good day for biographical details. "Come to think of it," Abe said, "I don't want to go over early times again—my effective mother educated at Johns Hopkins, top of her class. And my dumbhead father held it against me that I didn't make Phi Beta Kappa. In what mattered I had top grades. For the required courses B's and C's were good enough. Still, no matter how well I did—invited to Yale or Harvard to lecture—my dad to the end threw it in my face that I hadn't made Phi Beta K. His mind was a sort of Georgia swamp—Okefenokee with neurotic lights playing over it. A failure, of course he was, but with some hidden merit—so well buried it could never be found again."

Then Ravelstein stopped and said, "I think I'd rather go along the rue St. Honoré this morning. . . ."

"Or what's left of the morning."

"Rosamund will sleep in. We wore her out with last night's glamour—a beautiful lady at dinner with three desirable men. You'd only be a bother to your wife before one o'clock. I'd like your advice about a sports coat at Lanvin. I told the salesman I'd stop by in the A.M. I'm a little dopey this morning—I was nodding just now. Being torpid is a condition I especially dislike. . . ."

We left the penthouse. The moment was well chosen because several floors below the elevator stopped and Michael Jackson and his people got in. There he was in one of his spangled costumes, gold on black—a tight fit. His curls were fresh and his slim smile was chaste. In spite of yourself you studied him for signs of facial surgery. His air I thought was wistfully transitional. Golden boys coming to dust, like chimney sweepers.

Ravelstein, who was as big as any of the bodyguards—even bigger but certainly not so strong—loved this brief moment of contact. He was like that—the pleasure of a moment consumed him.

On the main floor, the guards cleared a way for Jackson as if they were swimming, doing the breaststroke. There were lots of people in the lobby. The big crowd was outside, in the street beyond the police barrier. But we were pressed together and held back behind braided gilt cords. The star walked out delicately waving to the hundreds of shouting groupies. Abe Ravelstein didn't at all mind being behind the ropes. Paris today was Paris as it should be. The kings who had laid out Versailles directed the architects to build the magnificent public spaces of the capital. These, today, were Ravelstein's setting. He was the grandee in the new order of things, carrying his credit cards and checks, willing to spend his dollars—if there had been a better hotel than the Crillon, Abe would have gone there. These days, Ravelstein was a magnificent man. The bills were paid by credit card and charged to his account at Merrill Lynch. Ravelstein seldom checked his statements. From time to time, Nikki, who wasn't supposed to do it, looked them over. His only aim was to protect Abe. It was thanks to Nikki that a major swindler in Singapore was discovered. Someone there had used Abe's Visa card to run up a $30,000 tab. "The signature was an obvious forgery," said Abe, not too upset. "Visa took care of it. International electronic swindles are the order of the day. The crooks learn to get ahead of high technology like inventive bacteria that outwit the pharmaceuticals, while the brainy researchers in the labs figure out how to stay ahead. Little campus geniuses outsmarting the Pentagon."

On the rue St. Honoré, Ravelstein was perfectly happy. We went from one shop display to the next.

The French term for window shopping is *lèche-vitrines*—licking the plate glass. This requires perfect leisure, and our breakfast had used up most of the morning. Still we did linger over the displays of socks and neckties and made-to-order shirts. Then we walked a little faster. I said to Abe that these luxurious displays made me feel tense. Too many attractions. I couldn't bear to be pulled from all sides.

"I've noticed," said Ravelstein, "that since your marriage your dress standards have dropped. You once were something of a dude."

He said this with regret. From time to time he would buy me a necktie—never one that I would have chosen for myself. These gift-ties were something of a put-down, to remind me that I was becoming dowdy. But there was more in it than that. Ravelstein was a bigger man than me. He was able to make a striking statement. Because of his larger size, he could wear clothes with more dramatic effect. I wouldn't have dreamed of disputing this. To be really handsome a man should be tall. A tragic hero has to be above the average in height. I hadn't read Aristotle in ages but I remembered this much from the *Poetics*.

In the rue St. Honoré, loaded with all the glamour of French history and politics—with all the special claims made for French civilization—what came back to me was that old music-hall number called "The Man Who Broke the Bank at Monte Carlo." There is a *flâneur* who strolls in the Bois de Boulogne with an independent air. And he is debonair. And of course the people stare.

Things don't happen at all if they don't happen in Paris, or are brought to the attention of Paris. That bursting old furnace, Balzac, established this as a first principle. What Paris hadn't vetted didn't even exist.

Of course Ravelstein knew too much about the modern world to agree with this. Ravelstein was, remember, the man at the private command post of telephones with complex keyboards and flashing lights and state-of-the-art stereo playing Palestrina on the original instruments. France, alas, was no longer the center of judgment, enlightenment. It was not the home of cyberspace. It no longer attracted the world's great intellects and all the rest of that cultural *schtuss.* The French had *had* it. De Gaulle the human giraffe sniffing down his nostrils. Churchill saying about him that England's offense had been to help *la France.* The lofty military creature gazing on the treetops of the late-modern world could not suffer the thought that his country needed help.

Abe's mind was never short of items to fill out or document the times. "'France without an army is not France'—Churchill again." My taste in conversation was similar. I couldn't do it but I loved to hear it done. Ravelstein did it infinitely better. He took a special interest in Great Politics. In that line, of course, France today was bankrupt. Only the manner was left, and they made the most of the manner but they were bluffing, they knew they were talking twaddle. What they were still good at were the arts of intimacy. Eats still rated high—e.g., last night's banquet at Lucas-Carton. In every *quartier,* the fresh-produce markets, the good bakeries, the *charcuterie* with its cold cuts. Also the great displays of intimate garments. The shameless love of fine bedding. *"Viens, viens dans mes bras, je te donne du chocolat."* It was wonderful to be so public about the private, about the living creature and its needs. Slick magazines in New York imitated this but never got it right.... Yes, and then there was the French street life. "American residential streets are humanly nine-tenths barren. Here humankind is still acting up," said Ravelstein.

Ravelstein the sinner did have a taste for sexy mischief. He relished *louche* encounters, the fishy and the equivocal. For certain kinds of conduct, or misconduct, Paris was still the best place. If Ravelstein walking, smiling, expounding, stammered, it was not from weakness but from overflow. The famous light of Paris was concentrated on his bald head.

"How far is the joint we're going to?"

"Don't be impatient, Chick. You make me feel you always have something more important to do than what you're doing now."

I didn't defend myself—didn't even try. Our destination, Lanvin, was close by but we were detained en route by various shops. Optometrists always held Ravelstein up. He was familiar with every sort of frame. There he wasn't alone. According to a survey, the average American woman has three pairs of sunglasses. "O, reason not the need!"—poor Lear's defense of superfluities. Abe loved specs; he bought them also as gifts. He gave me the folding kind that go into a small case made for an outer pocket. He swore off contact lenses after he lost one in a spaghetti sauce he was cooking. Rosamund and I had been his dinner guests that evening, and jokes were made about a new kind of hindsight. —Or was a contact lens humanly digestible? As hard iron was said to be, for ostriches.

"What does this Lanvin jacket have that your twenty others haven't?" I wanted to say. But I knew perfectly well that in Abe's head there were all kinds of distinctions having to do with prodigality and illiberality, magnanimity and meanness. The attributes of the great-souled man. I didn't want to get him started. Neither did he want to get started, this morning.

Back in the Middle West, not so long ago, when he was still hard up and complained about his wardrobe, I took him downtown to Gesualdo, my tailor, to get him measured for a suit. In Gesualdo's loft he picked a bold-looking flannel from a good Scotch mill. We had three or four fittings and in my opinion the final product was very handsome. I spent a good piece of change on it. Just then I had a book on the low end of the best-seller list; it never rose past the middle but I was more than satisfied. A child of the Great Depression, I was happy with middling returns. My standards had been set in the meager thirties. Fifteen hundred bucks should have bought us a top-of-the-line suit. Even in my dude days (I had a very short fashion-plate phase) I had never gone beyond five hundred bucks for a suit. This, at the time, was what students who had just passed the bar exam were paying. When they later became partners, they stopped going to Gesualdo's. They found themselves classier tailors, the kind used by surgeons, professional athletes, and racketeers.

Ravelstein and I had it out about Gesualdo's suit. "Listen, Chick," Ravelstein said. "The real value of that suit was not in the cut of it—not the workmanship . . ."

"You and Nikki made fun of it when you put it on at home. You never wore it but once, to please me. . . ."

"I can't deny that I didn't think it fit for use."

"*Use* isn't the word. You two wouldn't have dressed a dummy in it."

Ravelstein, a chain smoker lighting another cigarette, twisted his trunk backward, perhaps to avoid the lighter flame, perhaps because he was laughing so hard. When he could speak, he said, "Well, it wasn't Lanvin. You wanted to do something for me. It was generous, Chick, and Nikki was the first to say it. But Gesualdo is way behind the times. He makes mafiosi-type clothes, not for the dons but for the soldiers, the lower-rank gangsters."

"So much for the way *I* dress."

"You have no interest in fashion. You don't care about name brands. You should have given me the dough you paid Gesualdo and then I would have raised the rest for a decently cut garment."

We were perfectly open with each other. You could speak your mind without offending. On either side there was nothing too personal, too shameful to be said, nothing too nasty or criminal. I did feel at times that he was sparing me his most severe judgments if I wasn't just then ready to stand up under them. I used to spare him, too. But it gave me tremendous relief to be as plain and clear with him as I would be with myself about weak or vicious things. In self-understanding he was well ahead of me. But every personal discussion turned finally into good, clean, nihilistic fun.

"Maybe an unexamined life is not worth living. But a man's examined life can make him wish he was dead" was what I said to him.

Ravelstein was overjoyed. He laughed so hard his eyes turned up to heaven.

But I'm not done yet with Paris in the Spring.

The gorgeous jacket at Lanvin was beautiful flannel, silky as well as substantial. The color was one I associated with Labrador retrievers—golden, with rich lights among the folds. "You see such jackets advertised in *Vanity Fair* and the other fashion slicks, and they're usually modeled by unshaven toughs with the look of rough trade or of downright rapists who have nothing—but nothing—to do, other than being seen in all the glory of their dirty narcissism." You don't even think of such a garment on an unwieldy intelligent man. A little fat in the chest, maybe, or with lover's handles at the waist. It's actually a pleasant thing to see.

I advised Ravelstein to buy this Lanvin jacket.

The price was $4,500 and he put it on his Visa Gold card because he wasn't sure offhand about his balance at the Crédit Lyonnais. Visa protects you from gouging; it guarantees you the legal rate of exchange for the day of the transaction.

In the street he asked how the color held up in full daylight. He was deeply satisfied when I said it was gorgeous.

Our next stop was Sulka's, where he looked over the custom-made shirts he had ordered. They were to be delivered to the Crillon, each one in a durable plastic box. We then went to the Lalique showrooms, where he wanted to look at lighting fixtures for his walls and ceilings at home.

"Let's set aside half an hour for Gelot the hatmaker."

At Gelot's I broke down and bought myself a green corduroy fedora. Abe said I had to have it. "I like the look of it on you. You can do with a little assertion. You don't make enough of yourself," he said. "You're too fucking modest, Chick. It's unbecoming because anybody who catches your eye sees that you're an overweening megalomaniac. If you're too stingy to do it I'll put it on my account. . . ."

"My parents had green sofas at home," I said. "Secondhand, but velvet. I'll pay for it myself. . . . I'm buying this for old times' sake."

"It may be too heavy for June."

"Well, I expect to be still alive in October."

He was wearing his new Lanvin jacket on the rue de Rivoli. The great Louvre and the parks were on our left. The arcades were full of tourists.

"The Palais Royal"—Ravelstein gestured loosely toward it—"was where Diderot walked late every afternoon and where he had his famous conversations with Rameau's nephew." But Ravelstein was by no means like the nephew—that music teacher and sponger. He was above Diderot, too. A much larger and graver person with an extensive training in history, especially the history of moral and political theory. I was always drawn to people who were orderly in a large sense and had mapped out the world and made it coherent. Ravelstein only sounded incoherent with his "thee-ah thee-ah"s. We had a buddy back in the States who liked to tell us, "Order itself is charismatic." Which is another way of saying "Music hath charms" et cetera.

And we happened just then to be talking about this charisma-man whose name is, or was, Rakhmiel Kogon. Rakhmiel was a dead ringer for the actor Edmund Gwenn, who played a Macy's Santa Claus in *Miracle on 34th Street*. But Rakhmiel was a non-benevolent Santa Claus, a dangerous person, ruddy, with a red-eyed scowl and a face in which the anger muscles were highly developed. He came down the chimney like Santa Claus, but his aim was to make trouble.

Ravelstein and I had no need for lunch—the Lucas-Carton ten-course banquet took away your appetite till dinnertime next day—but we sat down to drink some coffee. Ravelstein was on his second packet of Marlboro cigarettes, and at the Café de Flore, which he patronized regularly, he ordered *"un espresso trés serré."* At the Flore they packed it tight for him. But if his big fingers shook when he picked up the cup it was not because he had a case of nerves. What he had was an overflow of excitement. The caffeine was the least of it.

He said, "Rakhmiel was one of my teachers, early on. Then he taught at the London School of Economics. Then at Oxford, where he turned British. Always divided his time between the U.S. and England. He's a serious person, not comfortable with himself. But I do owe him a lot—like my present position. I was in exile in Minnesota and he got me the appointment I wanted . . ."

"Almost what you wanted . . ."

"That's true. I'm the only one with rank who doesn't have a name chair. After all I've done for the university . . . And the only chair the administration offers me is the electric chair."

But Ravelstein was unusually free from such preoccupations and grievances. And this is not the place for them. I may return to this subject later. I probably won't. Anyway, it isn't what I should be presenting here. I *said* I'd take a piecemeal approach to Ravelstein.

He was a curious man to watch at the table. His feeding habits needed getting used to. Mrs. Glyph, the wife of the founder of his department, told him once that he must never again expect her to ask him to dinner. She was in her own right a very rich lady, big on high culture and an entertainer of visiting celebrities. She had had R. H. Tawney at her dinner table, and Bertrand Russell, and some big-shot French Thomist whose name escapes me (Maritain?), and lots of literati, especially the French. Abe Ravelstein, then a junior faculty member, was invited to a luncheon to honor T. S. Eliot. Marla Glyph said to Abe Ravelstein as he was leaving, "You drank from your Coke bottle, and T. S. Eliot was watching—with horror."

Ravelstein told this on himself. And on the late Mrs. Glyph. She was born to huge wealth, her husband was a great orientalist. "People who are self-glamourized invent their peculiar significance as they go along," Ravelstein said. "Until they knit together a dazzling fantasy. They turn themselves into something like glorious dragonflies and whiz through an atmosphere of perfect unreality. Then they write essays, poems, whole books about each other . . ."

"Crude Jewish behavior at a lunch for a nob—a superimportant visitor . . . ," I said.

"And what will T. S. think of us!"

But somehow I can't believe that drinking from a Coke bottle was the whole story. (And what, to begin with, was a Coke bottle doing on the table!) Faculty wives knew that when Ravelstein came to dinner they would face a big cleaning job afterward—the spilling, splashing, crumbling, the nastiness of his napkin after he had used it, the pieces of cooked meat scattered under the table, the wine sprayed out when he laughed at a wisecrack; courses rejected after one bite and pawed to the floor. An experienced hostess would have spread newspapers under his chair. He wouldn't have minded. He didn't pay much attention to such things. Of course each of us has ways of knowing what is going on. Abe *knew*—he knew what to bring to full consciousness and what to brush aside. Objecting to Abe's table manners would be a confession of pettiness.

It amused Ravelstein to say, "She wasn't going to let any kike behave so badly at *her* table."

Professor Glyph, her husband, had no such prejudices. He was a tall, grave man. His manner was decorous but his real look seemed focused elsewhere, on objects more distant and even more amusing—more amusing than Ravelstein, I mean. His small eyes set wide apart were pleasant and tolerant; his hair, parted in the middle, was the hair of a learned gentleman, famous for his scholarship. His friends were mainly French, and prominent, with names like Bourbon-Sixte—either members of the Academy or short-listed for nomination. Glyph was pampered by his wife and her servants—a laundress, a cook, and a parlor maid. The Glyphs were no ordinary academic couple—they were at home in London as well as in Paris. In Saint-Tropez, or some such place, the Scott Fitzgeralds had been their close neighbors. Glyph and his wife were not your common name-droppers: They had been a rich American Jazz-Age couple. They had known Picasso and Gertrude Stein.

For some reason Ravelstein and I were talking about them at the Café de Flore. On especially enjoyable days I suffer an early afternoon drop—fine weather makes it all the worse. The gloss the sun puts on the surroundings—the triumph of life, so to speak, the flourishing of everything makes me despair. I'll never be able to keep up with all the massed hours of life-triumphant. I had never spoken of this to Ravelstein but he probably sensed it. At times he seemed to be intervening on my behalf.

"Glyph loved the Pont Royal—it was his favorite hotel. Very close by," Ravelstein said. "And I'll tell you—when Mrs. Glyph died, Glyph came to Paris to grieve for her. He brought her papers along. His idea was to publish a collection of her essays. And he sent for Rakhmiel Kogon to help him—Rakhmiel was in Oxford."

"Why did Rakhmiel come?"

"He owed the old man. From way back. Glyph had saved Rakhmiel from being thrown out on his ear. He protected him— gave him sanctuary. This was before Rakhmiel became what academic fuckheads call 'a towering figure.' He came to Paris, anyway, and was also at the Pont Royal, though not in a suite. And every morning he reported to work on Marla Glyph's papers. Every morning Glyph would say, 'I have a cold, and Marla would not have wanted me to work today.' Or else, 'I must have my hair cut. Marla would say I am past due.' Or he would make an appointment with a Rochefoucauld or with a Bourbon-Sixte, while Rakhmiel organized her notes and read her crazy essays. But he was all the time drawn back to her journal. Because he was often mentioned there: *'Again that frightful little Jew, R. Kogon.'* Or, *'I do my best to tolerate Herbert's repulsive protégé Kogon, who gets Jewisher and viler and more unbearable by the day—with that brassy tomcat Jew face . . .'"*

"Kogon told you this himself?" I said.

"You bet he did. He couldn't help but be amused. He said she was

such a Verdurin—a relentless social climber. When they're cultivated, such people have something more to exclude Jews from."

"But no serious person could take Mrs. Glyph seriously," I said.

"Did you know her, Chick?"

"I turned up just after she died. Glyph, a good man, unusually
generous, would say 'my late wife' and then, for laughs, he'd add
that she never was punctual. The second was a charmer—some
people choose better as they go along. She turned out to be strong,
generous, and clever. Once he invited me to dinner and he asked on
the phone in his formal French style whether I objected to *gens de
couleur.*' The guest was a gorgeous woman from Martinique—the
wife of some famous art historian. Was it *the* Rewald who wrote the
book on Cézanne?"

"You've always been lucky. You seldom make the most of your
luck," said Ravelstein.

I was used to this. Ravelstein believed that I was gifted and bright
but uneducated, naïve and passive—inward. He said that when I
was in the right company I was an inspired conversationalist and
he told the students that there was no important subject I hadn't
thought about. —Yes, but what had I done about all these big
topics?

By following my suggestion Ravelstein had become very rich.
And Rosamund after last night's celebration had said to me, "It was
meant to be a great occasion. All the thanks and affection in Abe
went into the Lucas-Carton symposium—dining, drink, and conversation Athenian-style." She had been one of Ravelstein's learned
groupies. She was good at Greek. To study with Ravelstein you had
to read your Xenophon, Thucydides, and Plato in Greek.

While I laughed at the way she described her teacher, I agreed.

She was unlike most other observant persons in that she also thought clearly. This was one of Rosamund's talents. But she also loved Ravelstein. She was one of his great admirers.

Abe went for his third *espresso serré* when the waiter set it down; Ravelstein's big, unskillful hand gripped the little cup as he carried it to his mouth. I would have given big odds on the outcome if a bet had been offered. Brown stains appeared on the lapel of his new coat. It was unpreventable—a fatality. He was still drinking the espresso; his head was far back. I kept my mouth shut, turning away from the large brown blot on the Lanvin coat. Another sort of man might have sensed at once that something had happened—someone, perhaps, who took money more seriously and who would feel somehow the responsibility involved in the wearing of a $4,500 garment. Ravelstein's neckties from Hermès or Ermenegildo Zegna were dotted with cigarette burns. I tried to interest him in bow ties. I said they would be protected under his chin. He saw the point, but he wouldn't buy ready-mades: He had never learned to knot a "papillon" (as he called it). "My fingers are too unsteady," he observed.

"Ah, well," he said, when he at last saw that he had soiled his Lanvin lapel. "I've fucked up again."

I didn't laugh at his remark.

A decision had to be made at this point. The coffee spill was funny, it was pure Ravelstein. He himself had just said so. But I did not treat it as a comic incident. I suggested in a somewhat stifled manner that the stains might be removed. "The valet service at the Crillon probably can do it."

"You think so?"

"If they can't, it can't be done anywhere."

You had to be something of a specialist to follow the movements of his mind. You had to distinguish between what people had been taught that they ought to do and what they deeply desired to do. According to certain thinkers, all men were enemies; they feared and hated one another. There was a war of all against all, in the state of nature. Sartre has told us in one of his plays that hell is "the others"—Abe detested Sartre, by the way, and despised his ideas. Philosophy is not my trade. True, I had studied Machiavelli and Hobbes at school, and I suppose that I could bluff my way through a quiz show. I was, however, a quick study, and I had learned quite a lot from Ravelstein because I was devoted to him. I "cherished" him, as one of my acquaintances had taught me to say.

Obviously, my purpose in mentioning the Crillon's valet service was to comfort Abe for spilling the Flore's strongest coffee on his brand-new jacket. But Abe didn't want me to console him for being what he was. He would have thought better of me for laughing at his sputtering reckless slobbering, his gauche eager tremors. He liked broad comedy, old vaudeville routines, wounding remarks, brashness, and raw fun. So he didn't think well of my weak, liberal, let's-make-it-all-better motive—my foolish kindness.

Abe took no stock in kindness. When students didn't meet his standards he said, "I was wrong about you. This is no place for you. I won't have you around." The feelings of the rejects didn't concern him. "Better for them if they hate me. It'll sharpen their minds. There's too much therapeutic bullshit, altogether."

He said that all kinds of creatures imposed on me and wasted my time. "Read any good book about Abe Lincoln," he advised me, "and see how people bugged him during the Civil War about jobs, about war contracts, franchises, consular appointments, and mad military ideas. As president of all the people he thought he was obliged to talk to all these parasites, creeps, and promoters. All the while he was standing in a river of blood. War measures made him a tyrant—he had to cancel the habeas corpus writ, you know. There was a higher thee-ah thee-ah need. He had to keep Maryland from joining the Confederacy."

Of course my needs were different from Ravelstein's. In my trade you have to make more allowances, taking all sorts of ambiguities into account—to avoid hard-edged judgments. All this refraining may resemble naïveté. But it isn't quite that. In art you become familiar with due process. You can't simply write people off or send them to hell.

On the other hand, as Ravelstein saw, I was willing to take risks—abnormally willing. "Humongous risks" was how he put it. "It's hard, all-in-all, to find a less prudent person than you, Chick. When I consider your life, I begin to be tempted to believe in a *fatum*. You have a *fatum*. You really are one for sticking your neck out. And maybe the thee-ah neck is not all that sticks out. But what I want to say is that your guidance system is extremely defective."

But it was just this absurdity that Ravelstein liked. "You never do the safe thing if there's a risky alternative. You're what people would call feckless, in the days when such words were still in use. Of course we're good and fed up with personality profiles, or defects. One reason why violence is so popular may be that psychiatric insights have worn us out and we get satisfaction from seeing them blown away with automatic weapons, or exploding in cars, or being garroted or stuffed by taxidermists. We're so sick of having to think about everybody's problems—Grand Guignol mock-destruction isn't good enough for the bastards."

He liked to raise his long arms over the light gathered on his bald head and give a comic cry.

It occurs to me that this account of mine will lead to charges of misanthropy. Ravelstein was anything but a misanthrope or a cynic. He was as generous as they come—a reservoir, a source of energy for the students he accepted. Many came with the good democratic premise that he should oblige them all and share his ideas with them. Of course he refused to let himself be used, enjoyed—tapped by idlers. "I'm not the pipe at Saratoga Springs, where the Bronx Jews came in summer with cups to drink life-giving water for free—a remedy for constipation or hardening of the arteries. I'm not a free commodity or public giveaway, *am* I! Incidentally the wonder-working water turned out to be carcinogenic. Bad for the liver. Worse for the pancreas." He laughed at this—not with pleasure.

If these characters hadn't come by bus and train to drink Saratoga water they would have eaten or drunk something just as deadly in Flatbush or Brownsville. How can you tabulate the endless dangers of tobacco, of food preservatives, asbestos, the stuff the crops are sprayed with—the *E. coli* from raw chicken on the hands of the kitchen employees. "Nothing is more bourgeois than the fear of death," Ravelstein would say. He gave these little anti-sermons in a wacko style. He reminded me of the rag-doll dancers, clowns of the twenties who waved their tattered, nerveless long arms and painted huge smiles on their powdered faces. So that Ravelstein's serious preoccupations "coexisted," to borrow a word from twentieth-century politics, with his buffoonery. Only his friends saw this side of him. He could be correct enough on serious occasions, not as a concession to academic fussbudgets but because there were real issues to be considered—matters related to the purpose of our existence: say, the correct ordering of the human soul—and there he was as stable and earnest as any of the deepest and greatest of teachers. Ravelstein was vigorous and hard. Although even while teaching one of his Platonic dialogues he allowed himself to cut a caper.

He sometimes said, "Yes, I play the *pitre.*"

"The straight man."

"The buffoon."

We had both lived in France. The French were genuinely educated—or had been so once. They had taken a bad beating in this century. However, they had a real feeling for beautiful objects still, for leisure, for reading and conversation; they didn't despise creaturely needs—the human basics. I keep making this pitch for the French.

On any street you could buy a baguette, a pair of underpants *taille grand patron,* or beer or brandy or coffee or *charcuterie.* Ravelstein was an atheist, but there was no reason why an atheist should not be influenced by the Sainte-Chapelle, should not read Pascal. For a civilized man there was no background, no atmosphere like the Parisian. For my part I had often felt myself hustled and despised by Parisians. I didn't see Vichy solely as a product of the Nazi occupation. I had ideas of my own about collaboration and fascism.

"I don't know whether it's your Jewish edginess or your unnatural need for a friendly welcome," said Ravelstein. "Or maybe you feel the Frenchies are ungrateful. I don't believe it's hard to prove that Paris is a better place than Detroit or Newark or Hartford."

It was a minor disagreement involving no big principles. Abe had excellent friends in Paris. He was well received by the *écoles* and *instituts* where he lectured on French subjects in his own sort of French. He himself had studied in Paris years ago under the famous Hegelian and high official Alexander Kojève, who had educated a whole generation of influential thinkers and writers. Among these Abe had quite a few buddies, admirers, readers. In the States he was controversial. He had more enemies at home than any normal person could want, especially among social scientists and philosophers.

But I have only the limited knowledge of these things that a non-specialist can have. Abe Ravelstein and I were close friends. We lived on the same street, and we were in almost daily contact. I was often invited to attend his seminars and to discuss literature with graduate students. In the old days there was still a considerable literary community in our country, and medicine and law were still "the learned professions," but in an American city today you can no longer count on doctors, lawyers, businessmen, journalists, politicians, television personalities, architects, or commodities traders to discuss Stendhal's novels or Thomas Hardy's poems. You occasionally do come across a reader of Proust or a crank who has memorized whole pages of *Finnegans Wake.* I like to say, when I am asked about *Finnegan,* that I am saving him for the nursing home. Better to enter eternity with Anna Livia Plurabelle than with the Simpsons jittering on the TV screen.

I wonder what terms to apply to Ravelstein's large, handsome apartment—his Midwestern base. It wouldn't be right to describe it as a sanctuary: Abe was in no sense a fugitive. Nor a solitary. He was actually on good terms with his American surroundings. His windows gave him a huge view of the city. He seldom had to use public transportation in his latter years, but he knew his way around, he spoke the language of the city. Young blacks would stop him in the street to ask about his suit or his topcoat, his fedora. They were familiar with high fashion. They talked to him about Ferre, Lanvin, about his Jermyn Street shirtmaker. "These young dudes," he explained, "are lovers of high fashion. Zoot suits and such crudities are things of the past. They're extremely savvy about automobiles, too."

"And maybe about twenty-thousand-dollar wristwatches. And what about handguns?"

Ravelstein laughed. "Even black women stop me in the street to comment on the cut of my suits," he said. "They're intuitively responsive."

His heart warmed toward such connoisseurs—lovers of elegance.

The admiration of black adolescents helped Ravelstein to offset the hatred of his colleagues, the professors. The popular success of his book drove the academics mad. He exposed the failings of the system in which they were schooled, the shallowness of their historicism, their susceptibility to European nihilism. A summary of his argument was that while you could get an excellent technical training in the U.S., liberal education had shrunk to the vanishing point. We were in thrall to the high tech, which had transformed the modern world. The older generation saved toward the education of its children. The cost of a B.A. had risen to $150,000. Parents might as well flush these dollars down the toilet, Ravelstein believed. No real education was possible in American universities except for aeronautical engineers, computerists, and the like. The universities were excellent in biology and the physical sciences, but the liberal arts were a failure. The philosopher Sidney Hook had told Ravelstein that philosophy was finished. "We have to find jobs for our graduates as medical ethicists in hospitals," Hook had admitted.

Ravelstein's book was not at all wild. Had he been a noisy windbag he would have been easy to dismiss. No, he was sensible and well informed, his arguments were thoroughly documented. All the dunces were united against him (as Swift or maybe Pope expressed it long ago). If they had had the powers of the FBI, the professors would have put Ravelstein on "most wanted" posters like those in federal buildings.

He had gone over the heads of the profs and the learned societies to speak directly to the great public. There are, after all, millions of people waiting for a sign. Many of them are university graduates.

When Ravelstein's outraged colleagues attacked him, he said he felt like the American general besieged by the Nazis—was it at Remagen? When they demanded his surrender, his answer was "Nuts to you!" Ravelstein was upset, of course; who wouldn't have been? And he couldn't expect to be rescued by some academic Patton. He could rely on his friends, and of course he had generations of graduate students on his side as well as the support of truth and principle. His book was well received in Europe. The Brits were inclined to look down their noses at him. The universities found fault, some of them, with his Greek. But when Margaret Thatcher invited him to Chequers for a weekend, he was *"aux anges"* (Chequers was heavenly: Abe always preferred French expressions to American ones; he didn't say "a chaser" or "a womanizer" or "ladies' man"—he said *"un homme à femmes."*). Even bright young left-wingers were strongly for him.

At Chequers, Mrs. Thatcher called his attention to a painting by Titian: a rearing lion caught in a net. A mouse was gnawing at the cords to set the lion free. (Is that one of Aesop's fables?) This detail had been lost in the shadows for centuries. One of the greatest men of the century, the statesman Winston Churchill, with his own brushes had restored the mythic mouse.

When he returned from England, Abe told me all about it in his own parlor (a drawing room it was not). He had paintings of his own, done by minor but good French artists. Some were quite handsome. The largest was a Judith with the head of Holofernes, a very bloody picture. She's got Holofernes by the hair. His eyes are upcast, half closed, her look is calm, pure, and saintly. I sometimes think he never knew what hit him. There are worse ways to go. I would now and then ask Ravelstein why he had chosen *this* painting to dominate the parlor.

"No particular statement is being made," he said.

"Everything we see we translate into Freud's language. Now, which is being trivialized, his vocabulary or our observations?"

"You can always refuse to be co-opted," said Ravelstein.

He was not big on what Americans call "the visual arts." The canvases were there because walls were meant for paintings and paintings for walls. His apartment was luxuriously furnished, and the right pictures had to be hung. When the money began to come in he replaced all his "old" things. They weren't old at all. They were earlier, cheaper purchases. Even when he had no more than his university salary to live on he had bought expensive sofas, good Italian leather furniture on money borrowed from his friends. When he rose to the top of the best-seller list, he gave the old stuff away to Ruby Tyson, the black woman who came in twice weekly to wash up and do the dusting. He made the delivery arrangements for her of course, he paid for the trucking. He urgently needed the space and things couldn't be moved out fast enough to suit him.

I would say Ruby's duties were very light. She polished Ravelstein's silver, she washed the blue-and-white Quimper dinner service and the Lalique crystal plate by plate, glass by glass. She didn't do any ironing—his shirts were laundered by American Trustworthy Home-delivery Service. They cleaned his suits as well. He did lots of business with Trustworthy. All but his neckties. Those were sent via air express to a silk specialist in Paris.

New rugs and furniture continually arrived—all the replaced dining-room suites, china cabinets, bedsteads were probably handed on by Ruby to her daughters and grandchildren. She was a religious old woman, very formal Southern-style when she answered the telephone. She was a loyal presence in the household. He was perfectly clear about her and had no illusions about being admitted to intimacy, received into the soul of a respectable old black person. Besides she had worked in the university neighborhood for more than half a century and had much to tell him about the closets of academic households. She fed Ravelstein's appetite for gossip. He hated his own family and never tired of weaning his gifted students from their families. His students, as I've said, had to be cured of the disastrous misconceptions, the "standardized unrealities" imposed on them by mindless parents.

Certain difficulties of presentation arise here. You don't want to confuse Ravelstein with the campus "free spirits," common enough in my own student days. The job of such people was to make you aware of the bourgeois upbringing from which your education was supposed to free you. These liberated teachers offered themselves as models, sometimes seeing themselves as revolutionaries. They spoke youth gibberish. They wore ponytails, they grew beards. They were Ph.D. hippies and swingers.

Ravelstein had no such act—nothing you could easily imitate. You couldn't begin to be like him without study, without learning, without performing the esoteric labors of interpretation he had gone through under *his* late master, the famous, controversial Felix Davarr.

I try at times to put myself into the shoes of a gifted young man from Oklahoma or Utah or Manitoba invited to join a private study group in Ravelstein's apartment, coming up in the elevator, arriving to find the door wide open and getting his first impressions of Ravelstein's habitat—the big antique (sometimes threadbare) Oriental carpets, the wall hangings, classical figurines, mirrors, glass cabinets, French antique sideboards, the Lalique chandeliers and wall fixtures. The living-room sofa of black leather was deep, wide, low. The glass top of the coffee table in front of it was about four inches thick. On it, Ravelstein sometimes spread his effects—the solid-gold Mont Blanc fountain pen, his $20,000 wrist watch, the golden gadget that cut his smuggled Havanas, the extra-large cigarette box filled with Marlboros, his Dunhill lighters, the heavy square glass ashtrays—the long butts neurotically puffed at once or twice and then broken. A great amount of ashes. Near the wall on a stand, sloping, an elaborate many-keyed piece of telephone apparatus—Abe's command post, expertly operated by himself. It saw heavy use. Paris and London called almost as often as Washington. Some of his very close friends in Paris phoned to talk about intimate matters—sex scandals. Those students who knew him best tactfully withdrew when he signaled with the fingers below his cigarette. He asked keen, low questions, and when he was listening his bald head was often drawn back on the leather cushions, his eyes sometimes upcast, glazed with absorption, mouth falling slightly open—his feet in the loafers coming together sole to sole. At all hours he was playing Rossini CDs at top volume. He had an extraordinary fondness for Rossini and for eighteenth-century opera as well. Baroque

Italian music had to be performed on the original ancient instruments. He paid top prices for his hi-fi equipment. Speakers at $10,000 apiece he did not consider too expensive.

Above him and below, three stories of the apartment building, like it or not, had to listen to Frescobaldi, Corelli, Pergolesi, to the "Italian Maiden in Algiers." When neighbors knocked to complain, he smiled and said that without music you couldn't swallow what life offered, and that it would do them good to submit and listen. But he promised to have more insulation blown in between the floors, and indeed he did bring in a soundproofing engineer. "I spent ten thousand on kapok insulation and still the rooms are not *insonoriseés.*" But when the neighbors were listed for him one by one there wasn't a single tenant he was able to care about. He annotated his reasons and was prepared to explain his grounds. He had a line on each of the neighbors—little bourgeois types dominated by secret dreads, each one a shrine of *amour propre,* scheming to persuade everyone else to endorse his image of himself; flat, reckoning personalities (a better term than "souls"—you could deal with personalities but to contemplate the souls of such individuals was a horror you wanted to avoid). Nothing to live for but foolishness, vainglory—no loyalty to your community, no love for your *polis,* devoid of gratitude, with nothing you would lay down your life for. Because, remember, the great passions are antinomian. And the great figures of human heroism looming tremendously over us are very different from the man in the street, our "normal" commonplace contemporary. Ravelstein's appraisal of the people he dealt with daily had this background of great love or of boundless rage. He would remind me that "rage" was in the first line of the *Iliad—menin Achileos.* Here you see the main, bearing beams of Ravelstein's deeply honest belief. The greatest heroes of all, the philosophers, had been and always would be atheists. After the philosophers, in Ravelstein's procession, came poets and statesmen. The tremendous historians like Thucydides. The military geniuses like Caesar—"the greatest man who ever lived within the tides of time"—and, next to Caesar, Marc Antony, briefly his successor, "the triple pillar of the earth" who valued love above imperial politics. Ravelstein went for classical antiquity. He preferred Athens but he respected Jerusalem greatly.

These were some of his fundamental assumptions, and the foundations of his teacher's vocation. If these are left out of my account of his life we'll see only his eccentricities or foibles, his lavish, screwy purchases, his furnishings, his vanities, his gags, his laugh-paroxysms, the *marche militaire* he did as he crossed the quadrangle in his huge fur-lined coat of luxurious leather—I knew only one other such coat. Gus Alex, a hit man and a hoodlum, wore a long, beautifully tailored mink coat on Lake Shore Drive where he lived and where he walked his little dog.

It used to be said now and then that his favorite students got a "charge" out of Ravelstein—that he was funny, a hoot. The charge, however, was only superficially funny or entertaining—a vital force was transmitted. Whatever the oddities were, they fed his energy, and this energy was spread, disseminated, bestowed.

I am doing what I can with the facts. He lived by his ideas. His knowledge was real, and he could document it, chapter and verse. He was here to give aid, to clarify and *move,* and to make certain if he could that the greatness of humankind would not entirely evaporate in bourgeois well-being, et cetera. There was nothing of the average in Ravelstein's life. He did not accept dullness and boredom. Nor was depression tolerated. He did not put up with low moods. Troubles when he had them were physical. His dental problems at one time were severe. He was persuaded at the university clinic to have implants put in; these went through the gums into the sockets, into the bone of the jaw. This operation was bungled and he suffered agonies at the hands of the surgeon. He walked the floors all night. Then he tried to get the implanted posts pulled out, and this was even more painful than the driving in.

"This is what comes of taking a cabinet maker's approach to the human head," he told me.

"You should have gone to Boston for this. Boston oral surgeons are supposed to be the best."

"Never put yourself in the hands of any lousy specialists. You'll be sacrificed on the altar of their thee-ah *technics*."

He was impatient with hygiene. There was no counting the cigarettes he lit in a day. Most of them he forgot, or broke. They lay like sticks of chalk in his CEO glass ashtrays. But then the organism was imperfect. His biological patchiness was a given—faulty, darkened heart and lungs. But to prolong his life was not one of Ravelstein's aims. Risk, limit, death's blackout were present in every living moment. When he coughed you heard the sump at the bottom of a mine shaft echoing.

I stopped asking Abe about the implants in his jawbone. I assumed that there were pangs now and then, and I thought of them as part of the psychophysical background.

Irregular in his habits and his hours, he seldom had a full night's sleep. Class preparation often kept him up. To lead his Oklahoma, Texas, or Oregon students through a Platonic dialogue, you needed exceptional skills as well as esoteric knowledge. Abe was not a late riser. Nikki on the other hand watched Chinese kung fu thrillers all night long and often slept until 2 P.M. Both Abe and Nikki were basketball fans. They seldom missed the Chicago Bulls on NBC.

When an important game was played, Ravelstein invited his graduate students to his apartment. He ordered pizza. Two delivery boys, carrying stacks of boxes, kicked at his door. The entry hall was filled with the hot smells of oregano, tomatoes, toasted cheese, pepperoni, and anchovies. Nikki presided over the cutting, using a sharp rolling blade. Slices were handed out on paper plates. Rosamund and I ate sandwiches made by Ravelstein with eager, unsteady hands and cheerful shouts. There was something like a demonstration of extraordinary skill in the serving of the drinks, as though he had halted in the middle of a high wire with a tray of overfilled glasses. You didn't want to banter with him then.

The portable phone was usually sticking out of Abe's pocket. I can't remember what call he was expecting just then. Maybe one of his sources had inside information about President Bush's final decision to end the war in Iraq. I have an impression somehow of the President—long-faced, lean, and tall—intermittently interrupting the pregame action on the basketball court. Vast banks of spectators, full of light, all brilliantly colored, Michael Jordan, Scottie Pippen, Horace Grant filling the net with warm-up shots. Mr. Bush equally tall but without beauty in his movements. It may not have been Iraq at all, but another crisis. You know how television is: you can't tell the wars from the NBA events—sports, superpower glamour, high-tech military operations; this was keenly felt by Ravelstein. If he spoke of Machiavelli and the best way to deal with a defeated enemy it was because he was a teacher through and through. There were flashes also of General Colin Powell and of Baker, the

Secretary of State. And then in the stadium the brief dimming of the vast lights—and after that the dramatic return of full illumination.

All of this put you in mind of the mass displays organized and staged by Hitler's impresario, Albert Speer: sports events and mass fascist rallies borrowed from each other. Ravelstein's young men were well up on basketball. In Michael Jordan, of course, they had a genius to watch. Ravelstein felt himself deeply and vitally connected with Jordan, the artist. He used to say that basketball stood with jazz music as a significant black contribution to the higher life of the country—its specifically American character. No less than bullfighters in Spain or tenors in Ireland or Nijinskys in Russia were the guards and forwards in the U.S. On that evening, in any case, President Bush had given the U.S. a military triumph; and Ravelstein, commenting on the black American servicemen, said what a credit they were to the country and to the U.S. military— how well-spoken they were on TV and how expert technically, how well they knew their jobs. For this he gave the Pentagon high marks.

For reasons of all sorts, Ravelstein was big on soldiers. He spoke with deep feeling about the American pilot shot down over North Vietnam who battered and bruised his own face, who deliberately broke his nose on the wall of his prison cell. This he did when he was told that he would have to appear with other prisoners on Ho Chi Minh's TV in order to denounce U.S. imperialism.

At his basketball parties, Ravelstein passed pizza slices among his graduate-student guests, his bald head swiveling toward the busy, colored TV screen behind him. His lot, his crew, his disciples, his clones who dressed as he did, smoked the same Marlboros, and found in these entertainments a common ground between the fan clubs of childhood and the Promised Land of the intellect toward which Ravelstein, their Moses and their Socrates, led them. Michael Jordan was now an American cult figure—small boys saved his apple cores as relics. A children's crusade might be possible even in the present age. Jordan, the papers said, had "bionic" powers. He could suspend himself in the air out of the reach of blockers, and you could trace his deliberations in his actions, with time enough to change hands while he soared—a man who earned $80 million a year, not a cult figure but a hero who moved the hearts of the masses.

Inevitably Ravelstein was seen by the young men he was training as the intellectual counterpart to Jordan. The man who introduced them to the powers and subtleties of Thucydides and analyzed the role of Alcibiades in the Sicilian campaign as no one else could—a man who expounded the *Gorgias* to his seminar, literally in sight of the steel mills and the ash heaps and street filth of Gary, its ore boats coming and going across the water—could also hang in the air, levitating just like Jordan. A man of idiosyncracies and kinks, of gobbling greed for penny candies or illegal Havana cigars, was himself a Homeric prodigy.

Ravelstein the host coming now with a cheese platter, saying, "What about a chunk of this Vermont cheddar . . . ?" ineptly brought the cheese knife, with uncontrollable nervous discharges in his fingers, down on the five-pound round of Cabot's supersharp.

When the cellular telephone in his trouser pocket rang, he drew apart to exchange a word or two with somebody in Hong Kong or Hawaii. One of his informants was calling in a bulletin. There were no security violations. Top secrets he neither heard nor asked to hear. What he loved was to have the men he had trained appointed to important positions; real life confirming his judgments. He'd go aside with his portable phone and then he'd return to tell us, "Colin Powell and Baker have advised the President not to send the troops all the way to Baghdad. Bush will announce it tomorrow. They're afraid of a few casualties. They send out a terrific army and give a demonstration of up-to-date high-tech warfare that flesh and blood can't stand up to. But then they leave the dictatorship in place and steal away . . ."

It gave Ravelstein the greatest satisfaction to have the inside dope. Like the child in the Lawrence poem sitting under a "great black piano appassionato," "in the boom of the tingling strings," while the child's mother plays.

"Well, that's the latest from the Defense Department . . ."

Most of us knew that his main source was Philip Gorman. Gorman's academic father had strongly objected to the Ravelstein seminars in which Philip was enrolled. Respectable professors of political theory had told old Gorman that Ravelstein was off the wall, that he seduced and corrupted his students. "The paterfamilias was warned against the bugger-familias," Ravelstein said.

Of course old Gorman would be too rigid to be grateful that his son did not go into business administration, Abe said. "Well, Philip is right now one of the Secretary's closest advisers. He has a powerful mind and a real grasp of great politics, this kid, whereas statisticians are as common as minnows."

Young Philip was one of the boys Ravelstein had educated over a span of thirty years. His pupils had turned into historians, teachers, journalists, experts, civil servants, think-tankers. Ravelstein had produced (indoctrinated) three or four generations of graduates. Moreover, his young men were mad for him. They didn't limit themselves to his doctrines, his interpretations, but imitated his manners and tried to walk and talk as he did—freely, wildly, pungently, with a brilliancy as close to his as they could make it. The very young ones—those who could afford the prices—also bought their clothes at Lanvin or Hermès, had their shirts made on Jermyn Street by Turnbull & Asser ("Kisser & Asser," as I revised it). They smoked with Ravelstein's erratic gestures. They played the same compact discs. He cured them of their taste for rock and they now listened to Mozart, Rossini, or, farther back, Albinoni and Frescobaldi ("on the original instruments"). They sold their collections of the Beatles and the Grateful Dead and listened instead to Maria Callas singing *La Traviata*.

"It's only a matter of time before Phil Gorman has cabinet rank, and a damn good thing for the country." Ravelstein had given his boys a good education, in these degraded times—"the fourth wave of modernity." They could be trusted with classified information, the state secrets they naturally would *not* pass on to their teacher who had opened their eyes to "Great Politics." You could see the changes their responsibilities had made in them. Their heads looked more firm and mature. They were absolutely right to withhold in-formation. They knew what a gossip he was. But he himself had very important secrets to keep, information of a private, dangerous nature which only a few could be trusted with. Teaching, as Ravel-stein understood teaching, was tricky work. You couldn't afford to let the facts be generally known. But unless the facts *were* known, no real life was possible. So you made your choices with a jeweller's touch. There were two people in Paris who knew him intimately and three on this side of the Atlantic. I was one of them. And when he asked me to write a "Life of Ravelstein," it was up to me to interpret his wishes and to decide just to what extent I was freed by his death to respect the essentials—or the slant given by my temperament and emotions to those essentials, my swirling version of them. I suppose he thought it wouldn't really matter because he'd be gone, and his posthumous reputation couldn't matter less.

Young Gorman, you may be sure, edited the information he gave to Ravelstein. He wouldn't have gone beyond the facts in tomorrow's press release. But he knew what pleasure it gave his old prof to hear the inside dope, so he briefed him out of respect and affection. He also knew that Ravelstein had masses of historical and political information to update and maintain. This went as far back as Plato and Thucydides—perhaps as far back as Moses. All those great designs of statesmanship—going back through Machiavelli via Severus or Caracalla. And it was essential to fit up-to-the-minute decisions in the Gulf War—made by obviously limited pols like Bush and Baker into a true-as-possible picture of the forces at work—into the political history of this civilization. When Ravelstein said that young Gorman had a grasp of Great Politics, something like this was what he had in mind.

At every opportunity, on any reasonable pretext, Ravelstein zipped across the Atlantic to Paris. But that didn't mean he was unhappy with the urban Midwest. He was attached to the University, where he had taken his degree under the great Davarr. He was an American through and through.

I had grown up in the city, but Ravelstein's people hadn't arrived from Ohio until the end of the thirties. I never met the father, whom Ravelstein described to me as a toy ogre, a huffy little man, and a neurotic disciplinarian. One of those small-time tyrants who control their children with demented screams, in some crazy nonstop family opera.

The University accepted high school kids who could pass its entrance exams. Ravelstein was admitted when he was fifteen years old and then was free from his father and from a sister he disliked almost as much. As I have said, he was fond of his mother. But at the University he was rid of all the Ravelsteins. "My real mental life began here. For me there was nothing better than the student rooming houses where I bunked. I never could see what was so disgraceful about 'stiffening in a rented house,' as Eliot wrote. Do you croak better on your own property?"

Still, without being envious (I never knew Ravelstein to envy anybody), he had a deep weakness for pleasant surroundings and liked to think of living in one of the tony flat buildings formerly occupied by the exclusively WASP faculty. When he returned to the University as a full professor after two decades on lesser campuses, he wangled a four-room apartment in the most desirable building of all. Most of his windows looked into the dark courtyard, but beyond he could see the campus to the west with its gothic, Indiana limestone spires, labs, dormitories, office buildings. He could stare at the tower of the chapel—a kind of truncated Bismarck Colossus with bells that boomed over and beyond the University compound. When Ravelstein became a national figure (an international one as well—his Japanese royalties alone were, he said with wild pleasure and no modesty, "ferocious"), he moved into one of the best apartments in the place. Now he had views in all directions. The late Madame Glyph, who put him down for drinking from a Coke bottle at her T. S. Eliot luncheon, had not been better situated.

Curiously enough, there was a monastic-retreat tone to his place. You entered under low vaulted ceilings. The lobby was paneled in mahogany. The elevators were like confession boxes. Each apartment had a small flagstone entry hall, and a gothic light fixture overhead. On Ravelstein's landing there was often a piece of furniture on its way out, displaced by some new purchase or other—a chest of drawers, a small armoire, an umbrella stand, a Paris painting about which he was beginning to have doubts. Ravelstein could not compete with the Glyphs' collection of Matisses and Chagalls, begun in the twenties. But in the kitchen he went far beyond them. From a restaurant supply company he had bought an espresso machine. It was installed in the kitchen, it dominated the sink, and it steamed and fizzed explosively. I refused to drink his coffee because it was made with chlorinated tap water. The huge commercial machine made the sink unusable. But Ravelstein had no use for sinks—it was only the coffee that mattered.

He and Nikki slept on Pratesi linens and under beautifully cured angora skins. He was perfectly aware that all this luxury was funny. Under charges of absurdity he was perfectly steady. He was not going to have a long life. I'm inclined to think he had Homeric ideas about being cut down early. He didn't have to accept confinement in a few dead-end decades, not with his appetite for existence and his exceptional gift for great overviews. It wasn't the money alone—his great best-seller windfall—that made it possible; it was his ability proven in the mental wars—the positions he held, the fights he provoked, his disputes with Oxford don classicists and historians. He was sure of himself, as de Gaulle had said about the Jews. He loved polemics.

Rosamund and I lived just up the street in a building that reminded you of the Maginot Line. Our rooms weren't as splendid as Ravelstein's monastic-luxurious apartment. They were boxy, but I had been looking for shelter just then. I was bombed out—evicted after twelve years of marriage from what had been my uptown home, and I was lucky to find sanctuary in one of the concrete pill-boxes down the way from Ravelstein, about fifty yards from his wrought-iron midwestern gothic gate and his uniformed door-man.—We had no doorman.

What I had were some fifty years of walking these sun-striped pavements, past buildings once occupied by friends. Now here, where a Japanese theologian was the tenant today, a Miss Aber-crombie had lived forty years ago. She was a painter who had mar-ried a pleasant hippie burglar whose specialty was to entertain company by re-enacting second-story break-ins. On every one of the surrounding streets there were front rooms where friends had lived—and at the sides, the windows of bedrooms where they died. There were more of those than I cared to think about.

At my age, you don't want to be too tender-minded. It's different if you lead an active life. And I am active, on the whole. But there are gaps, and these gaps tend to fill up with your dead.

Ravelstein credited me with a kind of simpleminded seriousness about the truth. He said, "You don't lie to yourself, Chick. You may put off acknowledgment for a very long time but in the end you do own up. It's not a common virtue."

I am by no means a professor, although I've been around the Uni-versity community for so many decades that some of the faculty think of me as a longtime colleague. And when I walked out on one of those sun-printed days shortly after I had returned to the Uni-versity neighborhood, the weather dry, cold, clear, and high, I met an acquaintance named Battle. He was a prof, an Englishman who strode about the freezing streets in an old thin topcoat. A man in his sixties, he was big, ruddy, fleshy, his huge chilled face as thick as sweet red pepper. His hair was dense and long, and he sometimes reminded me of the Quaker on the oatmeal box. He had energy enough to keep two men warm. Only his raised shoulders acknowledged that the temperature was well below freezing—the shoulders up, and the hands thrust down into his coat pockets—all but the thumbs. His feet were set close together. He was not what we used to call "a sport" but he always wore classy shoes.

Battle was said to be a man of immense knowledge. (I had to take people's word for this—how would I know about his command of Sanskrit and Arabic?) He was not an Oxbridge type. He was a product of one of England's redbrick universities.

In a case like his you couldn't simply mention that you had run into a prof named Battle whose long hair made hats superfluous. In World War II, Battle had been a paratrooper, and a pilot as well. He had ferried de Gaulle across the Mediterranean once. Besides which, he had been a notable tennis player in civilian life. He had also taught ballroom dancing in Indochina. He was very quick on his feet, an astonishing runner who had chased and caught a mugger. He punched the mugger so hard in the guts that the cops had to send for an ambulance.

Battle, one of Ravelstein's favorites, was fond of good old Abe. But to say how he, Battle, saw Ravelstein was well-nigh impossible. There were no clues as to what went on behind that powerful forehead. Full of force it came down to the bristling overhang of a superorbital ridge intersecting the straight line of his nose and matching the tight parallels of his lips—the mouth of a Celtic king.

He might have been trained as an Olympic-class weightlifter. This was a very strong man—but to what end was he strong? Battle brushed aside his natural gifts. Subtlety was what he aimed at—hidden, complex, bold, secret Machiavellian moves. His purpose might be to frustrate a departmental chairman by influencing an indifferent dean to pass a word to the provost, et cetera. No one would ever suspect such conspiracies existed, much less care to discover who was behind them. Ravelstein, who explained all this to me, incoherent with laughter and crying "thee-ah, thee-ah," said, "He comes to discuss all kinds of personal, highly personal thee-ah things with me but never mentions those other operations."

With a little encouragement Ravelstein would reveal Battle's confidences—or anyone else's. He would say, quoting a late friend of ours, "When I do it, it's not gossip, it's social history."

What he really meant was that idiosyncrasies were in the public domain, to be enjoyed like the air and other free commodities. He wasted no time on psychoanalytic speculation or the analysis of everyday life. He had no patience with "this insight bullshit" and preferred wit or even downright cruelty to friendly, well-meant interpretations of the conventional, liberal kind.

In the cold, sunny street—his face all folds in the whipcrack cold—Battle said, "Is Abe receiving visitors, these days?"

"Why not? He's always glad to see you."

"I didn't say it right. . . . He's always polite to Mary and me."

Mary was a plump, witty, short, smiling woman. Ravelstein and I were particularly fond of Mary.

"Well, if you are welcome and he's nice to you, what's the question?"

"He's not in the best of health, is he?"

"He's one of those tall, strong, always ailing men."

"But isn't he more ailing than usual?"

Battle was testing me, hoping for hints about Ravelstein's condition. I wasn't about to tell him anything, though I knew he liked Ravelstein—looked up to him, somehow. With odd people I can go along so far and no farther. Each frosty breath through Battle's dramatic nostrils rushed more red into his face. The color went down as far as the accordion pleats under his chin. He seldom wore a hat. His black hair seemed to keep the back of his neck warm enough. He wore a tango dancer's shoes. I sympathized with his eccentricities. It seemed to be a mixture of hold-tight delicacy and flyaway brutality.

The Battles, man and wife, valued Ravelstein highly. They felt for him. You could be certain that they had frequent conversations about him.

"Well," I said, "he has had a series of infections. The shingles hit him hard."

"Herpes zoster. Of course," said Battle. "Inflammation of the nerves. Horribly messy and painful. It often hits the spinal and cranial nerves. I've been around such cases."

His words made me see Ravelstein. I saw him lying silent under his down quilt. His darkened eyes were recessed. His head was set on its pillows. His posture suggested rest. But he wasn't getting any rest.

"Got over that one, did he?" said Battle. "But hasn't he been hit by another? Something new?"

There was another. This next infection was called Guillain-Barré by the neurologists when they finally identified it. It hadn't yet been diagnosed, just then. Abe had flown back from Paris for a dinner in his honor given by the mayor. Black tie and celebrity speeches—just the kind of occasion that Ravelstein, long starved for recognition, couldn't say no to. In Paris, where he intended to spend his sabbatical year, he had taken an apartment on an avenue of embassies and official residences very close to the Elysée Palace. The police were always around, and coming home at night presented a problem, since Abe couldn't find the time to waste at the bureaucratic Hotel de Ville applying for a *carte de séjour,* so that when the cops stopped him for his identity papers he had none to show and there were long midnight discussions. He referred the police to the Marquis of Such and Such, his landlord. There was something to be said for everything that happened in these streets. Even the inconveniences in Paris were on the highest level. Compared to his real troubles, these Corsicans (Ravelstein believed that all *flics*—French cops—came from Corsica, that no matter how close they shaved, their chins still bristled) remained in every respect entertaining.

The long and the short of it was that Ravelstein made a fast flight home to attend the mayor's banquet for him and came down with a disease (first discovered by a Frenchman) that sent him to the hospital. The doctors put him in intensive care. They were giving him oxygen. His visitors were let in no more than two at a time. He said hardly anything. Occasionally he gave me a stare of recognition. His big eyes were concentrated in that bald, cranial watchtower of his. His arms, never well developed, quickly lost such muscle as they had had. In the early days of the Barré virus he wasn't able to use his hands. Still he managed to convey that he needed to smoke.

"Not with an oxygen mask, you won't. You'd blow up the whole joint."

Somehow I found myself stuck always in the cautionary role,

speaking up for the commonest sort of common sense to people who took pride in brushing off prudence. Was it others who were forever putting me in this position, or was I at bottom exactly like that? I thought of myself, at hyper-self-critical moments, as the bourgeois *porte parole*. Ravelstein was aware of this flaw of mine.

Nikki and I were not unlike, in this respect. Nikki was far more sharp and critical. When Ravelstein bought a costly rug from Sukkumian on the North Side, Nikki shouted, "You paid ten grand for all these holes and loose threads—because the holes prove it's a genuine antique? What did he tell you, that this was the carpet they rolled Cleopatra in naked? You really are one of those guys, as Chick always says, who thinks money is supposed to be thrown from the rear end of an express train. You're on the observation platform of the Twentieth Century scattering hundred-dollar bills."

Nikki had been telephoned and told that Ravelstein was sick again. He was still at his hotel school in Geneva, and we learned that he was returning immediately. Nobody questioned the strength of Nikki's attachment to Abe. Nikki was perfectly direct—direct, by nature, a handsome, smooth-skinned, black-haired, Oriental, graceful, boyish man. He had an exotic conception of himself. I don't mean that he put on airs. He was never anything but natural. This protégé of Ravelstein's, I thought—or used to think—was somewhat spoiled. I was wrong, there, too. Brought up like a prince, yes. Even before the famous book that sold a million copies was written, Nikki was better dressed than the Prince of Wales. He was more intelligent and discerning than many better-educated people. He had, what is more, the courage to assert his right to be exactly what he seemed to be.

This, as Ravelstein pointed out, was not a posture. There was ab-

solutely nothing in Nikki's appearance that was decorative or theatrical. He doesn't look for trouble, mind you, but "he's always
ready for a fight. And his sense of himself is such that . . . he'll fight.
I've often had to hold him back."

He would sometimes lower his voice in speaking of Nikki, to say
that there was no intimacy between them. "More father and son."

In matters of sex, I sometimes felt Ravelstein saw me as a throw-
back, an anachronism. I was his close friend. But I was the child of
a traditional European Jewish family, with a vocabulary for inver-
sion going back two millennia or more. The ancestral Jewish terms
for it were, first, *Tum-tum,* dating perhaps from the Babylon captiv-
ity. Sometimes the word was *andreygenes,* obviously of Alexandrian,
Hellenistic origin—the two sexes merged in one erotic and perverse
darkness. Mixtures of archaism and modernity were especially appealing to Ravelstein, who could not be contained in modernity and
overflowed all the ages. Oddly enough, he was just like that.

He came out of intensive care unable to walk. But he quickly recovered partial use of his hands. He had to have hands because he
had to smoke. As soon as he was installed in his hospital room he
sent Rosamund out to buy him a pack of Marlboros. She had been
his student, and he had taught her all that a student of his was required to understand—the foundations and assumptions of his esoteric system. She understood, of course, that he had only just begun
to breathe on his own again and that smoking was damaging, dangerous—it was almost certainly forbidden.

"You needn't tell me that it's a bad idea to smoke now. But it's
even worse not to smoke," he said to Rosie, when he saw her hesitate.

Of course she understood, having taken every last course he offered.

"So I went down to the vending machine and brought up six packs of Marlboros," she told me.

"If you hadn't done it, ten other messengers would have," I said.

"They sure enough would."

At the hospital his best students—the inner circle—came and went, gathered, chatted in the waiting room.

On the second day after release from intensive care, Ravelstein, who hadn't recovered the use of his legs, was once more on the telephone with friends in Paris, explaining why he would not be coming back just yet. The apartment had to be given up. His aristocratic landlords would have to be approached with tact to return the *dépôt de garanti*. Ten thousand dollars. Maybe they'd cough it up, maybe not. He could understand their feelings, he said. Those were the most beautiful, the most distinguished rooms he had ever lived in, he said.

Ravelstein didn't count on recovering his deposit, though he was highly connected in French academic circles. He had lots of important connections in France—and in Italy as well. He knew perfectly well that there was no legal way to recover his earnest money. "Especially in this instance, because the tenant is a Jew, and there's a Gobineau in the landlord's family tree. Those Gobineaus were famous Jew-haters. And I'm no mere Jew but, even worse, an American one—all the more dangerous to civilization as they see it. Anyway, they will let a Jew live on their street, but he *should* pay for it."

In an off moment, weakened by the disease, eyes only half open and in a voice in which the words were unclear and the tones had to carry most of the meaning—several days when his speech was like his narrowed gaze—he kept trying to tell me something. What he was trying to say at last became clear—that he was even now arranging for a BMW to be sent over.

"From Germany?"

So it seemed, though he didn't actually say that it was being shipped. I had the impression that it was already on a freighter in mid-Atlantic. Maybe even unloaded and being trucked to the Midwest.

"It's for Nikki," Ravelstein said. "He feels he should have something outstanding and entirely his own. You can see that, can't you, Chick? In addition, he may have to drop out of his Swiss school."

This was not put to me as a question. I could see it well enough. For one thing, if you were dressed—as Nikki was—by Versace, Ultimo, and Gucci, you didn't want to use public transportation. But having satisfied my quirky need for humor with such an observation, I was now able to be real. The reality was that Ravelstein had barely squeaked by, that he was still on what doctors called "life supports," that his lower body was still paralyzed, his legs were not working, and that if and when paralysis was overcome there were still other infections waiting to be reckoned with.

"Now tell me, thee-ah Chick, how do I look to you?"

"The face?"

"Face, head. You have a peculiar eye, Chick. And don't hold back."

"You look like a ripe honeydew melon, on the pillow."

He laughed. His eyes narrowed and glinted; he took a peculiar satisfaction in my mental ways. He saw this kind of remark as a sign of higher faculties in operation. About the car he said, "The agency was trying to sell me on some wine-colored BMW. I prefer the chestnut one. Over there is a chart of the colors—" He pointed, and when I handed it to him he flipped it open. Bar after bar of enamel strips. Soberly studying the samples, I said that the wine color wouldn't do.

"You're never wrong in a matter of taste. Nikki thinks so, too."

"That's nice, but I never thought he was noticing."

"The clothes you wear may not be the latest, but you did have the makings of a dude, Chick—in a former phase, and in a limited way. I remember your Chicago tailor, the one who did a suit for me."

"You hardly wore it."

"I wore it home."

"But then it disappeared."

"Nikki and I laughed ourselves silly over the cut of it. Perfect for Las Vegas or on a politician for the annual Democratic machine gathering at the Bismarck Hotel—don't be hurt, Chick."

"I'm not. I don't invest much sensitivity in my suits."

"Nikki always says your taste in shirts and neckties is perfect. Kisser & Asser."

"Of course, Kisser & Asser."

"Yes!" said Ravelstein, and closed his eyes with satisfaction.

"I don't want to tire you," I said.

"No, no." Abe's eyes were still shut. "I'm still alive to bandy wise-cracks. You do me more good than a dozen intravenous drips."

Yes, and he could rely on me. I was present, too, at the hospital window. *Ad sum,* as you would answer roll call at school—or *ab est,* as we said in unison when a seat was empty.

The city presented mile upon mile of late-autumn bareness—the cold hardening of the ground, the branching boulevards, the painted-desert look of the apartment houses, the paling green of the parks—the temperate zone and its seasons, cranking away. Winter coming.

When the telephone rang again I picked it up; I was going to screen him from callers. But the BMW woman was on the line and he wanted to talk to her. "Let's go through this checklist," he said to her. "You're sure we're going to get the stick-shift . . . ? Automatic transmission won't do."

With extras, the car would cost eighty thousand bucks.

"Of course there'll be safety bags for the passenger's seat as well as the driver's?"

". . . Now about the interior color—the kid-leather upholstery. The CD deck set in the trunk should be able to play six discs! Eight! Ten!

"And the door locking and unlocking with an electronic switch? We don't want to fuck around with keys. I can't give you a certified check, I'm in the hospital. I don't care if it is company policy. I have to have delivery no later than Thursday. Nikki—Mr. Tay Ling is arriving from Geneva Wednesday night. So all the paperwork has got to be done. No, as I thought I told you, I'm in my room at the hospital. Thee-ah thee-ah! one thing I can assure you is that it's not a mental hospital. You have my account number at Merrill Lynch. What? You certainly have done a fast credit check on me, Miss Sorabh—is it spelled *bh* or *hb*?"

There may have been as many as a dozen consultations daily. "Nikki is such a stickler," he said. "And why shouldn't everything be perfect? I want him to be pleased one hundred percent—the engine, the body, all the electronic stuff. Everything in place. Stabilizers equilibrated. It used to be the Harmonious Blacksmith—now it's the harmonious computers. There won't be any baroque operas in the new car. Only Chinese jazz, or whatever."

Nikki, as I well knew, was exacting. This was evident even from his casual relations with people. And it must follow with objects as well.

"I don't want to look as if I were taken in by BMW owing to this illness. I must try to anticipate how Nikki will react. In his quiet way, he's extremely fussy," said Ravelstein. "It's only natural. He shares my prosperity, of course. But not long ago he said how much he'd like a sign from me—some big gesture. It's not just my prosperity, it's *our* prosperity."

I didn't invite him to go into particulars. Since he and I were close friends, it was up to me to do my own thinking about Nikki's place in his life. I believed that I was alert enough to understand. Though maybe I wasn't. Ravelstein often made me doubt my abilities.

I said, "All the warranties you're getting, it would take a month to read them."

"You make it sound like the Stations of the Cross," Ravelstein said, smiling.

"You and Nikki are safe with this giant German corporation. It's like bourgeois royalty. I wonder, did they use slave labor during the war?"

Because his arms were wasted, Ravelstein's hands looked unnaturally big as he lit one of the cigarettes Rosamund had brought him. Then as he put it down in the ashtray and waved away the smoke, I was aware that someone had entered the room.

It was Dr. Schley—Ravelstein's cardiologist. He was my cardiologist too. Dr. Schley was short and slight, but his slightness was not

a sign of weakness. He was stern. He was backed by his seniority in
the hospital—its chief heart-man. He didn't say much. He didn't
have to.

"Do you realize, Mr. Ravelstein, that you're just out of intensive
care? Only hours ago you weren't even able to breathe. And now
you're pulling smoke into your weak lungs. This is most serious,"
Schley said, with a cold side-glance at me. I should not have allowed
Ravelstein to light up.

Dr. Schley, too, was entirely bald, white coated, and his stetho-
scope, sticking out of his pocket, was gripped like a slingshot by his
angry hand.

Ravelstein didn't answer. He declined to be intimidated—but he
wasn't yet strong enough to fight back. On the whole he cared little
for doctors. Doctors were the allies of the death-dreading bourgeoisie. He was not about to change his habits for any doctor, not
even for Schley, whom he respected. As Rosamund understood
when she went to buy the cigarettes, Abe would do what he had always done. He'd never play the valetudinarian.

"I ask you, Mr. Ravelstein, to give up your cigarettes until your
lungs are stronger."

Ravelstein answered nothing, he only nodded his head. But not
in agreement. He wasn't even looking at Dr. Schley—he looked
past him. Schley wasn't his primary physician. The primary was Dr.
Abern. But of course Schley was part of the team; more than that,
he was one of its leaders. As for me, Schley liked me well enough—
in my place. You would never hear Dr. Schley say as much, but if you
were any good at mental sonics you got the message soon enough.
Ravelstein was a major figure in the highest intellectual circles. It
wouldn't be too much to say that Ravelstein was genuinely impor-

tant. By contrast I was good enough, of my sort. But it was a far from important sort.

Generally Schley talked to me about keeping up the quinine level in my system to control my heartbeat. I was subject to fibrillations and sometimes short of breath. The big doses of Quinaglute he prescribed deafened you, I was to discover down the line. Anyway my minor cardiac complaint was virtually all that connected me to Schley. Ravelstein, on the other hand, fascinated him. He saw Ravelstein as a great fighter in the cultural and ideological wars. After Abe had given his sensational Harvard speech, telling the audience that they were elitists disguised as egalitarians—"Well!" Dr. Schley said to me. "Who else had the learning, the confidence, the authority to do this! And so easily, so naturally!"

As for Ravelstein, he would never simply *have* a doctor. He had to know what to think about everyone with whom he had to do. He had a relentless curiosity not only about the students he attracted but also tradespeople or high-fidelity engineers or dentists or investment counselors, barbers and, of course, physicians.

"Schley is the boss doctor here," he said. "The single most influential one. He's the one who makes policy. He polices all the departments and refers patients to his own people—just as he's done for me. But then there's his domestic life . . ."

"I never thought about his home life."

"Have you ever met his wife?"

"Never."

"Well, by all reports it's a women's kingdom over there. The wife and daughters are absolutely in control. His real life is here in the clinics and labs."

"Is that so? It's often the case with strict people. . . ."

"Like yourself, Chick. You ought to know, you've plenty of experience in that line."

I said, "One more case of the son of man having no place to lay his head."

"Well, don't go feeling sorry. You set it up yourself, all of it. Nothing to complain about," said Ravelstein.

I couldn't dispute this. All I could say was that the doctor had no friend, no Ravelstein, to set him straight.

"Poor Schley becomes more and more medically correct," Ravelstein went on. "His wife is a toughie, and then there are the two unmarried daughters. Activists, all three of them, busy with causes like feminism, environmentalism. So the doctor is a tyrant in the clinic and the odd man out at home."

"I made him furious too," I said. "A real friend would have taken your cigarette away!"

I wasn't telling Ravelstein anything he didn't know. He didn't miss much.

The BMW 740 was ready—delivered an hour before Nikki arrived. He came immediately to the hospital. Ravelstein was still unable to walk and had only the partial use of his arms and of his hands. He could smoke, he could dial numbers on the telephone—otherwise he was, in the French expression he preferred, *hors d'usage*. As soon as Nikki arrived, Rosamund and I left and waited outside.

After a time Nikki came out with tears on his face. He very seldom discussed Ravelstein with me or other friends. He accepted us because we had been vetted by Abe. We were the people Abe talked to about matters he, Nikki, was not interested in. Of course, Nikki had his own views of each and every one of us. And Abe had learned to take his judgments seriously.

"You have to go down right this minute and take possession of your new car," Rosamund said.

We went below with him and saw Nikki get behind the wheel. The company driver had waited and given him a briefing, Nikki later explained, about all the special features of the glamourous 740. I glanced at the switches and lights of the control panel—it looked like the cockpit of a fighter plane. The whole thing was beyond me—I couldn't have turned on the defroster or released the hood.

Ravelstein of course wanted to divert Nikki from the medical facts with this tremendous toy. He only partially succeeded. There was a certain pleasure in sliding into the driver's seat, but Nikki told me that he wouldn't be going back to Switzerland. All this was now on hold. He'd have to drop the hotel training course.

When the time came to go home, Abe said he didn't want to ride in an ambulance. He said that Nikki would drive him in the new 740. Dr. Schley's position was that since Ravelstein couldn't walk, couldn't sit up, he'd have to be wheeled out on a gurney. Abe said there was no need for gurneys or stretchers or ambulances. Students and friends would transfer him from a wheelchair to the 740.

Schley put his foot down on this. He wouldn't sign Abe out, he said. Abe submitted in the end and they lifted him, bedding and all, onto the gurney. He was silent throughout, but not sullen or rancorous. He didn't have the sullenness or moodiness of the sick.

The 740 was already garaged. A phone call would bring it to the door within minutes.

I was re-reading the Keynes memoirs that Ravelstein had recommended as the model I should follow. There was always a book to fill up the hours in the lounge of the intensive care unit, or when the patient was asleep or silently reflecting—seeming to sleep. While waiting for the ambulance I sat in the courtyard of Ravelstein's apartment building with Rosamund, reading J. M. Keynes.

The question at issue in Keynes's memoir was the release of gold by the Germans in 1919 to finance the purchase of food for the blockaded, starved cities. The commission charged with the execution of the Armistice convention had its seat at Spa, the fashionable watering place on the Belgian frontier, which had been the Grand Headquarters of the German Army. Ludendorff's villa was there, and the Kaiser's villa and Hindenburg's—you felt at once that Keynes was writing esoterically for his Bloomsbury intimates, not for the newspaper-reading masses.

The Belgian ground was haunted, he said. "The air was still charged with the emotions of that vast collapse. The spot was melancholy with the theatrical Teutonic melancholy of black pine woods." I was greatly interested to learn that Keynes held Richard Wagner directly responsible for World War I. "Evidently the Kaiser's conception of himself was so molded. And what was Hindenburg but the bass, and Ludendorff but the fat tenor of third-rate Wagnerian opera?"

There was, however, a danger that Germany might drift into Bolshevism. With starvation and disease rising, mortality figures were damaging to the Allies, Lloyd George told the Conference. Clemenceau in answering "saw that he must needs concede a good deal." "Must needs" was an expression that now had vanished, I told Rosamund.

But the French still objected to the German proposal to pay for their food in gold. Clemenceau claimed German gold for reparations. One of the French ministers, a Jew named Klotz, declared that the starving Germans should be allowed to pay for rations in any other way, but not in gold. It was impossible for him to go further without compromising his country's interests, "which (puffing himself out and attempting an appearance of dignity) had been placed in his charge."

Lloyd George—why am I drawn back to this again and again? I can't explain why I am so affected by it—now turned on M. Klotz with hatred, Keynes writes. "Do you know Klotz by sight?—a short, plump, heavy moustached Jew, but with an unsteady, roving eye, and his shoulders a little bent in an instinctive deprecation. Lloyd George had always hated and despised him. And now saw in a twinkling that he could kill him. Women and children were starving, he cried, and here was M. Klotz prating and prating of his 'gooold.' He leant forward and with a gesture of his hands indicated to everyone the image of a hideous Jew clutching a money bag. His eyes flashed and the words came out with contempt so violent that he seemed almost to be spitting at him. The anti-Semitism, not far below the surface in such an assemblage as that one, was up in the heart of everyone. Everyone looked at Klotz with a momentary contempt and hatred; the poor man was bent over his seat, visibly cowering. . . . Then, turning, he [Lloyd George] called on Clemenceau to put a stop to these obstructive tactics; otherwise, he cried, M. Klotz would rank with Lenin and Trotsky among those who had spread Bolshevism in Europe. The Prime Minister ceased. All round the room you could see each one grinning and whispering to his neighbor 'Klotsky.'"

Another Jew, this one in the service of the German government, was Dr. Melchior. He was not so well connected with his delegation as Keynes; Keynes was at the side of Lloyd George and against Herbert Hoover whenever breadstuffs, pork products, or financial arrangements were discussed. Melchior seemed to feel as Keynes did. In Keynes's account Melchior is "staring, heavy lidded, helpless looking . . . like an honorable animal in pain. Couldn't we break down the empty formalities of this Conference, the three-barred gate of triple interpretations, and talk about the truth and the reality like sane and sensible persons?"

Germany was hungry, France had almost bled to death. The English and the Americans really intended to furnish food. There were tons of pork waiting for Herbert Hoover to order delivery to begin. "I allowed that our recent actions had not been such as to lead him to trust in our sincerity; but I begged him [Melchior] to believe that I, at least, at that moment, was sincere and truthful. He was as much moved as I was, and I think he believed me. We both stood all through the interview. In a sort of way I was in love with him. . . . He would speak with Weimar on the telephone and would urge them to give him some discretion. . . . He spoke with the passionate pessimism of a Jew."

The place where I sat reading, where Rosamund and I waited for the ambulance to bring Ravelstein home, was a small courtyard inside the wrought-iron gates. A stone pool, shrubs, grass—there were even shade-flowers. Frogs and toads would have done well here, but you'd have had to import them. Where would they have come from? There were no frogs in the miles of rubble that surrounded this sanctuary. The courtyard was something like a decompressing chamber. For some of the professor-tenants it may have recalled the grotto-retreats built by English gentlemen in the eighteenth century. You wanted some protection from the brute facts. To be fully aware of both the sanctuary and the slum, you had to be a Ravelstein. "Out *there,*" he would say, laughing, "the cops will tell you not to stop at a red light. In no-man's-land, it could be the end of you to stop." You must not be swallowed up by the history of your own time, Ravelstein often would say. He quoted Schiller to the same effect: "Live with your century but do not be its creature."

The architect who put a little Alhambra arcade here, with water pipes and shade plants had much the same idea: "Live in this city but don't belong to it."

Rosamund, who was sitting beside me on the edge of the stone basin, did not feel shut out when I was reading.

It had taken Ravelstein some time to get used to seeing Rosamund and me as a married pair. There was a kind of oddity about that because he took an unusual interest in his students, and Rosamund was one of them. He would have said, if asked about this, that given the sort of education they were getting, with its unusual emphasis "on the affects"—on love, not to beat around the bush—it would have been irresponsible to pretend that the teaching could be separated from the binding of souls. That was his old-fashioned way of putting it. Naturally there was a Greek word for it, and I can't be expected to remember every Greek word I heard from him. Eros was a *daimon,* one's genius or demon provided by Zeus as a compensation for the cruel breaking up of the original androgynous human whole. I'm sure I've got that part of the Aristophanic sex-myth straight. With the help of Eros we go on, each of us, looking for his missing half. Ravelstein was in real earnest about this quest, driven by longing. Not everyone feels that longing, or acknowledges it if he does feel it. In literature Antony and Cleopatra had it, Romeo and Juliet had it. Closer to our own time Anna Karenina and Emma Bovary had it, Stendhal's Madame de Rênal in her simplicity and innocence had it. And of course others, untaught, untouched by open recognition have it in some obscure form. This was what Ravelstein was continually on the watch for, and with such a preoccupation he was only a step from arranging matches. Doing the best that could be done with these powerful but incomplete needs. A good palliative for the not-always-conscious pain of longing had a significant importance of its own. We have to keep life going, one way or another. Marriages must be made. In adultery men and women hope for a brief reprieve from the lifelong pain of privation. What made adultery a venial sin in Ravelstein's judgment was that the pain of our longings drives us so mercilessly. "Souls Without Longing" had been the working title of his famous book. But for most of mankind the longings have, one way or another, been eliminated.

—How have I gotten so far afield?

I am bound as an honest observer to make plain how Ravelstein operated. If he cared about you it was in this perspective that he would sketch you. You wouldn't have believed how much thought he devoted to each and every case, the closeness with which he observed the students he had accepted for higher or esoteric training, those willing to break with the orthodox social science majority which dominated the profession. If students followed Ravelstein, they would find jobs hard to get. So you had to think how to provide for the young people who were chosen. Professionally speaking, they had made an erratic choice. Ravelstein often asked my opinion. "What if Smith were to pair up with Sarah? He's got some queer tendencies but he'll never be a queer. Now Sarah is a very serious young woman—disciplined, hard-working, loves her books. No genius but she's got a lot going for her. She may have just the touch of masculinity that would make young Smith happy."

He was so accustomed to thinking up arrangements of this sort that he apparently had had something in mind for me after Vela divorced me. My mistakes were so clear that I couldn't be trusted to do anything right. He had accurately prophesied seven or eight years ago, "Vela will soon be through with you. She's off to conferences all over the world. She's never home for as much as a week. Whereas you've got the uxorious tendency, Chick. And all you've got to live with now are her clothes hanging in the closet. It's only to be respectable that she needs a husband. I don't think men are her top preference. But she's an odd case; she's got the makings of a beauty but she's not a beauty, no matter how she dresses and makes up. Now you as an artist, Chick, spotted her as having something to do with beauty. It's a fact that she has beautiful eyes but, closely looked at, she's got some sort of European military correctness about her. And when she inspects you, you just don't make the grade with her. Mentally speaking, she comes toward you but then walks away as fast as her high heels will carry her. She's an odd one, Chick. But you're pretty odd yourself. Artists fall in love, of course, but love isn't their primary gift. They love their high function, the use of their genius, not actual women. They have their own sort of driving force. Now Goethe of course had his *daimon,* he talked about it to Eckermann all the time. And in old age he fell in love with a very beautiful young thing. But of course this falling in love was *dérisoire*—a pure absurdity . . ."

This was his way of laying open a subject—not entirely flattering, but then he never flattered anyone, nor did he level with you in order to put you down. He simply believed that a willingness to let the self-esteem-structure be attacked and burned to the ground was a measure of your seriousness. A man should be able to hear, and to bear, the worst that could be said of him.

But some time before, in her wonderfully polished but also clumsy not-of-this-world way, Vela had already begun divorce proceedings. It appeared that she had retained a lawyer as much as a year earlier. This lawyer, a woman who belonged to a tremendous downtown law firm, knew to a nickel what my assets were, and Vela's demand was for twenty-five percent of my bank account, tax-exempt. She went downtown regularly to have her hair and her eyebrows done and to shop for dresses and shoes. Often she lunched with a friend—or with her lawyer.

We had no domestic routines at all. What we had was a loose arrangement—a household, not the locus of married love or even affection. When supplies ran low, Vela went to the supermarket and bought up a storm—apples, grapefruits, meats for the freezer, cakes, tapioca puddings for dessert, canned tuna and tomato herrings, onions, rice, dry breakfast cereals, bananas, salad greens, cantaloupes. I tried several times to teach her how to choose a melon by sniffing it at the bottom, but evidently she didn't want to be seen doing anything out of line for a person of beauty and delicacy. She bought bread and rolls, soap powder for the dishwasher, steel wool for the pots. Several hundred dollars' worth of groceries were then delivered in cardboard boxes. After shopping, she didn't return to the apartment but drove on to the university. I took delivery at home and stacked the fridge and the kitchen shelves. I stomped the cartons flat and took them down in the elevator. I was on friendly terms with the super and didn't want to bother him with the trash.

Kerrigan, the poet and translator who lived with his mother-in-law a floor above us, asked me one day why I had to dispose of my own junk and when I explained my relationship to the superintendent he said, "Everybody but you gets respected." My answer was that this might be true but that the super had to be spared and that the man tacitly indicated that he needed his dignity to be acknowledged. And that I would rather lug the flattened cartons below than have to think about his demand for esteem.

Toward the last, without realizing how near the end-zone was, I was still trying to puzzle out Vela, to get a handle on her motives. She preferred deeds to words, conceding that she couldn't compete with me verbally, and one day when I was reading a book (my regular diet of words) she wandered into the room entirely nude, came to my bedside and rubbed her pubic hair on my cheekbone. When I responded as she must have known that I would, she turned and left me with an air of having made her point. She had won hands down without having to speak a word. Her body spoke for her, and very effectively too, saying that the end was near.

There was nothing in the book I had been reading in bed that was of the slightest use to me. Nor could I go in pursuit of Vela to ask, "What does this behavior mean?" The large apartment was divided into zones—she had hers, I had mine. I'd have to go looking for her—and she would anyway refuse to discuss the message just delivered.

So I turned to Ravelstein. I phoned to say that I needed to talk to him right away and I drove across the city, a distance of twelve miles. I had worked this out—eight blocks to the mile as laid out by the original planners or founders.

Arriving, I for once accepted Ravelstein's offer of a cup of his coffee. I needed something strong to drink. I knew of course what a passion he had for the kind of incident I was about to describe. The freaky improvisations of creatures under stress—the more bumptious they were, the more he cherished them.

"In the nude, hey? She was making a statement, as they say. And what was your impression? What was she telling you in her untutored way?"

"It's my impression that she was saying she was no longer available."

"The kiss-off, eh? And you weren't expecting it—or were you, in your bones, aware it was coming?"

"Certainly I saw it coming. She and I could never make a go of it."

"But I wonder whether there are facts which might have escaped you, Chick. I don't blame you for demanding that she should behave as a wife ought, according to your lights. But they have lights, too, the women. She has a considerable reputation in her own field. She's a high-grade scientist, they tell me, and she may not feel like cooking your dinner—clocking in at five o'clock to peel the potatoes."

"She grew up in a starving country . . ."

"In the eyes of the world it's a big deal to be a chaos physicist—I don't know what it's about but it's considered highly prestigious. Only *you* give her no credit."

"She came to tell me that her body would no longer be available. To communicate any considerable matter she preferred actions to words. When she broke the news of our decision to marry to her mother, she waited until boarding time at the airport the day of Mama's return flight to Europe and at the last possible moment said, 'I've decided to marry Chick.' The old girl hated me. Vela let it be thought that she loved her mama, but in fact she crossed her in every way possible."

"But the opposite is true?" Ravelstein asked.

"I don't know the true answer, nor does anyone else know it. People go to the trouble of organizing a view of themselves and the view gives them the consistency or the appearance of consistency society seems to require. But Vela really has no organized view. . . ."

"Okay, okay," said Ravelstein. "But your idea was that she would come to love you. She'd love you because you are lovable. But this Vela of yours reserves her intellect for physics. The idea of leading a warm family life is her number one antipremise. So from this we pass to the supermarket, where Vela buys a few hundred dollars' worth of chow and has it delivered in boxes by young criminals who have parole officers keeping an eye on them. You can cook this shit yourself, and eat it by your lonesome, and then scrub the pots. Just as your mother did after feeding her family a real meal, cooked with love. You thought that if you could get her to prepare your dinners with love she'd come to love you. So her comment on this is satirical; she sends you the groceries. Just as she belongs to a different universe altogether. And you belong to a third universe, the vanishing one of old-fashioned Jews. The soul of another is a dark forest, as the Russians say . . . you're fond of Russian sayings."

"Not just now, I'm not."

"Well, I grant you the Russians are not so humane as they want us to think. All those Eastern empires are police controlled."

"And the dark forest is the soul, but you can't expect to take refuge from the GPU there. I'm not in the mood for wit, though."

"I know," said Ravelstein. "She notified you that you have no more access to her body. Your lease has expired. But it was never meant to be permanent. People can't be expected to live without love or the simulacrum of love. A nice friendly sexual connection is what most have to settle for."

I didn't expect Vela to appear in court when the formalities were completed, but turn up she did in a high-buttoned jacket, more like heraldry than feminine dress, brass buttons from the throat to the knees, with the makeup and tight hair of a ballroom dancer. It is probably impossible to convey the messages she was emitting. I had had my chance, given with extraordinary queenly generosity, and it was obvious that I just didn't have what it took.

She had worked out an esoteric rationality which was utterly unknowable but based on eighteen-karat principles. All the same there was a lame side to her queenliness. If you thought you could say where she was coming from, you were mistaken. "It may have seemed that such a man (Chick) could be my husband, but that was an error—Q.E.D." She walked away in her curious stride, each step forward a dig—only the toes were involved. The heels were on their own. This was not in the slightest grotesque. It was curiously expressive, but no one would ever be able to say what it meant.

Rosamund had not been one of Ravelstein's stars but very good in her way. "She does the work as well as anybody. Her Greek is more than adequate, and she doesn't miss a thing, understands the texts perfectly well. Very nervous and unsure about herself. And she's very attractive, isn't she. Not a voluptuary type but genuinely pretty."

He didn't know it, but I had been, for once, ahead of him. I wasn't going to have Ravelstein vet Rosamund for me. I couldn't let him arrange my marriage as he did for his students. If he lacked all feeling for you, he didn't give a damn what you did. But if you were one of his friends it was a bad idea, he thought, for you to take things into your own hands. It troubled him greatly to be kept in the dark on any matter by his friends—especially by those he saw daily.

The ambulance bringing Ravelstein home from the hospital came softly to the curb, and Rosamund and I stood up. I closed the book I had been reading on the letter Keynes had written to his mother about his duties as Deputy for the Chancellor of the Exchequer on the Supreme Economic Council. In silence the wheeled stretcher came by quickly and I saw the smooth naked melon of Ravelstein's head preceding us through the Alhambra arches of the arcade and beyond the shade plants and the water trickling in the mossy basin. Nikki came hurrying after the stretcher through the brass-and-glass doors.

Rosamund and I took the passenger elevator to the top of the building. Mischievous kids pressed all the buttons so that often you stopped at every floor. The continual opening and closing of doors made a fifteen-minute trip of it, and when we reached the top Ravelstein was already in bed—but not in his four-poster. A hospital bed had been ordered, and above it a mechanic was installing a large triangle, equilateral, of tubular stainless steel. Ravelstein could use it to shift his weight. When he had to move to a chair for physical therapy, the base of the triangle was slipped under his thighs. As he weakly gripped the steel tubing the bosun's rig was raised very gradually by the small whirring machine at the foot of the bed. Suddenly you saw his wasted legs being drawn up, out of the sheets. And because he couldn't fully open his eyelids, the look of alarm was only half formed.

He might have been musing over matter, over the physical management of life, the innumerable ways there were to be damaged,
wounded, even killed—an unusual line of thought for him. A nurse
had suddenly appeared and the mechanic (a technician from the
hospital) stood by as her backup. Ravelstein was swung over the
side of the bed and lowered, very slowly, into the wheelchair. Dr.
Schley's aim was to get Abe on his feet to rebuild his muscles. The
long, long legs had no calves and on the white inner arms you could
see the veins. You couldn't help but think of the contaminated blood
in them. While the nurse tried to cover his genitals, he seemed to be
musing over a pressing question—perhaps whether it made sense to
struggle so hard for existence. It didn't, but he struggled nevertheless. He gripped the steel, which was probably very cold, the two
fists were close to his big ears, near the occipital hair that stuck out,
below the bald line. There are bald heads that proclaim their
strength. Ravelstein's head had been like that. But now it had become the vulnerable kind. I believe he knew what a picture he
made, "piped over the side" in a naval sort of rig, wide open to ter-
ror—to ridiculous hysteria. By now, however, he was detached
from his triangle and already sitting in the wheelchair; the triangle
slipped out from under him, and Nikki took him on a tour of the
flat. Rosamund and I followed from room to room.

Nothing had been disturbed. Maintaining the apartment were
the two ladies—the Polish woman Wadja, who did the real cleaning on Tuesdays, and black Mrs. Ruby Tyson (far too old for real
work), who let herself in on Fridays. Mrs. Tyson's function was to
keep up the dignity of the households where she worked. To
Wadja, Ravelstein was just another loud Jew—her savage imagination had pictured the money he controlled, and he was rowdy,
incomprehensible. Ruby understood him better: he was a professor,

a mysterious white personage. As nearly as any honky could, he took into account her problems with her prostitute daughter, her jailed criminal son, and with the other son whose HIV troubles and scrambled wives and children were too complicated to describe. On quiet afternoons he, Ravelstein, would sometimes listen, sympathetic, half dreaming, to Ruby Tyson's stories—really beyond his reach or interests. The old woman presented herself as quiet, dignified, and sadly reserved. You can imagine how Ravelstein would have listened; the chaos the life of such people must be. This good old woman had learned the white game from the deans, provosts, and other academic bureaucrats whose beds she made, and whose parlors she dusted. And, of course, their family problems, the esoteric, psychiatric secrets of their wives, she would tell Ravelstein by the hour. In his apartment she did nothing; most of the time for which he was charged she sat on a bar stool in the kitchen. Now and then she climbed down and baked a pie. The stout, strong, aggressive Wadja attended to the scrubbing and scouring. It was Wadja who moved the furniture, cleaned the toilets, ran the vacuum, scoured the pots, washed the crystal. Easily overheated, she took off her dress and her slip. She worked in a giant bra and swelling Zouave bloomers.

At the sight of him in the wheelchair Wadja's face was torn between compassion and irony—a cocked eyebrow. A mass of suspended comment slid down the pug-nosed slope of her face. Well, it was very bad! But then, he was a Jew as well. You sometimes heard her muttering "Moishala" as she wiped or polished objects. Feeble in the earliest days, Ravelstein greeted her with a lifted forefinger, saying to Nikki, "For God's sake, keep her away from the Lalique."

"She swishes the wine glasses under the tap," Ravelstein said to me. "She chips them on the faucet. I showed her the damage. She started to weep. She said she'd buy me new glasses from Woolworth's. I said, 'You know what those Lalique glasses cost?' When I named a figure, she grinned. She said, 'You jokum, Mister.'"

"You told her the price?"

"You can't help thinking these women are just as rough with men's penises," he would say. "Just imagine—if they were glass."

A certain amount of documentation might be offered at this point to show what I was to Ravelstein and Ravelstein to me. This was never altogether clear to either of us—the principals. Ravelstein would have seen no point in talking around this. He said he was more than satisfied that I could follow perfectly well everything that was said. When he was sick, we saw each other daily and we also had long telephone conversations as close friends should. We were close friends—what else needs to be added? In my desk drawers I find folders containing pages and pages about Ravelstein. But these data only *seem* to go into the subject. There are no acceptable modern terms for the discussion of friendship or other higher forms of interdependence. Man is a creature who has something to say about everything under the sun.

Ravelstein was willing to lay it all out for me. Now why did he bother to tell me such things, this large Jewish man from Dayton, Ohio? Because it very urgently needed to be said. He was HIV-positive, he was dying of complications from it. Weakened, he became the host of an endless list of infections. Still he insisted on telling me over and over again what love was—the neediness, the awareness of incompleteness, the longing for wholeness, and how the pains of Eros were joined to the most ecstatic pleasures.

This is as good a moment as I will ever find to recall that, from my side, I was free to confess to Ravelstein what I couldn't tell anyone else, to describe my weaknesses, my corrupt shameful secrets, and the cover-ups that drain your strength. As often as not he thought my confessions were wildly funny. Funniest of all were the thought-murders. Perhaps I gave them a comic twist, unwittingly. Anyway, he thought they were uproarious and he said, "Did you ever read Dr. Theodore Reik, the famous Kraut psychoanalyst? He said a thought-murder a day keeps the psychiatrist away."

That I was hard on myself, Ravelstein took, however, to be a favorable sign. Self-knowledge called for severity, and I was always willing to go to the mat with that protean monster, the self, so there was hope for me. But I would have liked to go further. My feeling was that you couldn't be known thoroughly unless you found a way to communicate certain "incommunicables"—your private metaphysics. My way of approaching this was that before you were born you had never seen the life of this world. To grasp this mystery, the world, was the occult challenge. You came into a fully developed and articulated reality from nowhere, from nonbeing or primal oblivion. You had never seen life before. In the interval of light between the darkness in which you awaited first birth and then the darkness of death that would receive you, you must make what you could of reality, which was in a state of highly advanced development. I had waited for millennia to see this. Then when I had learned to walk—in the kitchen—I was sent down into the street to inspect it more closely. One of my first impressions was of the huge utility-pole timbers that lined the street. They were beaver-colored, soft and rotted. On their crosspieces or multiple arms they carried many wires or cables in an endless falling relay, soaring, falling again and soaring. On the fixed sag and flow of the cables the sparrows sat, flew off, came back to rest. Along the sidewalks, the faded bricks revealed their original red at sunset. You rarely saw an automobile in those days. What you saw were hansom cabs, ice wagons, beer drays, and the huge horses that pulled them. I knew people by their faces—red, white, wrinkled, spotted, or smooth; smiling or violent or furious—their eyes, mouths, noses, voices, feet, and gestures. How they bent down to amuse or question or tease or affectionately torment a small boy.

God appeared very early to me. His hair was parted down the middle. I understood that we were related because he had made Adam in his own image, breathed life into him. My eldest brother also combed his hair in the same style. Between the senior brother and me there was another brother. Senior to all of us was our sister. Anyway . . . this was the world. I had never seen it before. Its first gift was the gift of itself. Objects gathered you to themselves and held you by a magnetic imperative that was simply there. It was a privilege to be permitted to see—to see, touch, hear. This would not have been impossible to describe to Ravelstein. But he would have answered dismissively that Rousseau had already covered the same turf in his *Confessions* or his *Reveries of a Solitary Walker.* I didn't feel like having these first epistemological impressions anticipated or dismissed. For seventy-odd years I had seen reality under these same signs. I had the feeling, too, that I had to wait for thousands of years to see, hear, smell, and touch these mysterious phenomena—

to take my turn in life before disappearing again when my time was up. I might have said to Ravelstein, "It was my one turn to live." But he was too close to death to be spoken to in such terms and I had to surrender my wish to make myself fully known to him by describing my intimate metaphysics. Only a small number of special souls have ever found a way to receive such revelations.

Further childish penetrations of the external world: On Roy Street in Montreal a dray horse has fallen down on the icy pavement. The air is as dark as a gray coat-lining. A smaller animal might have found its feet, but this beast with its huge haunches could only work his hoofs in the air. The long-haired Percheron with startled eyes and staring veins will need a giant to save him, but on the corner a crowd of small men can only call out suggestions. They tell the cop he's lucky the horse fell on Roy Street, easier to write in his report than Lagauchettierre. Then there is a strange and endless procession of schoolgirls marching by twos in black uniform dresses. Their faces white enough to be tubercular. The nuns who oversee them keep their hands warm within their sleeves. The puddles in this dirt street are deep and carry a skim of ice.

In children this impression—real reality—is tolerated by adults. Up to a certain age nothing can be done about it. In well-to-do families it lasts longer, perhaps. But Ravelstein might have argued that there was a danger of self-indulgence in it. Either you continue to live in epiphanies or you shake them off and take up trades and tasks, you adopt rational principles and concern yourself with society, or politics. Then the sense of having come from "elsewhere" vanishes. In Platonic theory all you know is recollected from an earlier existence elsewhere. In my case, Ravelstein's opinion was that distinctiveness of observation had gone much further than it should and was being cultivated for its own strange sake. Mankind had first claim on our attention and I indulged my "personal metaphysics" too much, he thought. His severity did me good. I didn't have it in me at my time of life to change, but it was an excellent thing, I thought, to have my faults and failings pointed out by someone who cared about me. I had no intention, however, of removing, by critical surgery, the metaphysical lenses I was born with.

This is one of the traps that a liberal society sets for us—it keeps us childish. Abe would probably have said, "It's up to you to make a choice. Either you continue to see as a child, or else."

So once again Ravelstein was recovering from still another sickness and learning for what seemed the tenth time how to sit up. Nikki learned to operate the triangle-lift, and when Ravelstein began to improve Rosamund and I followed Nikki as he guided the wheelchair. Ravelstein with his eyes half shut dropped his head to one side. With Nikki pushing he rolled through the large apartment—meant for happier, more normal souls. But this was his kingdom, with all its possessions.

Rosamund, with tears in her eyes, asked me whether he would ever be himself again.

"Can he fight off the Guillain-Barré? I'd say the odds are on his side," I said. "Last year, he had the shingles—herpes something-or-other. He fought those shingles off. That one, he won."

"But how many times can you do that?"

"Everything is just as you left it," Nikki was saying to Ravelstein.

The carpets and hangings, Lalique fixtures, pictures, books, and compact discs. He had sold his collection of old phonograph records, a large and choice one, to keep pace with technological advances. He had CD catalogues arriving from London, Paris,

Prague, and Moscow offering the latest Baroque recordings. The telephones of what Nikki and I called the "command post" were disconnected. Only the instrument in Nikki's bedroom was, as he said, "operational." In this city of millions there couldn't have been another apartment like this one—with priceless antique carpets everywhere and, on the kitchen sink, a hissing espresso machine of commercial size. But Ravelstein could no longer operate it. Over the mantelpiece Judith was still holding the head of Holofernes by the hair. His mouth open. Her eyes turned to heaven. The painter wanted you to think of Judith as the simple daughter of Zion, a natural chaste beauty, even though she has just cut off a fellow's head. What was Ravelstein's view of all this? There were very few indications in his private quarters of Ravelstein's sexual preferences. One had no reason, in any respect, to suspect him of irregularities of the commoner sort—the outlandish seductive behaviors of old-fashioned gay men. He couldn't bear the fluttering of effeminate men.

On these wheelchair tours of his apartment what he was feeling was stingingly apparent: What will happen to all this when I am gone? There's nothing that I can take with me into the grave. These beautiful objects which I bought in Japan, in Europe, and New York, far and wide, with so many deliberations and discussions with experts and friends. . . . Yes, Ravelstein was going down. You might not have guessed, seeing him in his rolling chair, tucked into the plaid with a wide stooped back and the honeydew-melon head tipped far to the side, how physically impressive he was, and how little his quirks, tics, and idiosyncrasies, and recent infections counted. Years ago, visiting my country house in New Hampshire, Ravelstein asked whether I had any proprietary feeling for the fieldstone house, the old maples and hickory trees, the gardens. The truthful answer was that though I liked them all well enough, I did not identify myself as the owner of these acres and objects. So that if the worst were to happen and a local armed militia were to descend on me and drive me out as a Jewish alien, their offense mainly would be against the Jew, not against the landowner. And in such a case my concern would be for the U.S. Constitution, not for my investment. The rooms, the rocks, the vegetation had no hold on my vital organs. If I were to lose it, I'd live on elsewhere. But if the Constitution, the legal foundation of it all, were to be destroyed, we would return to the primal chaos, he used to warn me.

On that visit, Ravelstein had come down to see me from Hanover on Interstate 91, risking his life in a rented car. He was far too uncoordinated to be safe on the highways—he jittered at the wheel. He had no connection with vehicles except as a passenger, and was too nervous. And he disliked the country.

He said, repeating the opinion of Socrates in the *Phaedrus,* that a tree, so beautiful to look at, never spoke a word and that conversation was possible only in the city, between men. Because he loved to talk, to think while talking, to lean backward while the bath of ideas overflowed—he instructed, examined, debated, put down errors, celebrated first principles, mixing his Greek with a running translation and stammering madly, laughing as he embroidered his expositions with Jewish jokes.

In the country he never set off on his own across a field. He *looked* the woods and meadows over but had no other business with them. Somehow Rousseau, who was so fond of fields and woods, was at the back of Abe's mind. Rousseau botanized. Plants, however, were not Ravelstein's dish. He'd eat a salad but he couldn't see the point of meditating on it.

He had come to the country to see me, and the visit was a concession to my unaccountable taste for remoteness and solitude. Why
did I want to bury myself in the woods? It was a safe assumption
that he had examined my motives from more angles than I could
ever think up if I brooded over them for an aeon. It is also possible
that he was curious about my then-wife Vela—those were the pre-
Rosamund days—still trying to understand why I had married such
a woman. Now *there* was a question for you. He had real intelligence, you see, a working, persistent mind, whereas I was only occasionally, fitfully, intelligent. What he thought out, and thought
through, sat upon a foundation of tested principles. —How shall I
put it? . . . As birds went he was an eagle, while I was something
like a flycatcher.

He knew, however, that I could understand his principles—they
didn't even need to be explained to me. If he had a single illusion it
was that somehow I was capable of accepting correction, and he
was a teacher, you see. That was his vocation—he taught. We are a
people of teachers. For millennia, Jews have taught and been
taught. Without teaching, Jewry was an impossibility. Ravelstein
had been a pupil or, if you prefer, a disciple of Davarr. You may not
have heard of this formidable philosopher. His admirers say that he
is a philosopher in the classical sense of the term. I am no judge of
such things. Philosophy is hard work. My own interests lie in a different direction altogether. Within my mental limits I think of the
late Davarr with respect. Ravelstein talked so much about him that
in the end I was obliged to read some of his books. It had to be done
if I was to understand what Abe was all about. I used to run into
Davarr on the street, and it was hard to imagine that this slight person, triply abstracted, mild goggles covering his fiery judgments,

was the demon heretic hated by academics everywhere in the U.S. and even abroad. As one of Davarr's chief representatives, Ravelstein was hated, too. But he didn't at all mind being the enemy. He was anything but faint-hearted. I didn't much care for professors as a class. They haven't had much to offer us in the unbearable century now ending. So I thought, or used to think.

It is pleasant to consider the week of Ravelstein's country visit. Quiet New England in long, narrow frames—sunlight, greenery, the bed of orange-red poppies next to the red-and-white peonies.

Glancing through the venetian blinds (he separated and widened the slats with shaking fingers) he saw the blossoms—just then the azaleas were coming into bloom—and found it all very well but the drama of the season lacked real interest. Not to be compared to the human drama.

He asked, "Is your wife always like this?"

"Like what?"

"'*What,*' the man says. Fourteen hours a day bolt upright with her books and papers, Vela shut away in her country-cupboard room."

"I see what you mean. Yes. That's the way she is about her chaos physics."

"To sit without budging—without even breathing. You never see her breathe at all. How does she manage not to suffocate?"

"She's preparing her paper. She's supposed to attend a conference to comment on somebody's research."

"She must catch up on her breathing—in snatches. I've watched her," said Ravelstein, "and I don't think she inhales except in an underground way."

Of course he was exaggerating. But there were facts to support him. Moreover, he had maneuvered me into accepting his way of speaking about her. Before I could consider whether to agree or disagree he had already persuaded me. What he was suggesting was that I didn't have to accept Vela's behavior. When we went to the country she locked herself up in her room. Two solitudes were then created. That was what our summers in New England were like: under one sun, on one planet, there were these two separate existences. Vela was especially beautiful when she was silent. Silent, she seemed to be praying to her beauty. Ravelstein may have been aware of this.

He came to New Hampshire to be with me very briefly, and he immediately understood what I had gotten into. He detested the rural scene, but for my sake he put his life on hold. He didn't like leaving his city switchboard command post. To be cut off from his informants in Washington and Paris, from his students, the people he had trained, the band of brothers, the initiates, the happy few made him extremely uncomfortable.

"So this is how you spend your summers?" he said.

As often as possible he went to Paris for a week or, even better, for a month. Paris, he granted, was no longer what it used to be. Nevertheless he often quoted Balzac's statement that no event anywhere in the world *was* an event until it was observed, judged, and certified by Paris. Still, the good old days were gone. Czarinas and kings no longer imported poets or philosophers from Paris. When foreigners like Ravelstein spoke to a French audience on Rousseau, the lecture hall was packed. One could say that genius was still welcome in France. But very few French intellectuals got high marks from Abe Ravelstein. He did not care for foolish anti-Americanism. He had no need to be loved or pampered by Parisians. On the whole, he liked their wickedness more than their civility.

Paris (this is an important aside) was where Abe Ravelstein and Vela had their first falling out. He was there when she and I flew in to accept a prize given to foreign writers. We were staying at the Pont Royal Hotel. Impatient, in high spirits, keen to see me, Ravelstein called out from the anteroom and without waiting for an answer he rushed in. He intended to hug me—or Vela, if she should happen to be first. But she was in her slip and she wheeled round and ran, slamming the bathroom door. But Abe and I, happy to see each other again after so many months, hardly gave a thought to Vela, or to Ravelstein's impropriety in barging into the bedroom. He should at least have knocked. It was *her* bedroom, as she was to remind me.

I might have known from the dainty anger of her running that Ravelstein was guilty of an outrage. I was unwilling to take her notions of good conduct into account. She said afterward that she could never forgive him for blundering into her room. Why did he rush in without warning, before she was dressed?

"Well, he's impetuous," I said. "With a man like Ravelstein it's . . . it's one of his charms that he acts on impulse. . . ."

This didn't soften Vela. Every word I spoke to explain Ravelstein or to defend him went immediately into her retaliation stockpile to be fired back at me. "I didn't come to Paris to see your pals," she said. "Or to have them walk in on me when I'm half naked."

"You show more of yourself at the beach," I said. "In what the fashion minimalists call a bathing suit."

Vela dismissed this, too. "It's a different context and you have a right to make preparations. You talk to me in a very superior way, as if you are putting me down as an ignorant woman. You should please remember that I stand as high in my field as you do in yours."

"Of course you do. And even higher," I said.

I am accustomed to being downgraded by businesspeople, law-yers, engineers, Washington hotshots, various scientists. Even their secretaries, who get their notions of what matters from television, hide their smiles behind their hands and give one another the high sign when I turn up—some incomprehensible goofball.

So I allowed Vela to be as superior as she pleased, while Ravel-stein said I should have more proper pride and that it was phony of me to be so meek. But I wasn't inclined to go out of my way to de-fer to so many critics. I had a good grasp of reality and of my defects. I permanently kept in mind the approach of Death, who might at any time loom up before you.

Anyway, I should have anticipated that Vela would make a big thing of Ravelstein's "impropriety." She had been preparing to have it out with me over Abe, and his barging into our bedroom at the hotel gave her just the opening she was waiting for.

"I don't want to see him here again," she said. "I ask you also to remember that you promised to take me to Chartres."

"I said that I would. And of course I will take you—I mean, we'll go there together."

"And let's invite the Grielescus. They're old friends. Professor Grielescu will join us. Nanette wouldn't—she stopped taking such trips long ago. She doesn't like to be seen by daylight."

I had noted this myself. Mme. Grielescu had been a glamourous lady in her time one of those *jeunes filles en fleur* you read about long ago. Grielescu was a famous scholar, not exactly a follower of Jung—but not exactly *not* a Jungian. He was a hard one to place.

Ravelstein, who didn't bring wild charges against anybody, said that Grielescu was mentioned, by scholars who specialized in such things, as an Iron Guardist connected with the Romanian prewar fascist government. He had been a foreign service cultural official in the Nazi regime in Bucharest. "You don't like to think of such things, Chick," said Ravelstein. "And you're married to a woman who scares you. Of course you'll say she's a political ignoramus."

"About politics she understands very little. . . ."

"Naturally, she believes that a scientist must be above and beyond such stuff. But these are her pals. We may as well look straight at the facts."

I said, "I will admit that Radu Grielescu sets the standards for male conduct in those East European circles."

"You mean the courtly gentleman bullshit."

"Yes, that's more or less it. The considerate man, the only right kind, remembers birthdays, honeymoons, and other tender anniversaries. You have to kiss the ladies' hands, send them roses; you cringe, move back the chairs, you rush to open doors and make arrangements with the maître d'. In that set, the women expect to be petted, idolized, deferred to, or romanced."

"Those jerks playing *chevalier à votre service?*—Of course it's just a game. But the women get a kick out of it."

The trip from the Montparnasse Station to Chartres was fairly short. If I took Vela to view the cathedral, I'd prefer to do it on a market day in strawberry season. But Vela had no real interest in Chartres except to be taken there. She didn't give a shit about Gothic architecture or stained glass. She only wanted her will to be done.

"Vela sets all kinds of conditions for you to meet, doesn't she?" Ravelstein said. "Didn't she make you bring all her luggage?"

"That's true. I came via London."

"And she couldn't cancel some appointment back home, so you flew separately. And brought her party dresses . . ."

He didn't admire me for doing such errands. He made this super clear. The picture he had drawn of my marriage was anything but flattering. Writers don't make good husbands. They reserve their Eros for their art. Or maybe they just don't focus. As for Vela, he judged her even more severely. "Maybe I shouldn't have rushed into the bedroom." He granted that, but added, "There wasn't all that much to be seen. Anyway, I wasn't interested. She was far from exposed. She had on her slip, and all kinds of other stuff under that. So what's all the hue and cry?"

"Protocol," I explained.

Ravelstein disagreed. "No, no. Not protocol. It doesn't even look like protocol."

I don't often have a problem with words. What I meant to say was that she was simply not ready to be seen. Unless you had lived with her, you wouldn't know what she did in the morning with her hair, her cheeks, her lips (especially the upper lip)—the phases of her preparations. She had to be seen as a beautiful woman. But it was beauty-parade beauty, and required preparation at a West Point or Hapsburg hussar level. I will be suspected of prejudice. But I assure you that I am confronted with some very real oddities—I happen to be a serial marrier and I had here a problem of self-preservation.

Ravelstein said, "Doesn't Vela come from the Black Sea region?"

"What if she does?"

"The Eastern Danube? The Carpathians?"

"I can't place it, exactly."

"It's not too important," Abe said. "A grande dame on an Eastern European model. No modern Frenchwoman would put on such an act. Often people from Eastern Europe cling to France, they have no life at home, home is disgusting, and they need to see themselves in a French light only. This applies to somebody like Cioran or even our friend—your friend—Grielescu. They hope to turn into Frenchmen. But your wife is even more peculiar . . ."

I stopped him. It would leave me open to charges of disloyalty if I were to admit that she was indeed the very strange phenomenon he described. I saw her with the eyes of a lover. But not entirely. I also took a naturalist's view of her. She was a very beautiful woman. And I admitted also that certain aspects of her face reminded me of Giorgione. On a small map you could place Vela's origins in Greece or even Egypt. Of course a big-time intellect is a universal phenomenon, and Vela had a major league brain. The scientific part of it deserved particular respect. Ravelstein, however, held that examples of great personalities among scientists were scarce. Great philosophers, painters, statesmen, lawyers, yes. But great-souled men or women in the sciences are extremely rare. "It's their sciences that are great, not the persons."

I must drop Paris now and get back to New Hampshire.

A few days in the country led me to conclude that Ravelstein's visit was proof of his affection. He didn't care about the fields, trees, pools, flowers, birds: These wasted the time of a superior man. Why did he give up his bank of telephones, his restaurants, and all the conveniences and erotic attractions of New York or Chicago? Because he wanted to see firsthand what was going on between Vela and me in New Hampshire.

One day was enough. "I've been watching," he said, "and I see she's got you staked out on an anthill," he said. "Don't you ever do anything together? Hiking?"

"No, come to think of it."

"Swimming?"

"At odd times she jumps in the neighbor's pond."

"Barbecues, picnics, visitors, parties?"

"Not her cup of tea."

"She can't talk to you about her central interests . . ." Ravelstein's big face was now very close. Holding his breath, he silently led me to consider it all from his point of view: Why did I submit to an ordeal of daily tensions which would never end?

All that Vela needed, as she often said, was to sit in a quiet angle with a notepad and draw her diagrams, knees up, breath held, and immobile. But she was all the while also directing negative currents toward me. The beauty of this New Hampshire corner with great maples and centuries-old hickories—the periwinkles and mosses in the shaded corners signified . . . well, to Vela they signified very little. She concentrated on her great abstractions.

"How do you figure in this?" said Ravelstein. "Do you maybe represent all that any man will ever get from her . . . So the fascinating question is whether she concentrates on her science or on her witch-work, because in your ignorance that's how it must seem."

That seemed to be a fair way to state the case.

"The regular pattern for her," I said, "is to pack up her things every few weeks, including her party clothes, because there are social gatherings as well as hard sciences. She drives away in her white Jaguar and attends science conferences up and down the Eastern seaboard."

"Would you say that, apart from the hint of rejection, there is also some relief for you when she goes?"

Ravelstein could be sympathetic. But more often he speculated on my paradoxical oddities.

"What do you get out of this place?" he would say. "This is supposed to be your quiet green retreat where you think and work. Or at least advance your projects . . ."

I was generally open with him, and willing to entertain criticism. He took a genuine interest in the lives of his friends, in their characters, their deeper intimacies—their sexual needs or kinks: Often he surprised me by the selflessness of his observations. He did not try to promote himself over you in noting your faults. In a way, I was grateful to be observed by him, and I found myself speaking to him openly about my peculiarities.

I can offer a sample conversation.

"I grant you that this is a beautiful and peaceful place," said Ravelstein. "But can you explain what Nature does for you—a Jewish city type? You're not a Transcendentalist update."

"No. That's not my line."

"And to your country neighbors you're one of the beasts that should have been drowned in the Flood."

"Oh, absolutely. But I don't worry about fitting in or belonging to the community. It's the stillness all around that attracted me. . . ."

"We've had this conversation before. . . ."

"Because it's important."

"Life speeding away. Your days fly faster than the weaver's shuttle. Or a stone thrown into the air," he said like an indulgent parent, "and accelerating downward at the rate of thirty-two feet per second squared—a metaphor for the horrifying speed of approaching death. You'd like time to be as slow as it was when you were a child—each day a lifetime."

"Yes, and to do that you need some reserves of stillness in your soul."

"As some Russian puts it," said Ravelstein. "I don't know which one, but you always incline toward the Russians, Chick, when you try to explain what you're really up to. But in addition you have been working for years at the problem of arranging your life—your private life, that is. And that's why you turn out to be the owner of this house and those three-hundred-year-old maple trees, to say nothing of the green carpet meadows and the stone walls. The liberal politics of our country make it possible to be private and free, not molested in your personal life. But your hasting days fly on in full career—while your wife is determined to defeat your plan for peaceful fulfillment. There's got to be a special Russian expression for this thee-ah thee-ah constellation. I can see how she vamped you. She's a really classy looker, when she gets herself up, and she has a most sexy figure. . . ."

At first Ravelstein had been extremely careful not to offend Vela. He wanted us, for the sake of our friendship, to get on smoothly, and he was warm, markedly attentive when she spoke. He deferred to her. He did all this with a virtuoso air—like an Itzhak Perlman playing nursery tunes for a small girl. But his deeper judgment had to be set aside. When he rushed into the hotel bedroom in Paris he was still covered by the *entente cordiale* he had with Vela. He never lied to himself about the observations he made. He kept accurate mental records.

But he and I had become friends—deeply attached—and friendship would not have been possible if we hadn't spontaneously understood each other. On this occasion he leaned his bald head on the back of his chair. The size of his large, simpatico, creased pale face made me wonder at the power of the supporting muscles in his neck and shoulders because his legs had a minimum of muscle. Just enough to serve his purpose, or to do his will.

"It would have been so easy to make a sane connection. But you need an extreme challenge. So you find yourself trying to please a woman. But she refuses to be pleased—by you, anyway.

"Lucky for you," he went on, "you have a vocation. So this is just a side thing. It's not a genuine case of sex-slavery or psychopathology. Of Human Bondage, yes. But for you it's only marginal. You may simply be having fun, and diverting yourself in the pure green innocence of the White Mountains with these minor vices—sex tortures."

"Ever since you burst in on us in Paris she began to say that you and I were carrying on together."

He was stopped cold by this. In the silence I could see this unexpected "information" being processed by an apparatus—I mean this seriously—of great power. That Ravelstein was vastly intelligent is not a challengeable proposition. He was at the head of a school. To several hundred people here and in England, France, and Italy he was exactly that. He interpreted Rousseau to the French, Machiavelli to the Italians, et cetera.

After a pause, he said, "Ha! And by carrying on together does she mean what I think she means? After years of marriage? . . . How long have you been married?"

"Twelve whole years," I told him.

"Twelve! How pathetic," Ravelstein said. "Like a prison term you sentenced yourself to. You're even a faithful husband. You served day after day after day with no time off for good behavior or applying for parole."

"I was busy with absorbing work," I said. "In the morning she'd put on her clothes and her makeup and then check her hair, her face, and her figure in three different lighted mirrors—dressing room, bathroom, and guest toilet. Then she'd slam out of the front door. I had half a headache and half a heartache. This concentrated my mind."

"She doesn't know how to dress," said Ravelstein. "All those strange materials—what was it she was wearing last year? Ostrich hide?. . . . Finally she accuses you of having a corrupt sex affair with me. What did you say?"

"I laughed like anything. I told her I didn't even know how the act was done, and that I wasn't ready to learn, at my age. It seemed like a joke. Still she didn't believe me. . . ."

"She couldn't believe you," said Ravelstein. "It took too much out of her to invent even this pitiful accusation. Her mental range on that side is extremely limited—though I'm told she's very big in chaos physics."

It was from Abe's telephone network that this information must have come. The old expression "He has more connections than a switchboard" had now been buried under the masses of data heaped up by the wildly expanding communications technology.

Ravelstein had asked his friends everywhere for items about Vela, and he was prepared to tell me much more than I wanted to hear. So that I would clap my hands over my ears and squeeze my eyes shut. But you can't keep your innocence in this age. Nine-tenths of modern innocence is little more than indifference to vice, a resolve not to be affected by all that you might read, hear, or see. Love of scandal makes people ingenious. Vela was ingenious in her science and guiltless in her conduct.

You couldn't, as the intimate and friend of Ravelstein, avoid knowing a great deal more than you had an appetite for. But at a certain depth there were places in your psyche that still belonged to the Middle Ages. Or even to the age of the pyramids or Ur of the

Chaldees. Ravelstein told me about Vela's relationships with people I had never heard of till now. He said he was ready to name my rivals but I wouldn't listen. Since she didn't love me I had, with innate biological resourcefulness, holed up behind my desk and finished a few long-postponed projects—quoting Robert Frost to myself:

> *For I have promises to keep*
> *And miles to go before I sleep.*

At times changing this to:

> *For I have recipes to bake*
> *And far to go before I wake.*

The joke was on me, not on Frost—a sententious old guy whose conversation was mainly about his own doings, about his accomplishments and triumphs. It can't be denied that he was a self-promoter. He had PR genius. But he was a writer of rare gifts, nevertheless.

To hear about Vela's alleged misconduct was destabilizing. I lose my footing, I stumble when I remember what Ravelstein told me about her various affairs. Why were there so many conferences to attend in summer? Why didn't she give me phone numbers where she could be reached? Of course, he wouldn't have been interested in these facts if they hadn't been singular facts. As I have said, Ravelstein was crazy about gossip and his friends were given points for the racy items they brought. And it was not a good idea to assume that he would keep the lid on your confidences. I was not particularly disturbed about this. People are infinitely more clever than they used to be about pursuing your secrets. If they know your secrets they have increased power over you. There's no stopping or checking them. Build as many labyrinths as you like, you're sure to be found out. And of course I was aware that Ravelstein didn't care a damn about "secrets."

But since Ravelstein had a large-scale mental life—and I say this without irony, his interests really were big—he needed to know everything there was to know about his friends and his students, just as a physician pursuing a diagnosis has to see you stripped naked. The comparison breaks down when you remember that the doctor is bound by ethical rules not to gossip about you. Ravelstein was not so bound. When I was a kid in the thirties the notion of the "naked truth" was in the air. "Let's have the naked truth." An Englishwoman named Claire Sheridan wrote a memoir called *The Naked Truth*. It was appropriate that she should have visited revolutionary Russia, where she seems to have been on familiar terms with Lenin and Trotsky and many other prominent Bolsheviks.

But all this is mere background.

Let's get on with it.

Ravelstein, speaking still of Vela, said, "You make her an offering—beautiful country summers—but she doesn't care about this place, Chick, or she'd spend more time here. And so I find it curious that you should try so hard. However," he continued, "let me say what I see in all this. I see the Jew, the child of immigrants, taking the American premises seriously. You are free to do what you like, and can realize your wishes fully. It's your privilege as an American to buy land and build a house where you live in full enjoyment of your rights. It's true there's nobody here but yourself. So you have built this New Hampshire sanctuary where you're surrounded by your family mementos. Your mother's Russian samovar is a beautiful object. It's thee-ah thee-ah terribly handsome. But it's far far far from the city of Tula—Tula was for samovars as coals were to Newcastle. Thee-ah thee-ah Tula samovar has never been in such a foreign location of maximum deracination. As for you, Chick, you're making your total American declaration of rights. It's very brave of you to do it but it's also off the wall. . . . For miles around, you're the only Jew. Your neighbors have one another to rely on. Whom do you have—a gentile wife? You've got a theory—equality before the law. It's a big comfort to have constitutional guarantees on your side, and it's certain to be appreciated by other devotees of the Constitution itself. . . ."

He was enjoying himself. I didn't much mind. To be shown a pattern in my activities diverted me.

"I have to assume also that your tax bill is high. . . ."

"It certainly is. And there are new education assessments yearly."

He said, "I can imagine what sort of education they get here. Have you ever attended a town meeting?"

"Once I did."

"And your high-stepping wife?"

"She was there, too."

Before the cycle of obscure or new diseases began, Ravelstein and I had many fun conversations like the above. He seemed to think that I would value his opinion of my activities. Up to a point I did, in fact, find them useful. He said, for instance, that I was anything but risk-averse. And he asked, "I am fascinated by the marriages you've made—you remember Steve Brody, don't you?"

"The guy who jumped from the Brooklyn Bridge on a bet."

"That's him—one of those spirited people."

See Plato's *Republic,* especially Book IV. I did not study those great texts closely, but there wasn't the slightest hope of following Ravelstein's thoughts if you were ignorant of them entirely. I was not really intimidated by them. By now I am as much at home with Plato as with Elmore Leonard.

"There's nothing I say to you that you don't immediately understand," Ravelstein would sometimes declare, but it's possible that he had cultivated the art of conversation with good old Chick and would take special care to go slowly with him. And it's possible also that as a genius educator he knew how much traffic my mind would bear.

In New Hampshire he would press me again and again to repeat old jokes, old gags, and vaudeville routines. "Do me that Jimmy Savvo song." Or else "How does the furious husband bit go, again? The heartbroken man who tells his buddy 'My wife cheats on me.'"

"Oh, yes. And the buddy says, 'Make love to her every day. Once a day at least. And in a year that will kill her.'

"'No!' The guy is astonished. 'Is that the answer?'"

"'Once a day. That often, she'll never survive . . .'

"Then a sign is brought on stage. You may remember how that was done. An usher with a round cap and a double row of buttons would carry out a tripod with a sign. In bold print this sign read, 'Fifty-one weeks later.' And then the husband is pushed onstage in a wheelchair by the wife. He looks very weak. Muffled in blankets like an invalid. The wife is blooming. She is dressed for tennis and has the racket under her arm. She fusses over him, tucks him in, kisses him. His eyes are closed. He looks like death. She says, 'Rest, darling, I'll be back after my set—real real soon.' As she strides off the feeble husband brings his hand up to his face and behind his hand in a wonderful vaudeville whisper he says confidentially to the audience, 'She don't know it, but she's got only a week to live.'"

Ravelstein threw his head back at this. Shutting his eyes he flung himself bodily backward into laughter. In my own different style I did the same thing. As I've said before it was our sense of what was funny that brought us together, but that would have been a thin, anemic way to put it. A joyful noise—*immenso giubilo*—an outsize joint agreement picked us up together, and it would get you nowhere to try to formulate it.

In those days, Rosamund had a long ride on the elevated train. She crossed the huge breadth of the city, and she had the faces of her fellow passengers to train her thoughts and feelings on. She brought me the week's mail and the phone messages. For two years she had been my graduate-assistant, typing and faxing for me. Vela was condescending to her and would not even invite her to sit down. I would offer Rosamund a cup of tea and try to make her comfortable. Although slightly threadbare, Rosamund was ultra-neat, but Vela considered her a frumpy little thing. Vela's airs were grandly aristocratic. She bought herself very expensive costumes in strange materials like ostrich hide. One season she bought ostrich only—a large ostrich hat in bushranger style, with follicles from which the feathers had been pulled. She had an ostrich-hide bag slung over her shoulder and ostrich boots and gloves. On her full professor's salary, she had lots of money to spend. Her straight-profiled beauty was the only kind of beauty that mattered.

Vela said, "Your little Rosamund is dying to take care of you."

"I think she believes I'm happily married."

"In that case why does she always bring a bathing suit?"

"Because it's a long hot trip on the El and she enjoys swimming in the lake."

"No, it's because you can see her beautiful figure. Otherwise she'd go swimming at her own end of town."

"She feels safer here."

"You don't spend all your time dictating letters."

"Not all of it." I granted that.

"Well, what do you talk about—Hitler and Stalin?"

These, to Vela, were contemptible topics. Compared to chaos physics, they didn't even exist. And she was born, mind you, within an hour's jet flight of Stalingrad, but her parents had conspired to keep her impeccably innocent of the Wehrmacht and the gulags. Only her own esoteric studies mattered. Still, Vela curiously had a talent for politics. She made certain that people would think well of her. It was her wish that they should see her as a warmhearted, friendly, generous person. Even Ravelstein said of her, "People are flattered by her attentions. She buys the most expensive birthday presents."

"Yes. It's a funny thing how she attracts acquaintances and turns them away from me. I don't feel like getting into a spending contest."

"What are you trying to tell me, Chick, that she's some kind of space alien?"

I was familiar now with Ravelstein's ideas on marriage. People are beaten at last with their solitary longings and intolerable isolation. They need *the* right, *the* missing portion to complete themselves, and since they can't realistically hope to find that they must accept a companionable substitute. Recognizing that they can't win, they settle. The marriage of true minds seldom occurs. Love that bears it out even to the edge of doom is not a modern project. But there was, for Ravelstein, nothing to compete with this achievement of the soul. Scholars deny that Sonnet 116 is about the love of men and women but insist that Shakespeare is writing about friendship. The best we can hope for in modernity is not love but a sexual attachment—a bourgeois solution, in bohemian dress. I mention bohemianism because we need to feel that we are liberated. Ravelstein taught that in the modern condition we are in a weak state. The strong state—and this was what he learned from Socrates—comes to us through nature. At the core of the soul is Eros. Eros is overwhelmingly attracted to the sun. I've probably spoken of this before. If I speak of it again it's because I am never done with Ravelstein and he was never done with Socrates, for whom Eros was at the center of the soul, where the sun nourishes and expands it.

But in some respects I thought better of Vela than Ravelstein did. He was not vulnerable to her sort of charm. I on the other hand continued to see what others saw in her—crossing a room, dressed very expensively, so rapidly planting her toes that her heels hardly ever touched the ground. She had original notions about walking, talking, shrugging, smiling. American acquaintances thought that she was the soul of European gracefulness and elegance. Rosamund herself thought so. I explained that under it all there was really a special kind of attractive clumsiness. But all the prestige, her reputation in her branch of physics, the fat salary she was paid, her inimitable toppling glamour, were too hard for any woman to compete with. Rosamund would say, "What an unusually beautiful woman she is—waist, legs and everything."

"True. But there's a hint of artificiality about it. Like a stratagem. Like a lack of affect."

"Even after such a long marriage?"

I had hoped to make it work with Vela because I had had earlier marriages. But I had more or less given up the fight and for a dozen years or so had made no claims on Vela. In the morning she would slam out of the house and I would turn to my tasks and spend my days at them. Ravelstein, from the other side of the city, checked in on the telephone for an hour or two. At least once a week Rosamund came by public transportation from Ravelstein's end of town. I often suggested that she hire a cab but she said that she preferred the El train. Rosamund said that George, her fiancé, thought the El was perfectly safe. The Transit Authority policed them more effectively here than in New York.

Picking up Ravelstein's habit I taught her the term *louche*—dubious. Nothing like a French word to neutralize an American danger.

Everything just then was going from bad to worse. I had come back after the funeral of my brother in Tallahassee in time to see my surviving brother, Shimon, on what turned out to be the last day of his life. He said to me, "You're wearing a beautiful shirt, Chick— that's got class, the red-and-gray stripe."

We were sitting together on the rattan sofa. His cancer-wasted face wore the usual pert look of good humor.

"But I hear you want to buy a diesel Mercedes. I advise you not to do it," he said. "It'll be nothing but trouble." He was vibrating with the final urgency or restlessness. It was all but over now, so I promised not to buy the diesel. Then he said, after a long exchange of silent looks, that he wanted to climb back into bed. He was too far gone to do this. He had been a ball player once with strong legs, but the muscle now was all gone. I watched from behind, trying to decide whether to intervene. He had nothing left to do his will with. And then his head twisted toward me and his eyeballs turned up—nothing but blind whites. The nurse cried out, "He's leaving us."

Shimon raised his voice and said, "Don't get excited."

This was what he said often to his wife and to his children when they differed or began to quarrel. Not to let things get out of hand was his function in the family. He was unaware that his eyeballs had rolled back into his head. But I had seen this in the dying and knew that he was leaving us—the nurse was right.

After his funeral in the very same week, a few days before my birthday, I was loud and angry, kicking at Vela's bathroom door when I remembered my brother's call for calm, very nearly the last thing he had said. So I left the house. When I came back that night I found a note from Vela; she was sleeping over with Yelena, another Balkan-French woman.

Coming home again the following night I found the house filled with large, colored stickum circles—the green identified my possessions, the salmon-colored were glued to hers. The apartment swirled with these large dots. Their colors were abnormal, something gassy or bilious about them; they were identified on the box they came in as "pastel shades." They produced a snowstorm effect—"a meum-tuum blizzard," as I said to Ravelstein.

A team of his students helped me to unpack in the new apartment after I had moved. Rosamund was among them. She was naturally interested in the books I had collected. In the movers' boxes were my college Wordsworth and my Shakespeare and Company

Ulysses with the curious errors made by Joyce's Parisian typesetters—not "give us a touch, Poldy. God, I'm dying for it," but "give us a tough," says Molly. All because two dogs are copulating in the street below. "How life begins," thinks Leopold Bloom. On this day he and Molly conceive their son, a child who does not live long. In every direction, the walls of life are tiled with such facts so that you can never account for them all, only note some of the more conspicuous ones. For instance, what Vela must have looked like when she plastered all those objects with pale green and orange stickum dots. To look at them would make you run out screaming. So why does one marry a woman whose final act as a wife is to apply hundreds if not thousands of labels? For that matter, why did Molly marry Leopold Bloom? Her answer was "Well as well him as another."

I had thought of Vela as a beauty impossible to rival. She had worn her skirts tightly tailored on the backsides. She had cavalry cruppers, together with a very fine bust, and the knocking of her heels when she entered a room were like military drums but gave you no clue to what she was feeling or thinking.

Vela had a stiff upper lip. I have always been inclined to give a special diagnostic importance to the upper lip. If there is a despotic tendency it will reveal itself there. When I examine a photograph it is my habit to isolate features. What does this forehead tell you, or the placement of those eyes? Or that mustache? Hitler and Stalin, the classic dictators of our century, wore very different mustaches. Hitler's lip, come to think of it, was extremely conspicuous. A curious fact: Vela's lip stung you when you kissed her.

She had a way of leading you, of showing you how to be a male. This tendency is more common among women than you might suppose. Either she had in mind men she had liked in the past, or she had some male principle of her own to follow, a Jungian masculine counterpart, her particular animus or inborn vision of a man—unconscious, of course.

Ravelstein had no patience for such stuff. He said, "This Jungian shtick comes straight from Radu Grielescu. Vela is a great pal of the Grielescu couple. You used to have dinner with them every other week. Of course you're a writer, you need to meet all kinds of people," said Ravelstein. "That's only natural for a man in your position. People from the sports world, from the movies, musicians, commodity brokers, criminals, too. They're your bread and butter, meat and potatoes."

"Then why shouldn't I dine with Grielescu and his wife?"

"No objection whatever, as long as you're aware of the facts."

"And what are the facts, in their case?"

"Grielescu is making use of you. In the old country he was a fascist. He needs to live that down. The man was a Hitlerite."

"Come, now . . ."

"Has he ever denied that he belonged to the Iron Guard?"

"It's never come up."

"You haven't brought it up. Do you have any memory of the massacre in Bucharest when they hung people alive on meat hooks in the slaughterhouse and butchered them—skinned them alive?"

One rarely heard Ravelstein speaking of such things. He would now and then refer to "History" in large Hegelian terms, and recommend certain chapters of the Philosophy of History as great fun. With him gloomy conversations on the "full particulars" were extremely rare. "You know Grielescu was a follower of Nae Ionesco, who founded the Iron Guard. Doesn't he ever mention this?"

"Now and then he does speak of Ionesco, but mostly he talks about his days in India and how he studied under a yoga master."

"That's his Eastern glamour fakery. You're much too soft on people, Chick, and it's not entirely innocent, either. You know he's faking. There's an unspoken deal between you. . . . Must I spell it out?"

As a rule, Ravelstein and I spoke plainly to each other. *Verbum sat sapienti est.* The Grielescus were socially important to Vela. I had a considerable gift for noting the phenomena and I was aware that Vela gave me good marks for being so polite to Radu and always on my best behavior with Mme. Grielescu. My small talk in French with Madame gave Vela great satisfaction. But Ravelstein was taking a very serious view of my relations with these people. When he was dying he seemed to feel it necessary to speak more openly about matters we had never felt it necessary to discuss.

"They use you as their cover," said Ravelstein. "You wouldn't have become chummy with those Jew-haters. But these were Vela's friends, and you put yourself out for them, and you gave Grielescu exactly what he was looking for. As a Romanian nationalist back in the thirties he was violent toward the Jews. He wasn't an Aryan— no, he was a Dacian."*

I knew all that, well enough. I was aware also that Grielescu had had a close connection with C. G. Jung, who saw himself as some sort of Aryan Christ. But what is one to do about the learned people from the Balkans who have such an endless diversity of interests and talents—who are scientists and philosophers and also historians and poets, who have studied Sanskrit and Tamil and lectured in the Sorbonne on mythology; who could, if closely questioned, tell you also about persons they had "known slightly" in the paramilitary Jew-hating Iron Guard?

The fact was that I enjoyed watching Grielescu. He had so many

---

*The Dacians were to Romania what the Aryans were to Germany.

tics. He was a fidgeting, pipe-digging, pipe-stuffing smoker, pushing wire cleaners into the stem of his briar or paring away at the carbon cake in the bowl. He was short and bald, but he let his back hair grow long; it bushed out over his collar. His scalp, wide-open as an estuary, was heavily veined; it looked congested. Very unlike Ravelstein's green-oval-melon baldness. While he dithered over his woolly-bear pipe cleaners Grielescu would continue to spell out some esoteric topic or other. His brows were bushy and his broad face was prepared for an exchange of ideas. But there was no exchange, for he was off inwardly on some topic from myth or history about which you had nothing to tell him. I didn't mind at all. I don't like the responsibilities that come when you have to do the talking. But everybody has something like a lawn of random knowledge, and it's very pleasant to have it kept watered and green for you. Sometimes Radu talked about Siberian shamanism; or then again it might be marriage customs in primitive Australia. It was assumed that you had come to listen or to learn from Radu. Mme. Grielescu had even arranged the parlor furniture with this in mind. "This was how he steered the conversation away from his fascist record," said Ravelstein. "But the record nevertheless shows what he wrote about the Jew-syphilis that infected the high civilization of the Balkans."

He turned out to be right. Grielescu had attached himself to the Nazis, not to the milder, Italian form of fascism. It's hard to say how political Mme. Grielescu had been. My guess is that in prewar days she was a stylish beauty, an upper-class flapper. You could easily picture her in a cloche hat stepping out of a limo. Women who wore good clothes and vivid lipstick generally had no politics. These European ladies monitored the social behavior of their husbands—the males of their set. Men existed to hold doors open and draw back dining-room chairs.

Mme. Grielescu was never altogether well. To judge by her wrinkles she was over sixty, unhappy about it but also very exacting with men—a walking manual of etiquette. It was impossible to guess what she knew about her husband's Iron Guard past. In the late thirties, when the Germans had conquered France, Poland, Austria, and Czechoslovakia, Grielescu became something of a cultural big shot in London and later he cut a figure in Lisbon under the Salazar dictatorship.

But by now his midcentury politics were dead and buried. When Vela and I dined out with the Grielescus the conversation was not about war and politics but about archaic history or mythology. The professor with a white silk turtleneck shirt under his dinner jacket pulled chairs out for the ladies and pinned their corsages for them. His hands shook. He fussed over the champagne. "He paid the bill in cash from a wad of fifties. No credit cards."

"I can't see him at the bank drawing money," said Ravelstein.

"Probably he sends his secretary to cash a check. Anyhow, he pays with clean, unwrinkled currency. He doesn't even count, he drops a bundle of green bills and makes a 'take it all away' gesture. Then he rushes to the other side of the table to light his wife's cigarette. There's all the gallantry, the *hommages,* a standing order at the florist's for roses, and the hand-kissing and bowing."

"All done in French. And there's a different standard for Americans. And you're a Jew, besides. The Jews had better understand their status with respect to myth. Why should they have any truck with myth? It was myth that demonized them. The Jew myth is connected with conspiracy theory. The Protocols of Zion for instance. And your Radu has written books, endless books, about myth. So what do you want with mythology, anyway, Chick? Do you expect to be tapped one of these days and be told that you have

℘

127

now become an elder of Zion? Just give a thought now and then to those people on the meat hooks."

Ravelstein and I endlessly discussed the Balkan fix I was in, but in continuing this narrative, I see that I have to begin by closing out Vela. She has to be disposed of for once and for all. This is not as simple as you might suppose. She was gorgeous and beautifully dressed and memorably made up. On the telephone she chirped like Papagena. Ravelstein was almost alone in describing her as a taste-less dresser. He saw her as a superior manager of the externals. In political terms it could be said that she was out to be elected by a landslide. But Ravelstein did not agree. "Once you begin to suspect her, the whole production falls apart," he said. "Too much rational planning." But then he added, "She was right to throw you out."

"Why do you say that?"

"Because you would have murdered her eventually." He didn't say this gloomily. To him the thought of such a murder was a good thing. It did me credit. "She had a sex-hex on you, so you had to be thinking of a violent death for her. She chose the worst moment possible, just after the deaths of both your brothers, to tell you she was filing for a divorce."

Ravelstein would frequently say to me, "There's something in the way you tell anecdotes that gets to me, Chick. But you need a real subject. I'd like you to write me up, after I'm gone. . . ."

"It depends, doesn't it, on who beats whom to the barn?"

"Let's not have any bullshit about it. You know perfectly well that I'm about to die. . . ."

Of course I knew it. Indeed I did.

"You could do a really fine memoir. It's not just a request," he added. "I'm laying this on you as an obligation. Do it in your after-supper-reminiscence manner, when you've had a few glasses of wine and you're laid back and making remarks. I love listening when you are freewheeling about Edmund Wilson or John Berryman or Whittaker Chambers when you were hired at *Time* in the morning and fired by him before lunch. I've often thought how well you deal with a story when you're laid back."

There was no way I could refuse to do this. He clearly didn't want me to write about his ideas. He had expounded those fully himself and they're available in his theoretical books. I make myself responsible for the person, therefore, and since I can't depict him without a certain amount of self-involvement my presence on the margins will have to be tolerated.

Death was closing in on him and it was transmitting the usual advance reminders, telling me first of all that in preparation for his end I should not forget that I was his senior by some years. At my advanced age my every third thought *should* be of death. But the odd thing was that I was now the husband of Rosamund, one of Ravelstein's students. And Ravelstein was such a paradoxical character, you see, that one of the effects of his friendship was to make me unaware of the oddity of my condition—in my seventies I was married to a young woman. "It's odd only when you view the thing from the outside," said Ravelstein. "She fell in love with you and that was why there was no stopping her."

In choosing me or setting me up to write this memoir, he obliged me to consider my death as well as his. And not only his death from shingles, Guillain-Barré, etc., but a good many other deaths as well. It was collection time for an entire generation. For instance: I was on the very day of this conversation sitting with Ravelstein in his extravagant, lavish bedroom. The drape was pulled aside from the east window and we faced the wide-open blue of the shoreless Lake.

"What do you think when we look in this direction?" said Ravelstein.

"I think of good old—or bad old—Rakhmiel Kogon," I said.

"He has more of a grip on you than he has on me," said Ravelstein.

Maybe so. Still, I couldn't look in that direction—eastward—without seeing Kogon's apartment building, and then you'd count upward or downward trying to locate the tenth floor, but you could never be certain that you were looking at the right window. Rakhmiel, who had figured since the forties in my life and since the fifties in Ravelstein's would be one of the crowd taking off at intervals. You never knew who would be next. He had had several kinds of major surgery: his prostate gland had been removed last year—Rakhmiel said he'd never had much use for it anyway. I did not feel myself to be in the threatened category for I'd fallen in love with a young woman and had married her. So I was not quite ready to deal with the departing contingent. It was one of those curious moments of illumination that I don't feel I can pass over. Rakhmiel was highly educated, but to what end? Every corner of his apartment was stuffed with books. Every morning, Rakhmiel sat down and wrote in green ink.

Rakhmiel was neither a large man nor a healthy one, but he was physically conspicuous just the same—compact and dense, high-handed, tyrannically fixated, opinionated. His mind was made up once and for all upon hundreds of subjects and maybe this was the sign that he had completed his course. I felt I was summing him up for an obituary. It is possible that I was trying to replace Ravelstein with Rakhmiel so that I wouldn't have to think about Ravelstein's death. I would much rather think of Rakhmiel's death. So I reviewed his life and his works for a sketch on him while Ravelstein lay on his pillow with eyes shut, thinking thoughts of his own.

Rakhmiel was, or had been once, a redhead, but the red hair had worn away and what remained was a reddish complexion—in medieval physiology, sanguine: hot and dry. Or, better yet, choleric. His face wore a police expression and he often looked, walking fast, as if he were on a case—on his way to serve a warrant or make a pinch. His conversation, I thought, had an interrogatory tone. Very articulate, he spoke in complete sentences, at high speed and very impatiently. When you came to know him better you would understand that there were two conspicuous foreign elements in his makeup—one German and the other British. The German part of him was Weimar-style toughness. I suppose I knew Weimar in its nightclub version. Postwar Europe of the twenties was sold on hardness. The war veterans were hard, the political leaders were hard. Hardest of all of course was Lenin, ordering hangings and shootings. Hitler entered the competition when he took power in the thirties. Immediately he had Captain Roehm and other Nazi colleagues shot. Rakhmiel and I would at one time discuss this sort of thing quite often.

Lots of bitter facts, too horrible for contemporaries to contemplate. We can't actually bring ourselves to acknowledge them. Our souls aren't strong enough to bear that. And yet one can't give oneself a pass. A man like Rakhmiel would feel obligated to face up to the fact that this viciousness was universal. He believed that everybody had his share of it. You could find these murderous impulses in any person of mature years. In certain cases, like Rakhmiel's own, you could identify them in your physical structure as equivalents not necessarily of war but of widespread Russian, German, French, Polish, Lithuanian, Ukrainian, and Balkan shameful enormities.

Well, there was the Germanic side of him. Then there was the Brit component. Rakhmiel, whose name translates as "Save me, God" or "Be merciful, God, unto me," had also modeled himself on English dons and in time became a don himself. He had been in England during the war. He was blitzed in London, where he was gathering and interpreting intelligence. Then he taught at the London School of Economics. Later he was an Oxford professor and divided his time between England and the U.S. He was the author of many learned books. He wrote daily, copiously, endlessly, and without hesitation, in his green ink. "The Intellectuals" were his principal subject, and in style he was Johnsonian. Sometimes he would remind you of Edmund Burke, but mostly it was Samuel Johnson whose tone you heard. I see nothing wrong with this. The challenge of modern freedom, or the combination of isolation and freedom which confronts you, is to make yourself up. The danger is that you may emerge from the process as a not-entirely-human creature.

The arts of disguise are so well developed that you are sure to undercount the number of bastards you have known. Not even a genius like Rakhmiel was able to conceal the storminess or, if you prefer, the wickedness of his nature. He had ideas of decency which went back to the novels of Dickens, but he had wicked REMs—I borrow the term from the sleep specialists—wide-awake rapid eye movements. He looked like an irritable and highly volatile English

132

clubman, very red in the face. In America, where people are not familiar with such types, his idiosyncrasies were bound to be misunderstood. People saw a dumpy, slightly paunchy but strong, short
man in very old tweeds. To be ill-dressed is a donnish tradition going back to the Middle Ages, and at Oxford and Cambridge you
still saw the holes in academic gowns patched with Scotch tape.
There was a noticeable sourness coming from Rakhmiel Kogon's
clothing. He looked like a tyrant, with the tyranny baked into his
face. This was not well dissembled with meekness and Christian
forbearance, or with civility. He wore a fedora when he went out
and carried a heavy stick—"to hit the peasants with," he used to
joke. And it was a joke, because his strong subject was civility. With
civility he had opened up a new vein and everybody in the university world was mining it.

Rakhmiel was anything but simpleminded. My belief is that
on the side he grew a little herb garden of good, generous feelings.
He hoped, especially when he was wooing a new friend, that
he could pass for a very decent man. He was also very learned.
When you first came into his apartment your respect for him grew.
On his shelves there were full sets of Max Weber and all the
Gumplowitches and Ratzenhofers. He owned the collected works
of Henry James and of Dickens and the histories of Gibbon's Rome
and Hume's England as well as encyclopedias of religion and
masses of sociology books. Useful for propping up windows when
the sash cord broke, I used to say. There was also the green ink. No
other color was used. The green was his exclusive trademark.

Ravelstein shouted with laughter when we came to this. He said,
"That's how I want to be treated, too. That's it. I want you to show
me as you see me, without softeners or sweeteners."

Ravelstein, after he had read my sketch of Kogon, said that I should have commented on his sex life—a major omission, he believed. He told me authoritatively, "You've missed it—Kogon is attracted to men." When I asked for some proof of this he said that So-and-so, a graduate student, swore up and down that one night when they had drunk too much, Rakhmiel tried to kiss him. It was hard to think of Kogon as a kisser and I said that never in a thousand years could I picture Rakhmiel forcing his way on someone. "Then you've been brainwashed," said Ravelstein. Nothing in this line was too improbable for him, but I failed in every attempt to visualize Rakhmiel kissing anyone. I couldn't even picture him kissing his old mother. He would shout at her without mercy and then he would say, "She's deaf. . . ." But I don't believe she was at all deaf, his bewildered mama.

Back from the hospital, Ravelstein was doing reasonably well. Of course he couldn't beat his infection but he said, "I'm in no hurry to die." His social life flourished. In his best days he flew like a hawk, as he himself said. "But now I flutter like those wild turkeys on your place in New Hampshire."

He could walk well enough, though his sense of balance was off.

He could also dress and feed himself, shave, brush his teeth (he wore an upper plate), tie his shoes, and run the steam-fizzing espresso machine—too big for the grooved enamel of the kitchen sink. His hands shook hardest when there was an extra-delicate operation to perform, like finding an eyehole with the tip of the shoelace. He was barely strong enough to wear his general-staff fur-lined suede coat that dragged on the ground when I helped him put it on. He could no longer reset his watch and had to ask Nikki or me to do it.

He was, however, still giving parties on nights when his team the

Bulls were on TV. And now and then he took his student favorites
to a dinner party at Acropolis on Halsted Street. The waiters there
gave him power handshakes and called out, "Hey, lookit, the Professor!" They urged him to drink olive oil neat, by the glass. "Too
late to save your hair, Prof, but still the best medicine."

We went also to a dining club downtown: Les Atouts—the
Trump Cards. There Abe had a longtime gentlemanly connection
with M. Kurbanski—accent on the *ban*. M. Kurbanski, the Serbian
owner-manager, went abroad several times a year. He was preparing to retire to a villa on the Dalmatian coast.

He had a fine full front—head and belly matching a very impressive wide, short-nosed, breath-held pale face. His hair was combed
straight back. He wore a cutaway coat. Altogether he gave Ravelstein the pleasure of feeling that he was dealing with a civilized
man.

Ravelstein would say to me, "What's your take on Kurbanski?"

"Well, he's a Franco-Serbian gentleman who offers local people
membership in his dining club east of Michigan Boulevard."

"What kind of war record has he got?"

"He says he fought the Germans. He belonged to the Maquis."

"They'd all tell you that. But I don't think he was a Communist,"
said Ravelstein. "To hear them describe it, they were all freedom
fighters on the mountaintops. What's your bottom-dollar hunch
about Kurbanski?"

"If he were up against it he could put a bullet through his head,"
I said.

"That's more like it. I agree with you. But under it all he's a superior maître d'," said Ravelstein.

"Who's going to dispute him if he claims he was a guerrilla in his
glory days and fought the Germans?"

"That's why he wears such a sad and distant look. So what's left?" Ravelstein said. "The Jewish question."

"Not to be a Jew was very desirable in those times, a big asset. One never knows. But the big thing with Kurbanski is being French."

"Yes. We come into his establishment and he chats us up in French. And this courtesy is possible, though we are Jews, because we can answer in acceptable French. . . ."

"I like to hear you when you're drunk, Chick, talking and sketching freestyle. You're right to insist that Kurbanski has a sad look. . . ."

Ravelstein had come to agree that it was important to note how people looked. Their ideas are not enough—their theoretical convictions and political views. If you don't take into account their haircuts, the hang of their pants, their taste in skirts and blouses, their style of driving a car or eating a dinner, your knowledge is incomplete.

"One of your best pieces, Chick, is the one about Khrushchev at the UN pulling off his shoe and banging it on the table. And almost as good is your sketch of Bobby Kennedy, when he was the Senator from New York. He took you along on his Washington rounds, didn't he?"

"Yes. For one whole week . . ."

"Now that was one of your sketches that held my interest," said Ravelstein. "That his Senate office was like a shrine to his brother—a huge painting of Jack on the wall. And there was something savage about his mourning. . . ."

"Vengeful, was what I said."

"Lyndon Johnson was the enemy, wasn't he. They had gotten rid of him by making him vice president—a kind of errand boy. But then he was Jack's successor. And Bobby needed arms to retake the White House. Full of hate. They were very handsome men, both brothers. Bob was half the size of Jack," Ravelstein said, "but an alley fighter. Most amusing of all were those walks from the Senate office building to the Capitol. Those were wonderful questions he asked you—like, 'Tell me about Henry Adams.' 'Brief me on H. L. Mencken.' If he was going to be President, he thought he should know about Mencken."

It thrilled Ravelstein to talk about celebrities. At Idlewild, once, he had spotted Elizabeth Taylor and for the better part of an hour tracked her through the crowds. It especially pleased him to have recognized her. Because she was so faded, it took some doing. She seemed to know that her glamour was gone.

"You didn't try to talk to her?"

"Uh-uhn."

"As a best-selling author you were on equal footing with other celebrities."

But no.

He and I were sitting, as we had sat for years, in his living room, and he was in his Japanese gown. It fell away from his body on all sides. His bare legs were like prize-winning marrows because his ankles were so swollen— "That fucking edema!" he said. The top half of Ravelstein was as lively as ever. But the disease was gaining on him, and he knew it as well as any doctor. Not only did he talk more about the memoir I was appointed to write but he had curious things to tell me. About the persistence of sexual feelings, for instance. "I've never gotten so hot," he said. "And it's too late in the day for partners. I have to ease myself...."

"What do you do?"

"A hand-job. What else is there? At this stage, I'm humanly out of the running."

The thought of it made me flinch.

"I'm fatally polluted. I think a lot about those pretty boys in Paris. If they catch the disease they often go back to their mothers, who care for them. My old lady is a poor thing, now. Last time I saw her I asked, 'Do you know me?' and she said, 'Of course. You're the fellow who wrote that famous best-seller everybody talks about.'"

"You told me that."

"Well, it's worth repeating. Her second husband is also in a finishing school for nonagenarians. I'll beat them both, though. At this rate, I'll reach the finish line before my mom. Maybe I'll be waiting for her."

"That's aimed at me, isn't it?"

"Well, Chick, you've often talked about the life to come."

"And you're a self-described atheist, since no philosopher can believe in God. But this is no belief with me. It's only that my amateur survey shows that nine people out of ten expect to see their parents in the life to come. But am I prepared to spend eternity with them? I suspect I'm not. What I'd prefer would be to be accepted to study the universe, under God's direction. There's nothing original about this, unless it is after all a tremendous thing to grasp the collective longing of billions of people."

"Well, we'll soon find out, you and I, Chick."

"Why? Do you see the signs of it in me?"

"I do, yes, to be frank about it."

As if he were ever anything else.

Oddly enough, I didn't mind hearing this from him. He might, however, have given a thought to Rosamund. He was at times not quite clear about my connection to her—naturally disoriented by his illness. He had assumed the role of the benevolent intercessor, counselor, arranger. This was, in part, due to the influences of Jean-Jacques Rousseau, the political theorist and reformer. But he had initially been drawn to Jean-Jacques by his strong belief in the love that knits persons and societies together. At times he might admit that Rousseau, the genius and innovator whose ideas—his great mind—had powerfully dominated European society for more than a century, was (almost necessarily) himself a nutcase. To get a bit closer to the principal topic here, he had been taken by surprise when he learned that in marrying Rosamund I had not bothered to consult him. I was willing to admit that he might know more about me than I myself knew, but I was not about to put myself in his custody and rely on him to run my life for me. It would also be unjust to Rosamund. I shan't make speeches here about dignity, autonomy, and all the rest of that. She and I had been together for something like a year before Ravelstein knew that we were what tabloid journalists would call "an item." I have to say, however, that when we did get married he was quite good-natured about it, showing no resentment. People were doing naturally what people always had done. The old continued to have one resurgence of foolishness after another, until the organism gave out altogether. I was perfectly willing to amuse him by being typical, true to form. In the final months he reviewed his opinions of his close friends and favorite students and found that he had been right about them all along. I had never told him that I had fallen in love with Rosamund because he would have laughed, and told me that I was being an idiot. It's very important, however, to understand that he was not one of those people for whom love has been debunked and punctured—for whom it is a historical, Romantic myth long in dying but today finally dead. He thought—no, he *saw*—that every soul was looking for its peculiar other, longing for its complement. I'm not going to describe Eros, et cetera, as he saw it. I've done too much of that already: but there is a certain irreducible splendor about it without which we would not be quite human. Love is the highest function of our species—its vocation. This simply can't be set aside in considering Ravelstein. He never forgot this conviction. It figures in all his judgments.

He often spoke well of Rosamund. He said she was earnest, hard-working, had a good mind. She was a pretty and lively young woman. Young women, he said, were burdened by what he called "glamour maintenance." Nature, furthermore, gave them a longing for children, and therefore for marriage, for the stability requisite for family life. And this, together with a mass of other things, disabled them for philosophy.

"There are young women who think they can keep a husband alive forever," he said.

"Do you think that covers Rosamund's case? I almost never think of my calendar-years. I'm forever hiking across the same plateau with no end in sight."

"There are significant facts that have to be lived with but you don't have to let them engross you."

When he referred to his sickness it was almost always in this oblique way. Ravelstein was making his final arrangements. Nobody volunteered to talk to him about them. The one exception was Nikki. But Nikki was, in a special sense, family. If Ravelstein had a family it would be an exotic one, because he had no use for families.

Nikki, the handsome Chinese prince, would inherit. The rest of us in one degree or another were not heirs but friends.

In the last months of his life Ravelstein did the things he had always done. He met his classes, he organized conferences. When it was beyond his strength to give lectures, he invited his friends to give them: Foundation money was always available. His bald head at the center of the front row dominated these events. When a lecture ended, he was invariably the first to ask a question.

This became protocol. Everyone waited for him to kick off the discussion. At the beginning of the fall term he was still quite active, though when I escorted him to the campus from the apartment he had to stop at every other corner to catch his breath.

I recall that flocks of parrots had descended on a clump of trees that grew edible red berries. These parrots, thought to be the descendants of a pair of caged birds that had escaped, built their long, sac-like nests in the lake-front park and later colonized the alleys. In these bird tenements that hung from utility poles, hundreds of green parrots lived.

"What are we looking at?" said Ravelstein, turning his outsized round eyes on me.

"We're looking at parrots."

"Sure we are, but I never thought I'd see the likes of this. What a noise they make."

"Well, there used to be only rats, mice, and gray squirrels—now there are raccoons in the alleys and even possums—a new garbage-based ecology in the big cities . . ."

"You mean the urban jungle is no longer a metaphor," he said. "It really jangles me to listen to these noisy green birds from the tropics. Doesn't the snow get them down?"

"It doesn't seem to."

Nothing got them down. The noisy green birds threshing and bickering in the leaves, scattering snow, gorging on berries held Ravelstein's attention longer than I had expected. He had little interest in natural life. Human beings absorbed him entirely. To lose yourself in grasses, leaves, winds, birds, or beasts was an evasion of higher duties. And I think the birds held his attention unusually long because they were not merely feeding, but gorging, and he was a voracious eater himself. Or had been one. His meals were now mainly social, conversational occasions. He was dining out nightly. Nikki couldn't cook for all the people who were flying in to see Ravelstein.

Abe was taking the common drug prescribed for his condition but he didn't want it to be known. I remember how much it shocked him when his nurse walked in—the room was full of friends. She said, "It's time for your AZT."

He said to me the next day, "I could have killed the woman." He was still enraged. "Don't they give those people any training?"

"They're from the ghetto," said Nikki.

"Ghetto nothing!" Ravelstein said. "Ghetto Jews had highly developed feelings, civilized nerves—thousands of years of training. They had communities and laws. 'Ghetto' is an ignorant newspaper term. It's not a ghetto that they come from, it's a noisy, pointless, nihilistic turmoil."

One day he said to me, "Chick, I need a check drawn. It's not a lot. Five hundred bucks."

"Why can't you write it yourself?"

"I want to avoid trouble with Nikki. He'd see it on the check stub."

"All right. How do you want it drawn?"

"Make it out to cash."

There was no need to ask Ravelstein to elaborate. "I've written the address out," he said, and handed me a slip of paper.

"Consider it done."

"I'll cut you a check."

"Don't give it a thought," I said.

I wondered whether some visitor hadn't pinched a cigarette lighter or some other *bibelot,* and Ravelstein was paying ransom. But I decided it wasn't worth pursuing. He had already told me about his sharp increase in sexual feeling. He'd say, "I feel hot, and what am I supposed to do with it? And some of these kids have a singular sympathy with you. They've got the complete picture. I would never have expected death to be such a weird aphrodisiac. I don't know why I'm unloading this on you. Maybe I think this is information you should have."

I have a life-time habit of putting things off. Of course I knew Ravelstein was in the end zone, that he didn't have long to live. But when Nikki told me that Morris Herbst was coming to town I felt I was on notice to pull myself together.

Ravelstein and Morris Herbst were on the phone every day. With Ravelstein's assistance, Morris, a widower, had managed to bring up two children. Ravelstein was, somehow, in love with their late mother, and spoke of her with singular respect and admiration. He described to me her "dramatic white face, black eyes, a beautiful and sexually open but not promiscuous nature." Nothing in the sexual line is prohibited anymore, but the challenge is to hold your own against the general sexual anarchy. Ravelstein admired Herbst's late wife, loved her. She was the one woman whose photograph he carried in his wallet. So it was entirely natural that he should be a second father to her children. He dug up scholarships and found campus jobs for them, vetted their friends, and made certain that they read the essential classics.

It was Nikki who told me about the photo of Nehamah. "It's there with the credit and Blue Cross cards," he said. "You know that he goes for people who have basic passions—who make the tears come to his eyes. With Abe that counts more than anything."

If Ravelstein didn't often talk about Nehamah Herbst the reason was that in the last months of her life, he and Morris had built a cult of sorts around her. Abe had spent much time with her in the final weeks, and she had spoken freely about secret and intimate matters. Though he couldn't be trusted to respect confidences, he never told me what he and Nehamah had talked about.

Nehamah's mother came over from Mea Sha'arim and begged her daughter to have an orthodox ceremony performed.

"What, on my deathbed?"

"Yes. For the sake of your children you must. I am here to save them."

But one almost never gets the real thing, Ravelstein sometimes said. What truly matters has to be revealed, never performed. But only a handful of human beings have the imagination and the qualities of character to live by the true Eros. Nehamah not only refused to see the orthodox rabbi her mother had brought to her deathbed, but never spoke to her again, and without her daughter's goodbye the old woman flew back to Mea Sha'arim. "Nehamah was pure and she was immovable," Ravelstein said in the low voice of infinite respect.

I am trying as well as I can to transmit the singular connection between Ravelstein and Morris Herbst. For thirty or forty years

they were in daily contact. "Now that there is moolah for every purpose, I have the satisfaction of being in touch, of talking to Morris
without a thought of the expense," Ravelstein told me. Anyway, he
never opened the telephone bills, Nikki said. Those were paid by
Legg Mason, the vast investment firm in the East that managed his
money. Abe told Nikki, who opened the mail, "I don't like the electronic printouts, I'm certainly not about to study them. Don't bring
anything up, don't hand me a statement unless the principal falls
below ten million." Here, Nikki's oriental reserve was blown away.
He couldn't stop laughing. "Not a penny less than ten big ones," he
said. He was open with me because I never pressed him—we never
spoke of money. He would have been—let's see, now, what would
he have been? "Affronted" is the suitable word. He had his own
kind of princely Asiatic mildness, but if you were to offend him
Nikki would tear your head off.

Morris Herbst, to get back to him, was at the top of Ravelstein's
guest list for every conference he organized. He was the first to be
invited and the first to accept. He read a paper at each and every one
of Ravelstein's events. He had a reflective, settled, stable air and
spoke deliberately without hurry or nervousness. With his square
white beard—no mustache—he had the look of a Michigan farmer
I had known fifty years ago. Herbst too had studied with Professor
Davarr, but without Greek he could never call himself a genuine
Davarr product. He taught Goethe, he had written a book about
Elective Affinities, but the curious fact was—and there were always
curious facts—he had a weakness too for cards and dice and was often in Las Vegas. Ravelstein had an extra-high regard for reckless
plungers. And I too had a good opinion of Herbst. I couldn't say
why. He gambled, he lost his head when he played Twenty-one, and

though he mourned his wife he also chased women, but he never made any false claims about himself.

Yes, he had kept the family, just as he promised Nehamah, but the children knew all the details of his womanizing, his love affairs. There was always some lady or other camping in the house after Nehamah died, and women telephoned him from all parts of the country. He had a calm manner—a four-square way of sitting tight. His white hair was both curly and wavy and his color high. He looked well but he owed his life to cardiac surgery. And when you put a question to him, you had to wait while he organized his answer. He might sit tight, considering his reply (several times I clocked him) for as long as five minutes. He was a sober and circumspect conversationalist. German-born, he specialized in German thinkers. He was never as keen on them as he was on women but since the death of his wife he had had one durable love affair with a woman whose none-too-patient husband had to put up with their long nightly telephone calls. Without the telephone, what would Morris's spiritual life have been? Ravelstein preferred the French expression. He said "I wouldn't call Morris a chaser. He's a real *homme à femmes*. If it's not a vocation, it's nothing."

Five years ago, the surgeons had told Herbst his heart was used up. He was wait-listed for a transplant with a very high priority. He had no more than a week to go when a motorcyclist from Missouri was killed in a crash. The boy's organs were harvested. Technically these transplants are an immense achievement. The human side of the thing is that Morris carries another man's heart in his chest. One might accept a skin graft from a compatible stranger. But the heart, we would be inclined to agree, is a different matter. The heart is a mystery. If you've seen your own heart on a video screen, as millions by now have done, convulsing and opening rhythmically, you may have wondered why this persistent muscle is so faithful in its function from the uterus to the last breath. This rhythmic gripping and relaxing blindly goes on. Why? How? And who was it now that prolonged Morris Herbst's life—a harum-scarum adolescent speed demon from Cape Girardeau, Missouri, about whom Herbst knew nothing. Nothing fits here except the old industrial slogan: "The parts are interchangeable." This brings modern reality home to us.

During the war, it often came home to me that the Russian troops driving Hitler's army back through Poland did it all on canned pork from Chicago.

Why pork? Well, it is appropriate in this case. Morris was a believing Jew—not fully orthodox but more or less observant. And this freestyle Jew owes his existence to the heart from the bosom of a young man who lost control of his bike—I don't know the actual circumstances of his death. All I really know is that surgical technicians took out the boy's heart and it now replaced the faltering heart in Herbst's breast. Herbst would tell me that it brought foreign impulses and sensations into his life.

I asked him what that meant.

Seated and circumspect, his hands on his knees, his pale look gone with the leaky heart that had been killing him, the white hair curled around his now ruddy face, he said about himself that just then he felt like the Santa Claus in the department store asking kiddies what they wanted for Christmas. Because at the center of his "physical plant" (his own term for it) his borrowed heart had taken over, and he felt that a different temperament had come with it— boyish, heedless, not just willing but glad to take a risk. "I feel a little like that fellow who calls himself Evel Knievel and jumps his Honda bike over sixteen beer barrels."

I understood this, oddly enough, because at the time I was being treated by a physical therapist who told me that the main organs of the body were surrounded by charged energies and that she, the therapist, was then and there in touch with my gall bladder. I said, "But I no longer have a gall bladder. It's been taken out."

"Sure, but those energies remain—and they'll be there as long as you live," she told me.

I bring this up, with a touch of agnosticism, because I was asked to believe that it was not the young man's heart alone that had changed bodies. The organs are also repositories of the shadows or the assertive impulses—anxious or happy as the case may be, and these had come into Herbst's body with the new heart. They now would need to come to terms with the forces of their new setting.

If this were a kidney or a pancreatic transplant it would be different. But the heart carries so many connotations; it's the center of man's emotions—his higher life.

At any rate, Morris, a German Jew, was saved by this Missouri boy. And I had to restrain myself from questioning him about a heart originally Christian or Gentile, with its shadow energies and its rhythms—how did it adapt itself to Jewish needs or peculiarities, pains and ideas? At this point I could not discuss the subject with Ravelstein. He was in no condition to turn his thoughts in that direction.

The most I dared to do was to ask Morris in the most tentative way about the transplant. He said that in all states when you were issued a driver's license you were asked to check a box agreeing or declining to be an organ donor. "In half a second the kid made an X—what the hell, why not! So the heart was flown east and the surgery was done at Mass General."

"And you don't know anything else about the kid?"

"Very little. I wrote a thank-you letter to his parents."

"What did you tell them, if you don't mind saying?"

"I told them, honestly, how grateful I was, and I came on as a straightforward American so they wouldn't have to worry that their boy's heart was keeping some foreign creep alive. . . ."

"It must give you second thoughts, on the road, when you're suddenly surrounded by a gang of young guys on bikes, with scarves, caps, and goggles."

"I'm always braced for that."

"Did the boy's family answer?"

"Not so much as a postcard. But they must be glad his heart is living on." He turned his face downward with a tentative look. His fingers spread on the temple propped up his head—as if he were looking for answers in the motif of Ravelstein's Persian carpet, or doping out a singular message there about the miraculous extension he was given. I had no hope invested in the carpet. I fell back on the language of big-city politics—a strange fix had been put in. And so life—that is, what one incessantly saw, the pictures produced by life—continued. This was related to something I had said to Ravelstein.

When he asked me what view I took of death, how I imagined it, I said that the pictures would stop. Evidently I saw as pictures what Americans refer to as Experience. I wasn't at the moment thinking of the pictures newly available, recently offered by technology—the kind of tour one now might take of one's digestive tract, or of the heart. The heart—only a group of muscles after all. But how tenacious they are, starting to beat in the womb, and going in rhythm for as long as a century. In Herbst's case it had petered out in his fifties, and the transplant would keep him going into his eighties.

He signed himself into the hospital once a year for tests. But by and large his life went on as before. He looked kindly, tolerant, open-minded. His benevolent, silent clock of a face with its clean, curly white border of beard was calm and healthy. He looked women over very closely, checked out their figures, their breasts, legs, their hairstyles. He was one of those men who appreciate, who can do justice to, the qualities of women. His appraisals didn't seem to make anyone uneasy. He took a disinterested pleasure in sizing women up. But his manner was quiet, he didn't make a production of it, and few were annoyed by his interest.

When Herbst arrived I made myself scarce. Friends for nearly half a century, Abe and Morris would have a world of things to say to each other. Ravelstein was calling from his bed, "Bring him here." The Pratesi sheets had been pulled out at the corners and the mink coverlet, beautifully cured and soft, had fallen to the floor. On the walls, the paintings somehow were never hanging straight. All the good antique pieces in the room were piled with clothing and with manuscripts and letters. The letters always made me think of the controversies he was involved in—the powerful unforgiving enemies he had made in the academic world. He didn't care a damn about any of them.

Herbst stooped at the bedside and hugged Ravelstein.

"Chick, pull up a seat for Morris, won't you."

I brought forward the round-backed leather Italian chair. You tended to forget that Herbst was kept alive by his transplant. He looked well enough to attend to normal needs. I half suspected for a moment that Ravelstein preferred him, his oldest friend, to be an invalid. But that thought was very brief. It was unlike Ravelstein to play around like that. He was dying, of course, but there wasn't going to be any sickroom business. He needed—he wanted—to talk.

I got out, leaving the friends together in what Ravelstein had furnished as a kind of bedroom fit for a man of his stature. Almost immediately I heard the two of them laughing loudly—they were telling each other the best (the crudest, the raunchiest) jokes they had heard lately. The solemn "last days of Socrates" atmosphere was not Ravelstein's style. This was not the time to be somebody else—not even Socrates. You wanted more than ever to be what you had always been. He wasn't about to fool away his declining hours being somebody else.

When they settled down for their private talk I went home and reported the day's events to Rosamund. She had been on the phone with the woman who was typing her dissertation. She'd be giving her doctoral lecture in a few weeks. She had studied for five years with Ravelstein, so that if I needed to know what Machiavelli owed to Livy I had only to ask this slender, handsome young woman with the long blue eyes. I cared little these days about Machiavelli's debts. What was more important and tremendously comforting to me was that there was nothing I could say to this woman that she wouldn't understand.

"Did Herbst arrive? They must have so much to say to each other."

"I don't doubt that they do, but they had a few dirty jokes to tell each other first. It's an odd occasion from any angle. There's Herbst with another man's heart beating away in his chest and Ravelstein has already said goodbye to him. In a way jokes are more suitable than a conversation on the soul and immortality. To find out what happens after you stop breathing you have to buy a ticket."

"To die?"

"Well, is there any other way to get the information?"

"Did Nikki tell you that Dr. Schley is sending Ravelstein back to the hospital?"

"I'm surprised," I said. "He's just learned to walk again. You thought he'd at least have a year more."

"Didn't you?" said Rosamund.

"Sure, but he wouldn't want it to just drag on. In the hospital he'll have more protection from friends and well-wishers."

"He's far more sociable than you, Chick. He enjoys company."

It was not merely a matter of company. People brought their problems to him as well, as if from his deathbed you could expect something approaching divine information.

The door to Ravelstein's bedroom stood open and I could see our friend Battle's long back-hair resting on his mountainous shoulders, and his natty, ankle-high boots. I didn't have his face fully before me but his wife was evidently crying. She was bent forward. Those couldn't have been anything but tears. I had great respect for Mrs. Battle and was very fond of her husband.

The Battles were Ravelstein fans. They never attended his public lectures and I doubt they read his books, but they took him very seriously. When Battle retired some years ago, he and his wife moved across the state line into the Wisconsin woods, living very simply, à la Thoreau. When they were in town Ravelstein liked to dine with them at our Serbian-French club.

I had made the discovery that if you put people in a comic light they became more likable—if you spoke of someone as a gross, belching, wall-eyed human pike you got along much better with him, thereafter partly because you were aware that you were the sadist who took away his human attributes. Also, having done him some metaphorical violence, you owed him special consideration.

After they had gone Ravelstein said to me (he was coiled up with some internal amusement) that the purpose of their visit was to get his advice.

"About what?"

"They came to talk to me about their suicide plans. They apologized for troubling me. At such a time . . ."

"I should think so," I said.

"Don't be too hard on them, Chick. With older people suicide fantasies are common enough. I think they were serious."

"*They* thought they were being serious."

"Because I'm dying I had the same thought, naturally. This is a hell of a time for people to be bringing me their problems. They put it in the 'just suppose' form. Did I think that in the abstract, at their time of life, and all the rest of it, they would be well advised . . . ?"

"A suicide pact?"

"Battle made the argument and she filled it out and added the sensible comment. They said I was the only person they trusted enough and who wouldn't be satirical with them."

"So you come to a man who would rather not die and you put your case for suicide to him."

"Battle has been hinting at it for weeks. He's a very intelligent person, but he has too much character to overcome. His character makes him inarticulate. She's the more sensible one, and she came wearing a plain blue suit with rows of buttons down the front. She's a little thing. Or is it the supersized husband that makes her look tiny? Anyway, she has a pretty, upward-looking small Brit face. I think that when kids look at her they must see a lovely, sympathetic face. . . ."

"So what's their complaint?"

"The complaint is that they're getting old. All educated people make the same mistake—they think that nature and solitude are good for them. Nature and solitude are poison," said Ravelstein. "Poor Battle and his wife are depressed by the woods. That's the first observation to be made."

"What did you tell them?"

"I said they had done right to take it up with me. More people should get advice when they're suicidal. They feel that way because there's no community, no one to talk to."

"Maybe it's their idea of a tribute—as if they were saying that life without their friend Ravelstein would lose its value," I said.

"Well, they're dear people," said Ravelstein. "They dreamed up this occult way of letting me know that I didn't have to go it alone."

"Obviously they talk about you all the time, and you may have become their absent referee."

"So that if I died they might as well be dead, too," said Ravelstein, but this was his way of making light of the subject. He loved gossip but the interest he took in people would be hard to describe. He had a curious intuitive ability but with him it wasn't so much analysis as it was divination that you sensed when he talked about personalities, or groped them out.

"What I said was that it was a mistake to make suicide a matter of argument or debate. To reason for or against life is kid stuff."

"You have great authority with both of the Battles, and if you said don't do it, they wouldn't do it."

"That's not my style, Chick, to lay down the law."

This was certainly untrue.

"They wanted to be taken seriously," he said. "But of course they weren't. They wanted to amuse me with their double-suicide routine."

That was more like it.

"I told them they had had a great love affair. A classic."

"And they shouldn't bring love into disrepute," I said.

"Something like that," said Ravelstein. "You've heard the story. After one dance with Battle, whom she had never met before, she left her husband. She stepped into Battle's arms and that was that. In that same instant, both parties recognized that their respective marriages were ended. . . . He was strong on the tennis court and on the dance floor but he was no seducer, and she was not an unfaithful wife. He said he would be waiting for her at the airport. . . ."

"Where was that again?"

"In Brazil. And they've had a happy life."

"I remember now. Their plane was struck by lightning. They had to land in Uruguay. So for many years they were together— forty years without a letdown. The Battles count on me to summarize things, so I obliged and told them their own story. Among millions or hundreds of millions of people they alone lucked out. They had a great love affair and decades of effortless happiness. Each amused the other with his or her eccentricities. How could they bear to cheapen it with a suicide . . . ? I could see that Mrs. Battle was hearing what she hoped to hear. She wanted me to make the case for continuing to live."

"But Battle was not completely satisfied—is that it?"

"That's right, Chick. He wanted a discussion about suicide and nihilism. I've often thought that suicide fantasies and murder fantasies balance each other in the mental economy of civilized people. Battle's not a professor through and through, but he feels a responsibility to square himself with nihilism. He doesn't know much about nihilism but it's in the air. He said something about successful people being prone to suicide—seeing through the illusions of success and doing away with themselves . . ."

"If you dislike existence then death is your release. You can call this nihilism, if you like."

"Yes. American-style—without the abyss," said Ravelstein. "But the Jews feel that the world was created for each and every one of us, and when you destroy a human life you destroy an entire world—the world as it existed for that person."

All at once Ravelstein was annoyed with me. At least he was speaking with an angry emphasis. Perhaps I was still smiling at the Battles and it might have seemed to him that I was dissociating myself from the view that you destroyed an entire world when you destroyed yourself. As if I would threaten to destroy a world—I who lived to see the phenomena, who believe that the heart of things is shown in the surface of those things. I always said—in answering Ravelstein's question "What do you imagine death will be like?"— "The pictures will stop." Meaning, again, that in the surface of things you saw the heart of things.

To the end, Ravelstein attracted lots of visitors. Few reached his bedroom—Nikki saw to that. But among those who mattered was Sam Pargiter, whose presence was oddly significant. He was one of my close friends. Through me he had read Abe's famous book and attended his public lectures and came also to some of our joint seminars. He highly valued Ravelstein's opinions and his jokes. With a large *No Smoking* sign behind him, Ravelstein lit cigarettes with his Dunhill flame as he lectured, saying, "If you leave because you hate tobacco more than you love ideas, you won't be missed." He said this with such comic sharpness and good nature that Pargiter then and there fell in love with him and asked me to introduce him to this witty man. I told Ravelstein that my friend Sam Pargiter wanted to meet him.

"Well, we'll make you a double team of totally bald friends," said Ravelstein. Ravelstein did not reproach me for this but it was clear from his way of putting it that since time was now very short I shouldn't bring him new acquaintances.

"Did you say he was a Catholic priest?"

"Once, he was," I said. "He applied for a release. He's a Catholic still. . . . You have a Jesuit friend yourself—Trimble."

"Trimble and I shared a flat in Paris and we often went out together. But he was a Davarr student like me and we spoke the same language."

"Well, I haven't discussed this with Sam Pargiter but you can be sure that he comes here because he's read you and you can be sure also that he would never try to pull off a ninth-inning conversion."

I discover, looking back, that I was curiously concerned with the people who came to see Ravelstein in his last days and, along the walls of the room, form the largely silent group of witnesses. He no longer had the strength to accept or reject visitors. Of some of them I could say that he didn't at all want them to be there. One of his long-time rivals, Smith, appeared with a new wife who coached the professor at the bedside, "Say that you love him. Go on—say it." And the man lamely said, "I love you," when it was perfectly plain that he loathed him. They loathed each other. Ravelstein broke through this impossible moment with a golden smile but he was no longer capable of intervening. Clearly Smith was angry with his latest wife. Nobody had the authority to order the Smiths to leave the bedside. So it was just as well that Pargiter, whose presences, as I was dying, I would have welcomed, was sitting by the door. Pargiter came to comfort or witness—very simply, to sit along the walls and do a job, largely tacit, of being there.

Those of whom he had a genuine need came regularly. The Floods, for instance, husband and wife, a couple to whom Ravelstein and Nikki were greatly attached. Flood was part of the university administration—community relations were his special responsibility. He represented the University at City Hall and supervised the campus security system—the university police reported to him. Scandal management was one of his assignments. He was a complex, feeling, earnest, and good-hearted man. God knows how many unpleasant matters he had taken care of for the University community. Nor did you have to belong to that community to be taken up by him. There was a Greek restaurant proprietor whose daughter's life Flood saved by arranging surgery at the last possible dangerous moment. All over the city he had a quiet reputation as "a man you could turn to in a pinch." He had done favors for Ravelstein and for me. At home, the Floods' doors, like Ravelstein's own, were open. People came and went with a minimum of challenge or formality. Gilda Flood and her husband very simply loved each other. More than any other human connection this naïve (but indispensable) one was valued by Ravelstein. One doesn't have to spell this out. I am simply noting the variety of visitors drawn to Ravelstein's bedside so that when he roused himself to look at them along the walls, he would be comforted to see people with whom he was familiar, with whom he had affinities—something like relatives—the nearest thing to family available.

Toward the end Ravelstein was often impatient with me. He had learned from Professor Davarr that modern people—and, in some ways, I was a modern person—made things too easy for themselves.

And it did them no harm to be called to account—to prune back the persistent overgrowth of delusion. So he could be direct without offense.

Often the dying become extremely severe. We will still be here when they're gone and it's not easy for them to forgive us. If I didn't deserve the ruler for opinion X, I clearly deserved a double rap on the knuckles for Y. The older you grow the worse the discoveries you make about yourself. He would have put to better use the years *I* was allotted. To acknowledge the plain facts is the least one can do. He thought I was being flippant about the sin of suicide when I said he had given the Battles a very Jewish answer. But then he relented, saying, "Anyway, you can credit me with having saved two lives."

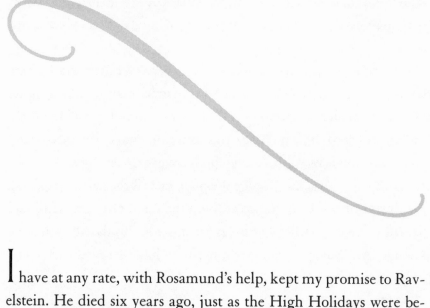

I have at any rate, with Rosamund's help, kept my promise to Ravelstein. He died six years ago, just as the High Holidays were beginning. When I said Kaddish for my parents, I had him in mind, too. And during the memorial service—Yizkor—I began even to give some thought to the memoir I had promised to write and wondered how I would go about it—how to deal with his freaks, quiddities, oddities, his eating, drinking, shaving, dressing, and playfully savaging his students. But that isn't much more than his natural history. Others saw him as bizarre, perverse—grinning, smoking, lecturing, overbearing, impatient, but to me he was brilliant and charming. Out to undermine the social sciences or other university specialties. He was doomed to die because of his irregular sexual ways. About these he was entirely frank with me, with all his close friends. He was considered, to use a term from the past, an invert. Not a "gay." He despised campy homosexuality and took a very low view of "gay pride." There were times when I simply didn't know what to make of his confidences. But then he had chosen me to do his portrait, and when he spoke to me he spoke intimately but also for the record. To lose your head was the great-souled thing to do. I suppose that even in this age people will understand the term "great-souled," though it is not the standing challenge it used to be. Ravelstein in any case counted confidently on my ability to describe him. "You can do it easy," he said to me. I agreed—more or less.

The rule for the dead is that they should be forgotten. After burial there is a universal gradual progress toward oblivion. But with Ravelstein this didn't altogether work. He claimed and filled a more conspicuous space in Rosamund's life as well as mine. She remembered a text from her schooldays that went "Associate with the noblest people you can find; read the best books; live with the mighty; but learn to be happy alone."

To Ravelstein this would have been the usual high-minded high-school kabibble.

Still, in his own shaggy way, Ravelstein had without question been one of those "noblest people." But for me the challenge of portraying him (what an olden-days' word "portraying" has become) by and by turned into a burden. Rosamund, however, believed that I was exactly right for the job. And in fact I went through a rehearsal of my own with death. But at that time we were only considering Ravelstein's death.

"It's just a matter of getting started," she said. "As he said, it's the *premier pas qui coûte*."

"Yes. Some French Ravelstein equivalent of bottled-in-bond or *sur papier timbre,* in perfect legal order, solemnized by the state."

"There it is—exactly the joke-tone he hoped you'd take. You can leave it to others to comment on his ideas."

"Oh, I intend to. I'm going to leave intellectual matters to the experts."

"All you need is to get yourself in the right position."

But as the months—years—went by, I couldn't for the life of me find this starting point. "It should be easy. 'Easily or not at all,' or as what's-his-name said, 'If it isn't like birdsong, it ain't right.'"

Rosamund occasionally answered, "Do Ravelstein and birdsong mix? Somehow they don't."

With exchanges of this sort, years went by, and it became apparent that I was unable to begin, that I faced a humongous obstacle. Rosamund no longer offered encouragement or advice. It was wise of her to let me be.

We continued, however, to talk almost daily about Ravelstein. It was I who recalled his basketball evening parties, the student dinners in Greektown, his shopping expeditions, and the racy but serious seminars he used to do. Another woman might have pressed me unpleasantly. "After all, he was a dear friend and you swore you'd do this," or, "In the life-to-come he's disappointed." But Rosamund understood all too well that I thought of this myself, and oppressively too often. I sometimes imagined him in his shroud, lying next to the father he had hated. Ravelstein used to say, "That hysterical man who beat my bare bottom and shrieked gibberish—and later, no matter how well I did he'd hold it against me that I never made Phi Beta Kappa. 'So you published a book and it was well received—but no Phi Beta Kappa?'"

Rosamund would only say, "If you did no more than this Phi Beta Kappa sketch it would cheer Ravelstein in the afterlife."

And my answer to this was, "Ravelstein didn't believe in an afterlife. And if he does exist somewhere, what possible pleasure could it give him to remember his dumbhead father or any part of what we call our mortal span? I'm the one who imagines seeing the dead parents on the other side. And brothers, friends, cousins, aunts and uncles . . ."

Rosamund often nodded. She admitted that she had a similar tendency. She sometimes added, "I ask myself what they're doing in the life-to-come."

"If you could take a poll on the subject you'd find that a majority of us expect to see their dead, whom they loved and continue to love—the very people they had, now and then, cheated and some-times despised or hated or habitually lied to. Not you, Rosamund, you're exceptionally honest. But even Ravelstein, a man who was too *hard* to have such illusions, said . . . He gave himself away when he told me that of all the people close to him I was the likeliest to fol-low him soon—to follow him *where?* Would I catch up with him, and would we see each other?"

"You can't build too much on remarks like that," said Rosamund.

"It's easy enough to argue that childish love is the source of these illusions. This is my way of admitting that half a century later I feel I haven't seen the last of my mother. Freud would have trashed this as sentimental and inane. But Freud was a doctor, and nineteenth-century doctors were rough on the sentiments. They'd say the human being represented chemical components worth about sixty-two-cents—they were severe rationalists and tough guys."

"But Ravelstein was far from simpleminded," said Rosamund.

"Of course he was. But let's go a step or two further—I'll let you in on a kinky thought. I wonder what might happen. If I were to write my memoir of Ravelstein there would be no barrier between death and me."

Rosamund laughed outright at this. "Do you mean that your du-ties would end, and there would be no reason to live on?"

"No, no. Luckily I'd still have you to live for, Rosamund. What I'm probably trying to say is that in Ravelstein's view I may have nothing more to do in this life than to commemorate him."

"That *is* an odd thought for anyone to have."

"He felt he was giving me a great subject—the subject of subjects. And that is an odd thought. But I've never assumed that I was a rational, modern person. A rational person wouldn't be meeting his dead in the gloaming—wherever the gloaming is."

"All the same," said Rosamund, "the fact that it's so persistent makes it something to reckon with."

"And why me? In less than a minute I can name five people better qualified."

"About his ideas, yes," said Rosamund. "But they mightn't have the color to put into it. Also—you two became friends late in life and, as a rule, older people don't form such attachments. . . ."

Perhaps she meant, also, that the old didn't fall in love. They weren't apt to blunder into the magnetic field where they had no business to be.

"For a year or two Ravelstein kept after me because Vela and I saw Radu Grielescu and his wife so often," I said to Rosamund.

"They entertained you?"

"They took us to good restaurants—the most expensive ones, anyway. Vela loved all the hand-kissing, bowing, fussing over the ladies, the corsages, and the toasting. She was terribly pleased. Grielescu put on such a show. Ravelstein was extremely curious about those evenings. He said that Radu had belonged to the Iron Guard. I paid no particular attention to this. I didn't get the drift, and that bothered Ravelstein."

"You didn't spot him for a Nazi?" Rosamund said.

"Ravelstein went a step further and told me that Grielescu about ten years ago had been scheduled to lecture in Jerusalem but that the invitation was canceled. Somehow even this didn't register with me. I must have been too busy to put it together. I do shut off my receptors sometimes and decide, somehow, not to see what there is to be seen. Ravelstein noticed that, naturally. I was the one who failed to notice.

"Ravelstein wanted to know just what Grielescu's line was like and I told him that at dinner he lectured about archaic history, he stuffed his pipe, and lit lots of matches. You grip your pipe to keep it from shaking, and then the fingers with the match tremble twice as hard. He kept stuffing the pipe with the rebellious tobacco. When it didn't stay stuffed, he didn't have enough thumb-power to pack it down. How could such a person be politically dangerous? His jacket cuffs come down over his knuckles."

Rosamund said, "My guess is that being seen in public with you was worth a lot to Grielescu. But this is how you do things, Chick: the observations you make crowd out the main point."

"That's exactly what Ravelstein eventually told me. And how curious it was that I let myself be used like that."

"You wanted to please your wife. You wanted her good opinion. And Ravelstein probably felt that you were letting yourself be conned. Taking the easy way out . . ."

"I suppose I said to myself that this was some Frenchy-Balkan absurdity. Somehow I couldn't take Balkan fascists seriously. When the check came, Radu sprang out of his chair to grab it. It became a game that I never once get the tab. And one of the things that got me was how he always paid with clean, unwrinkled, fresh-from-the-bank currency, and he never seemed to look at the amount of the bill. If you grew up in the Depression, you wouldn't miss such a thing."

"And you entertained Ravelstein with your descriptions."

"I tried to. But he waved away the pipes and mannerisms. He was waiting for me to come out of the fog."

"Well, you were his appointed biographer. That you were slow on the uptake couldn't have pleased him."

"Of course not. When he told me that Radu's invitation to Jerusalem had been canceled I didn't even ask for the particulars. I see that I missed the boat."

"Well, when he chose you to write about him he didn't think you had no faults," said Rosamund.

"About the basics we agreed as closely as we could, considering my ignorance," I told her. "He had the support of the classics. I certainly did not, but when I was wrong I didn't put my energy where my errors were. I learned later in life how foolish it was to insist that you had been right."

"You needed to be right and you couldn't get by and be right, also," said Rosamund.

"Vela's plan was that Grielescu should replace Ravelstein. In Paris, when Abe rushed into our room and surprised her in her slip, she ran for the bathroom—she had a strange way of running, hippity-hop on her tiptoes—and she locked the door. Then the time came when she told me we couldn't see Ravelstein anymore."

"That was very odd," said Rosamund. In speaking of Vela she was always proper and circumspect. "Was this when Vela sent for her mother? Did she bring her to Paris?"

"No, no. The old girl had died a couple years before this. Your hunch is right, though. She relied on her mother to cover the— what should I call them—the human relations. She had no such skills herself. Anyway, the old girl loathed me. Having a Jewish son-in-law poisoned her old age."

"Now you've put your finger on the real subject," said Rosamund.

"You've given lots of thought to all kinds of problems, except the most important one. You began with the Jewish question," she said.

"Of course that's what this conversation is circling—what it means to the Jews that so many others, millions of others, willed their death. The rest of humankind expelled them. Hitler was on record as having said that once he was in power he would have gallows, in rows, put up at the Marienplatz in Munich and the Jews, to the last Jew, would be hung there. It was the Jews that were Hitler's ticket to power. He didn't have, nor did he need, any other program. He became Chancellor by uniting Germany and much of the rest of Europe against the Jews. Anyway, insofar as this relates to Grielescu, I don't think he was a malevolent Jew-hater, but when he was called upon to declare himself, he declared himself. He had a vote and he voted. As Ravelstein saw it I refused to do the unpleasant work of thinking it all through."

"You didn't know where to begin?"

"Well, I had a Jewish life to lead in the American language, and that's not a language that's helpful with dark thoughts."

"Did you ever talk to Ravelstein about this power of viciousness?"

"I may have. Abe's character was far more cheerful than mine—a wide-open broad-daylight outlook. He was more like a normal person. But also he was anything but innocent."

"I did Thucydides with him," said Rosamund. "And I can remember what he had to say about the plague in Athens and the dumping of dead parents or sisters on the funeral pyres of strangers. But as for linking this with the masses of dead in the twentieth century—that wasn't something he did in class. Can you remember anything he might have said?"

"How do you suppose," I asked Rosamund, "that a man like Rav-

elstein might match up his existence—his daily awareness that he is
dying—with the fact that his attention now is drawn to the many
millions who were destroyed in this century. I am not thinking here
of the fighting men or of peasants, kulaks, bourgeois, or party members or those designated as people eligible for forced labor, for death
in the Gulags or fascist concentration camps—people easy to round
up and send away in cattle cars. These would not normally have attracted Ravelstein's attention. They were the usual 'losers,' people
whom governments had no reason to be concerned with—what
somebody called a 'quicksand society' which sucked its victims
down and drowned or suffocated them. The shortest way with such
people was to get rid of them, turn them into corpses. There were
also the Jews who had lost the right to exist and were told as much
by their executioners—'There is no reason why you should not die.'
And so from the Gulag in Russian Asia to the Atlantic Coast, there
was a record of destruction or something like a death-disseminating
anarchy. You had to think of these hundreds of thousands of millions destroyed on ideological grounds—that is, with some pretext
of rationality. A rationale had considerable value as a manifestation
of order or firmness of purpose. But the maddest forms of nihilism
are the most strict German military ones. According to Davarr, who
was a very great analyst, German militarism produced the extremest
and most horrible nihilism. For the rank-and-file this led to the
bloodiest and craziest kind of *revanchist* murderous zeal. Because it
was implicit in carrying out orders that all responsibility went back
to the top, the source of all orders. And everybody was thus ab-
solved. They were crazies through and through. And this was the
Wehrmacht way of getting around responsibility for their crimes.
Suppose there were civilian methods to attenuate guilty conduct,

Ravelstein told me. Adding, 'But here I'm talking through my hat.' On all topics he had firm views but toward the end, when he referred obliquely to his condition he was more often sad than ironic, wasn't he, Rosie?"

"He wouldn't let himself sink into sadness for long, either."

"Well, but there was a general willingness to live with the destruction of millions. It was like the mood of the century to accept it. In combat you were covered by the special allowances made for soldiers. But I'm thinking of the great death populations of the Gulags and the German labor camps. Why does the century—I don't know how else to put it—underwrite so much destruction? There is a lameness that comes over all of us when we consider these facts."

I date this particular conversation about two years after Ravelstein's death. After the Guillain-Barré he had worked very hard at walking and recovering the use of his hands. He knew that he had to surrender, to decline but he did it selectively. It didn't matter that he was unable to operate the coffee grinder, but he did need his hand skills for shaving, writing notes, dressing, smoking, signing checks. Few fail to recognize that if you don't apply yourself to recovery you're a basket case, a goner. On the morning of the day when he and I had come upon the parrot-filled holly bushes where the birds were feeding on red berries and scattering the snow, the hospital bed with the steel triangle was being dismantled and removed from Ravelstein's bedroom. "Thanks be to Somebody," he had said when it sank from sight in the freight elevator. "I never want to see that bosun's rig again."

He was walking independently—not yet altogether firm, but a Lazarus case if there ever was one. You're just back from the dead, and you run into an entire tribe of green parrots, tropical animals surviving a midwestern winter. Ravelstein grinned at me and said, "They even have a Jew look to them." Then, though he took almost no interest in natural science, he asked me once again how they had become so numerous. Suddenly I became the nature expert. So I described them again: those were slim sacks hanging from trees and from the crossbars of the timber, power-line supports. Like overstretched nylon stockings, those nesting tenements where eggs were hatched, drooped as much as thirty feet. "Those nests make you think of Eastside tenements," I said to him.

"Let's get Nikki to drive us over for a look. Where are the headquarters?"

"Jackson Park. But there's a big colony in an alley off Fifty-fourth Street."

But we never did go to see the parrot tenements, the swaying, layered tubes where they nested. Instead, Ravelstein told me when I next met him that he and Nikki were flying to Paris.

"But what do you want to do that for?"

I could see that I had asked a stupid and offensive question, and that Ravelstein was disappointed in me. But it was his way to cover for his closest friends. And it was natural that he should cover for me. "The people at the hospital tell me it's all right to go."

"Do they?" I said.

The doctors' reasoning was transparent. Although Ravelstein was dying he was still fit enough to fly. Paris was one of his great pleasures: He had close friends there and many kinds of unfinished human business. If he wanted so badly to go, why not let him? The doctors figured that a trip of ten days couldn't do much damage. For myself, twenty-five hours of air travel would have been too fatiguing, but Ravelstein would ride through the airports in wheelchairs and, unlike me, he flew first class. To go a bit deeper, I'm afraid I must admit that it seemed to me an unserious thing for a dying man to be doing. And nobody knew what "fit enough to fly" meant in a case like Ravelstein's. Was he flying in a 727, or were there powerful wings hidden under his coat?

And though I do think that Ravelstein was disappointed in me, I don't believe that he was surprised. It was a standing premise between us that there was to be nothing hidden or too shameful to confess, and there was nothing I couldn't tell Ravelstein. Partly this meant that there was scarcely anything he wouldn't have detected on his own. So he would have understood also that I looked down on Paris, rather. There is a Jewish freethinker's saying about Paris— *wie Gott in Frankreich.* Meaning that even God took his holidays in France. Why? Because the French are atheists and among them God himself could be carefree, a *flâneur,* like any tourist.

What I failed even toward the last to understand was that Ravelstein had a second, a supplementary life in Paris. He came back more cheerful from this brief farewell excursion, saying nothing about his French friends but with an air of having done what he should have done.

I was told, however, that Dr. Schley had now ordered Ravelstein to go back to the hospital for "further tests." Nikki confirmed this but added that the room Ravelstein wanted would be unavailable till early next week. On Sunday afternoon he gave a party—pizza and beer, picnic style, with paper cups and plates. He had bought new video equipment—*dernier cri,* he said (even I preferred that to "state-of-the-art")—and singers and instrumentalists were exhibited at full length and with a kind of tropical jungle-light immediacy. The film Ravelstein had chosen to run was one of his favorites—Rossini's *Italian Maiden in Algiers.* The panels on which the players and singers appeared were flat, thin, tall, wide, unendurably real—art re-armed by technology, as Ravelstein said. The faces of the singers colored like Venetian glass and the cameras taking you into their beautiful dark eyes and even into their teeth. Ravelstein in his camel-hair bathrobe was in his lounge chair admiring and explaining the new equipment—and also making fun of the ignorance of the laity. But he wasn't up to it and kept pressing the mute button to make himself heard. In the end it was simply too much for him, and Nikki helped him up and led him out, saying, "It's too much excitement. He thought he could skip his siesta just this once. But he can't."

The video on mute and Ravelstein himself, silent and perhaps reviewing the facts of disease and death from an unfamiliar angle, followed Nikki out. We led him back to his bedroom with its sleigh-bed and eiderdown silk quilts. When he lay back on the pillows I covered him with all the linens and the silks.

The apartment soon emptied. When latecomers turned up, Nikki pressed the button to hold the elevator door open and said, "Abe would have been so happy to see you but he's on all kinds of drugs and doesn't know whether he's coming or going."

Next day, when Ravelstein brought up the subject I said, "Nikki was very tactful. He wouldn't answer any questions. But the party folded pretty quickly."

"He never answers questions, does he. There are silent questions in every corner but he doesn't acknowledge them. That takes a certain amount of strength."

"He switched off the new video. I don't think I'd know how to do that."

During Ravelstein's last days at home I often kept him company in the morning. Because I lived in the same block and followed no regular schedule I would come by after breakfast. Nikki, whose usual bedtime was 4 A.M. would be fast asleep until 10, whereas Ravelstein dozed because he had no company and lay with his large knees asprawl. The doctors drugged (tranquilized) him, but this didn't stop him from thinking—considering various problems in their dawn-aspect. And even when he was dozing you could learn a lot about him by watching his peculiar Jewish face. You couldn't imagine an odder container for his odd intellect. Somehow his singular, total, almost geological baldness implied that there was nothing hidden about him. He would say—as usual preferring to say it in French—that he had had a *succès fou,* but now he was facing the cemetery.

Though I was his senior by some years he saw himself as my teacher. Well, that was his trade—he was an educator. He never presented himself as a philosopher—professors of philosophy were not philosophers. He had had a philosophical training and had learned how a philosophical life should be lived. That was what philosophy was about, and this was why one read Plato. If he had to choose between Athens and Jerusalem, among us the two main sources of higher life, he chose Athens, while full of respect for Jerusalem. But in his last days it was the Jews he wanted to talk about, not the Greeks.

When I commented on this change he was annoyed with me. "Why not talk about them?" he said. "In the South they still talk about the War Between the States much more than a century ago but in our own time millions were destroyed, most of them no different from you. From us. We mustn't turn our backs on them.

Moses communicated with God, who gave him instructions, and the connection has lasted for millennia."

Ravelstein went on for quite a while in this way. He said that the Jews had been used to give the entire species a measure of human viciousness. "You tell people that a new great era will begin if you abolish the ruling class or the bourgeoisie, if you rationalize the means of production, if you use euthanasia on the incurables. To minds so prepared you then propose that the Jews be destroyed. And they make a substantial start. They kill more than half of the European Jews—and you and I, Chick, belong to the remainder." These are not Ravelstein's actual words. I am paraphrasing. What he said was that we, as Jews, now knew what was possible.

"There's no telling which corner it will come from next—the French corner? No, no, not France. They had their glut of blood in the eighteenth century and they wouldn't mind if it happened, but they wouldn't be the ones to do it. But what about the Russians? The Protocols of the Elders of Zion were a Russian forgery. And not long ago you were telling me about Kipling."

"Yes, it was Kipling. A wonderful writer," I said. "But somebody put me on to a collection of his letters, and in one of them he was having an angry fit against Einstein. This was early in the century. He said that the Jews had already distorted social reality for their Jewish purposes. But not satisfied with that, Einstein was disfiguring physical reality with his relativity theory, and the Jews were trying to give a falsifying Jewish twist to the physical universe."

"You'll have to drop Kipling from your list of favorites, then," said Ravelstein.

"No, we can't afford to set up a Jewish Index. For one thing we could never impose it, not even on Jewish readers. Who could ever expect you to drop Céline? By the way, I lent you my copy of his pamphlet '*Les Beaux Draps.*' . . ."

"I never got around to it."

"You have a weakness for the nihilists," I said.

"I suppose it's because they don't tell a lot of high-minded lies. I like the kind who accept nihilism as a condition and live in that condition. It's the intellectual nihilists I can't stand. I prefer the sort who live with their evils, frankly. The natural nihilists."

"Céline recommended that the Jews be exterminated like bacteria. It's the doctor in him, I suppose. In his novels the influence of art is a restraint on him, but in his propaganda he's a killer out and out."

Here this conversation temporarily ended, for once again the quiet ambulance pulled up at Ravelstein's door and the attendants, familiar with the layout, rang the bell of the freight elevator. Ravelstein had been in and out of the hospital so often that he had arranged with himself to take no notice of it.

Dr. Schley had never discussed Ravelstein's illness with me. He was one of your super-earnest physicians—small, stiff, aquiline, efficient. Such hair as he had left was combed upward stiffly, Iroquois style. He owed me no medical explanations. I was not related to Ravelstein by blood. But by now Schley had seen that Ravelstein and I were very close and he began to pass me silent signals—what a Parisian lady I met decades ago in the ABC music hall taught me to call *chanson à la carpe*. Nobody else seemed ever to have heard this expression but I swore by it—two large fish amid clear bubbles silently communicating by opening their jaws. This was how Dr. Schley notified me that Ravelstein's days were numbered. And Rosamund, too, had said, "This could be Ravelstein's last ride to the hospital." I agreed. And Nikki, naturally, had reached the same conclusion. He put in very long hours, doing errands, taking phone calls. It was Nikki, not the nurses, who shaved Ravelstein with the electric razor while Ravelstein, eyes shut, lolled back his head to lift his chin. A small plastic cup under his nose supplied him with oxygen.

"It doesn't look too good, does it," said Nikki to me in the corridor.

"It doesn't, in fact."

"He has a message for his lawyer. And he told me to send for Morris Herbst."

Well, there was no recovery possible from this disease, as we all knew. When Ravelstein had last been hospitalized he had held impromptu seminars from his hospital bed, presiding brilliantly. The teaching-vaudeville was then still running. Even now his students were sitting in the visitors' lounge under the large skylight—waiting to be sent for—but although he would ask, by name, about one or another of them, he was no longer teaching, or holding court. The fact was that I could already see the early signs of approaching death in his movements—his head becoming a burden to his neck and shoulders, a change in color, especially under the eyes. His opinions were shortened, and there was less concern for your feelings, so that you were well advised to keep to neutral topics. He said about Vela, "You gave in—you tried to sell me a colored cutout of the woman like the cardboard personalities they used to hang in movie lobbies in the old days. You know, Chick, you sometimes say there's nothing you can't tell me. But you falsified the image of your ex-wife. You'll say that it was done for the sake of marriage but what kind of morality is *that*?"

"That's perfectly true," I said. He had me there, dead to rights. He might have added when I accused him of preferring nihilists to his "more principled" academic contemporaries that at least the nihilists weren't putting forward any petty-bourgeois deformities and falsehoods as examples of high principle and even beauty.

Nikki, Ravelstein's Chinese son who had nothing at all to do with these conversations, was there to wipe his face. Nikki stepped aside only for the technicians who x-rayed Ravelstein or took blood samples. Now and then I put my hand to my friend's bald head. I could see that he wanted to be touched. I was surprised to find that there was an invisible stubble on his scalp. He seemed to have decided that total baldness suited him better than thinning hair, and shaved his head as well as his cheeks. Anyway, this head was rolling toward the grave.

"Is it a dark day outside," Ravelstein asked me, "or am I in a gloomy mood?"

"It's not your mood. There's a thick cloud cover."

It wasn't like Ravelstein either to bother with the weather; the weather would adapt itself to whatever the people that mattered were thinking, and he would sometimes criticize me for "checking out the externals"—keeping one eye on the clouds. "You can count on nature doing what nature has been doing forever. Do you think you're going to rush in on Nature and grab off an insight?" he would say. But these bright moments seldom occurred now. More often he looked comatose—and Rosamund would anxiously whisper, "Is he still here?"

There were times when I couldn't answer with confidence. It had been repeatedly made clear that he couldn't survive, and he lay, irregularly breathing with a stand filled with medicine bottles near his head, ranged behind his large conspicuous ears. At times you thought that he preferred to doze his way into death. He would perhaps be following some line of thought he didn't care to discuss. He had devoted himself mainly to the two poles of human life—religion and government, that was how Voltaire had put it. Ravelstein didn't believe that Voltaire was intellectually serious, but now and then he did summarize things conveniently. And Ravelstein, nowadays, would have added that Voltaire, famous for the campaigns he fought—*"Ecrasez l'infame!"*—violently hated Jews. And there was yet another physical difference to note. Ravelstein's extended body was very large, he was nearly six and a half feet tall and his gown, which reached to the ankles of ordinary patients, ended just above his knees. Then his large underlip had an affectionate flexure but his big nose was severe. He was breathing through his mouth. His skin had the texture of cooked farina.

I could see that he was following a trail of Jewish ideas or Jewish essences. It was unusual for him these days, in any conversation, to mention even Plato or Thucydides. He was full of Scripture now. He talked about religion and the difficult project of being man in the fullest sense, of becoming man and nothing but man. Sometimes he was coherent. Most of the time he lost me.

When I mentioned this to Morris Herbst he said, "Well, of course he'll keep talking things out while there's a breath in his body left—and for him this is top priority, because it's connected with the great evil." I well understood what he meant. The war made it clear that almost everybody agreed that the Jews had no right to live.

That goes straight to your bones.

Other people have some choice of options—their attention is solicited by this issue or that, and being besieged by issues they make their choices according to their inclinations. But for "the chosen" there is no choice. Such a volume of hatred and denial of the right to live has never been heard or felt, and the will that willed their death was confirmed and justified by a vast collective agreement that the world would be improved by their disappearance and their extinction. Rismus, which was Professor Davarr's word for viciousness, hatred, determination to be rid of this intrusive population in furnaces or mass graves. We needn't go into this any further. But what persons like Herbst and Ravelstein concluded was that it is impossible to get rid of one's origins, it is impossible not to remain a Jew. The Jews, Ravelstein and Herbst thought, following the line laid down by their teacher Davarr, were historically witnesses to the absence of redemption.

So as he was dying, thinking of these questions, Ravelstein formulated what he would say but was not able to deliver his conclusions. And one of these conclusions was that a Jew should take a deep interest in the history of the Jews—in their principles of justice, for instance. But not every problem can be solved. And what *could* Ravelstein have done?

But anyway he wouldn't be here to do it. In that case what was the most significant suggestion he could make to friends? He began to talk about the approaching high holidays and directed me to take Rosamund to the synagogue. Herbst was certain that Ravelstein was indicating the way which was best for the Jews, who had nothing of greater value than this religious legacy.

Herbst and Ravelstein had been close as students forty years ago, and I could do worse than turn to Herbst for guidance. But if I began to ask questions, I would become involved in self-explanation and I had no stomach for this. Ravelstein was dying—he lay wrapped at full length, eyes shut. He was either asleep or thinking what had to be thought in these last days. My feeling was that he was trying to do all that could be done in these final moments— done, I mean, for the people under his care, for his pupils. Now I was too old to be a pupil, and Ravelstein didn't believe in adult education. It was far too late for me to Platonize. And what people called culture was nothing but a fancier term for their ignorance. Ravelstein sometimes said that I was a sleepwalker by choice, but this didn't mean that I was unteachable, just that it was up to me to decide when I would be ready to make my moves.

You might tell me something of great importance, and I would understand it well enough, but refuse entirely to take it in. This was no ordinary stubbornness.

Now there are few people you can discuss such matters with. Too bad about that. Since we are so often called upon for judgments, we naturally coarsen them by constant use or abuse. Then of course you see nothing original, nothing new; you are, in the end, no longer moved by any face, or any person. Now this was where Ravelstein had come in. He turned your face again toward the original. He forced you to reopen what you had closed.

I went so far one day as to dictate some notes on this subject and my then-secretary Rosamund made an unusual personal comment. She said, "I think I understand what you are talking about." I was persuaded by and by that it was really so.

Nikki, Ravelstein's heir and his chief mourner—the rivals were numerous—occupied his flat, just around the corner. There was a grassy space between his apartment building and ours where little kids tumbled and learned to throw and catch. From my bedroom window I looked across to what had once been Ravelstein's place. You saw the lights. There were no more parties. Worse still, Rosamund rightly said, "The whole neighborhood has become a cemetery. The community of your dead. You can't even take a walk without pointing out the doors and windows of old friends and acquaintances. We can't go around the block without your remembering old pals and girlfriends. Ravelstein was a dear friend—one in a million. But he would say that you were carrying an overload of depression."

She felt that we must move away. We had the house in New Hampshire and a three-year invitation by a university in Boston to give the courses (as well as I could, alone) that Ravelstein and I had given together. Rosamund and I were offered comfortable quarters in the Back Bay area. She would manage the move, I needn't worry about that. Since the Back Bay apartment was fully furnished, we could sublet the Midwest one. It would still be possible to come back if the East didn't suit us. And we needn't dread looking across the grassy lots straight into Ravelstein's windows.

"And as a special treat . . ." Rosamund held up the slick colored travel literature—sunny beaches, wooded hilltops, palm tress, native fishermen. A Caribbean holiday was what she was proposing. We'd unpack in Boston and dump the cardboard boxes in which our goods were packed. Then we'd fly to Saint Martin via San Juan. There we'd float idle, dream in the warm sea, recharging our vital batteries.

"Where did you get all that glamourous travel propaganda, Rosamund? Saint Martin, eh? Isn't that where the Durkins go?"

"Never mind. They're good friends. They can see exactly what you need."

"The West Indies will strip away all those layers of stress, and suddenly I'll be restored, and well and strong enough to write the Ravelstein memoir."

"I'm not suggesting a working holiday," said Rosamund. "I suppose you've been in the Caribbean."

"Yes."

"And you don't like it?"

"It's one huge tropical slum. . . . But I go mostly by Puerto Rico. Big gambling joints, a huge smelly lagoon, dark and muddy—unhappy welfare-looking native crowds. Then the Europeans arriving in charter flights. And what they carry home with them is the feeling that the Americans have made a mess of things and that Castro deserves the support of independent intelligent Scandinavians and Dutchmen."

But in the end Rosamund had her way. I discovered, however, in the early days of our marriage that, in having her way, she put my interests ahead of her own. The Durkins recommended a small apartment on the beach. The baggage was checked through—all the summer rags, papers, swimsuits, sunscreen, sandals, bug repellents. San Juan seemed more glamourous, around the seashore at any rate. We had time to kill between flights and we killed it at the bar of the grand hotel. There we sat beside a hard-drinking American who told us that his wife had been struck down by an unidentified disease. This man said that he commuted between Dallas, where he owned a business, and the great industrial-sized San Juan hospital where she was being treated. For some weeks she had been unable to speak, perhaps to hear—who could say. She was unconscious. She wouldn't, perhaps couldn't, open her eyes. "She don't respond. I feel like a damn fool, talking at her."

When our bus was ready, we left him at the bar. He looked a lot like a red sandstone bluff with an overhang of bleached grass. Rosamund couldn't bear to abandon him, so miserable—she is like that. But he didn't answer our goodbyes.

About half an hour later, landing in Saint Martin, we passed through the immigration hangar, a vast Quonset hut of corrugated green metal—everything in the tropics seemed to me to have a provisional character. Before an official counter under sizzling lights we lined up to pay a fee and have our passports stamped. Then we got into a cab and were driven to the French end of the island. Our landlady was short with us because we had kept her up so late. A little after we had gotten into bed a furious man arrived, kicked and punched her door, screaming that he would kill her. I said, "If the security-chain doesn't hold this may end in murder." But the cops came in a car with a flashing lamp on the roof and took him away.

"What do you think?" said Rosamund.

I remember saying that this might be normal for the climate. Gorgeous but unstable.

I refused to be captivated by the place. Maybe it was old age. I used to be a cheerful traveler but now I sniff at the linen when I lie down. Here I scented the detergent powder in the sheets and pillow cases, and the septic tank beneath the bathroom.

But we woke to a clear tropical morning with lizards and roosters. On the ocean, straight in front of us the yachts towed their dinghies. Planes at the airfield took off and landed. But the beach was fine, firm, broad, with a border of trees and flowering shrubs, and there were crowds of yellow moths traveling. On the inland side of the house there was a rich tree, heavy with a crop of limes. Behind was a steep hill.

For our morning coffee we walked to the far end of the main street. French of a sort was spoken in the bistros and bakeries. We sat on the terrasse taking in the sights. What was there to see here? Or to do? To begin with we'd buy the daily essentials. Then we'd swim. Waves were seldom seen in the bay. You could float on your back by the hour, or lie drying in the sand. Also, you could stroll along the waterline and inspect the topless women—sunning or exhibiting their breasts. Being natural, I suppose. But the eyes of these women informed you that if you spoke to them, they would not answer.

By the time we walked back, the lunch spots were opening. Ribs, chicken, and lobster were offered at about twenty grills that were crowded together, with flames spurting straight up, more flame than you needed for sensible cooking. Each and every joint had its own grinning tout, shouting, laughing and holding up live lobsters, swinging them by the antennae or the tail. If some part of the creature fetched loose and fell to the ground, that was part of the fun.

"Let's get away from this," said Rosamund. She complained about the barbecue smoke. It made her eyes smart. But what she couldn't bear was the torture of the lobsters. Back in New Hampshire when she saw salamanders in the road she picked them up and carried them to safety. I would say, "They may not want to be where you put them." It was wrong of me to tease her for her humane impulses. Tender-mindedness is an uncomfortable problem for all parties. The tender-minded leave it to the less feeling to say, "It's the law of life. We must eat. And aren't the crustaceans themselves cannibalistic?" But all this is evasion. You sprinkle your "interpretation" with schoolbook science. Do these armored lobsters regenerate the claws they lose? This seems to be why we have science classes, as a cover for our heartlessness. Or to refine it, at least. Polonius is at a dinner, not where he eats but is eaten by worms— the payoff for a lifetime of dinners.

You can't apply your humane tape measure to any effect. Before you can fend them off your dead suddenly have surrounded you. What would Ravelstein have said about this? He would have said, "Girlish queasiness." Meaning, perhaps, "She is a tender-minded human being and must work things out for herself. Such a matter has to be thought through by every adult. As for the red salamanders, perhaps they could go into a spaghetti sauce. . . ."

On Saint Martin we were at the lower—eastern—end of the bay, in a two-story house. Below us a tourist family from the North of France took over the garden. They were *en famille* while we had no special need of it. It was the beach that interested us, just beyond the low wall. We were about thirty feet from the water's edge. A glass-bottomed boat took tourists on a regular schedule to the coral reef just to the north.

I was grateful for the bay. It gave us an enclosure. I am thankful for boundaries. I am fond of having the lines drawn around me. I wasn't here to battle the seas but to swim and to float quietly. To open my mind to Ravelstein. Often Rosamund towed or carried me in water just shoulder-high. She put her arms under me and walked back and forth. She was not a strong young woman—she didn't have to be. Sea water seems more buoyant, you don't have to work to keep afloat, as you would in a lake or pond. Rosamund is slender in build, not skinny, not abrupt. She wears her brown hair down to the shoulders. It's like a limitless asset. Her long eyes turn out to be

blue, not the brown her dark hair would lead you to expect. The
music she sang as she sailed my body through the water was from
Handel's *Solomon*. We had heard it in Budapest a few months earlier. "Live forever," she sang. "Happy-happy Solomon." This cho-
rus sung by her single voice had the rustling sea water under it.
Lying on her forearms I saw the moths, pale yellow in slow spin-
ning clusters of hundreds. This must have been breeding time for
them. And over the main drag was a cloud of barbecue smoke, and
the touts, the children of Belial, laughing blinded by the sun would
be swinging live lobsters by the antenna to tempt the tourists.

I felt that I would never take this tropical paradise to my heart.
Instead, as Rosamund in her lovely voice sang "Live-for-ever," I
thought of Ravelstein in his grave, all his gifts, his endlessly diverting character, and his intellect entirely motionless. I don't suppose
that when he directed me to write an account of his life he expected
me to settle for what was characteristic—characteristic of me, is
what I mean, naturally.

Rosamund and I now changed places, and I carried her through
the water, the sand underfoot ridged as the surface of the sea was
rippled, and inside the mouth the hard palate had its ridges too.
"Shall we stop at Le Forgeron on the way home and reserve a table
for tonight? It's about five minutes away on the beach."

Roxie Durkin had given us a note to M. Bédier, who ran the joint.
Rosamund had already signed us up for dinner. In the matter of
restaurants you could trust the Durkins. They had seen a lot of Ravelstein in his last years. We had often dined together in Greektown
or at Kurbanski's club.

The Durkins had been very thoughtful. Only one favor they had
asked for in return. Durkin, a lawyer, had brought some fat vol-

umes to Saint Martin and he had forgotten to copy out several passages related to a case he would soon be trying. He had asked us, as a special favor, to look them up and send them by e-mail. Rosamund had several times reminded me of these bound volumes. The landlady had a servant carry them up to our small apartment.

That evening we walked to Le Forgeron along the cooling beach. Shoes and sandals were carried by Rosamund in a reticule. We put them on before entering the gate from the ocean side. There was water trickling pleasantly into the garden—vines and shrubs, flowers. Mme. Bédier, working in the kitchen, took no notice of us. M. Bédier looked at Roxie's pleasant familiar note without real interest. He was a large, bald, thick-built man, organized physically with a kind of violence. His message, if it could be put in words, would have run: "I am prepared to do everything a customer [*un client*] may desire but I am under tremendous pressure and may blow up at any time." He was the sole waiter, and the place was filling up. There was no other helper. His wife did all the cooking. But the tourists, one was given to understand, were not their social equals.

I was aware of the influence of Ravelstein when I made such a sketch. It may as well be admitted that he often figured in daily events. This was because of the power of his personality. It was also because his life had more inner structure than mine, and I had become dependent on his power of ordering experience—it may be that he also wanted to persist. And for his part, he also needed me. Also, many people want to be rid of the dead. I, on the contrary, have a way of hanging on to them. My persistent hunch—it should be clear by now—is that they are not gone for good. Ravelstein himself would have dismissed such notions as childish. Well, perhaps they are. But I am not arguing a case, I am simply reporting. I know one loses mental respectability by acknowledging such fantasies. Even I, you see, yield to accepted opinion. But there may be simple explanations for the persistence of Ravelstein in my daily life. When he died I began to see that it had become my habit to tell him what had happened since we last met.

Nevertheless he had strange ways of turning up, and I shan't pretend that he didn't come in obliquely from wherever it was that he continued to exist. This should not take the form of a discussion of life-after-death. I am not inclined to argue. It's only that I can't sit on information simply because it's not intellectually respectable information.

Now—what did M. Bédier of the Forgeron recommend tonight? The red snapper, served cold with mayonnaise. Rosamund ordered some other fish. Neither dish was well cooked. The snapper at room temperature was clammy. The mayonnaise was like zinc ointment.

"How is it?" Rosamund asked.

"Underdone."

Tasting it, she agreed that it wasn't cooked through. It was raw at the center.

"Tell the *patron* about it. You can speak to him in French."

"His English is better. People don't like to be trapped in dummy conversations. Why should he chat me up in French? I can take a Berlitz course, he'll think."

I could not finish the snapper. Dinner was endless.

Rosamund said, "It's an off night—they can't cook such bad food in a beautiful location like this."

You couldn't serve inedible dinners by this warm, still tropical water, with a moon to back up the setting. A restaurant ten minutes by foot from your apartment would have been a bride's dream—no shopping, peeling, cooking, serving, washing, or garbage disposal.

Toward midnight there was a lull in the air traffic. I had very soon learned how many privately owned planes came into the local airfield—a revelation of the wealth and the piloting skills of a considerable population of Americans, Mexicans, Venezuelans, Hondurans, and even Italian and French sportsmen—people who liked their reality to follow their thoughts. One thought of a place and in a matter of hours one could be in that place. In the sixteenth century, Spanish sea journeys lasted sometimes for months. Today you could play golf in Venezuela and dine the same evening in the Yucatan. Back to Pasadena in the morning, in time to catch the Orange Bowl.

When you begin to entertain such thoughts about people rich enough to buzz around and lay out their itineraries and figure gas mileage—very soon you may recognize that the air-hours fatigue you will feel is *your* fatigue.

The fact was that Bédier of the Forgeron had infected me.

When I complained of tiredness and low energy, Rosamund told me that it was the accumulation of fatigue aggravated by worry and grief. She, too, was still grieving for poor Ravelstein, destroyed by his reckless sex habits. Rosamund did not dismiss your complaints—she gave them her full attention without irritability. She said that holidays often began with such burdensome and heavy feelings. She stroked my face affectionately and told me I must catch up on my sleep.

I did just that but felt no better. The toxin carried by the fish was heat resistant, I was to learn, and more boiling or baking could not neutralize it. As it was explained to me later in Boston, the cigua toxin was quickly excreted by the body but not before it had radically damaged the nervous system. Very much like Ravelstein's Guillain-Barré syndrome. Among the first symptoms is a sudden distaste for food. I even disliked the look of it. I came to loathe all food odors. For dinner I could eat only cornflakes with a bit of milk. I kept telling Rosamund that this was all to the good. I was losing unwanted weight. Like everyone in the U.S., I said, I was grossly overfed.

The French family in the apartment below had come from Rouen to be easy and hang loose, unbuckled in the tropics. They swam in the smooth sea; so did Rosamund and I. We dried ourselves on the beach, chatting pleasantly. But the odors rising from their kitchen were becoming unbearable. I said to Rosamund, "What kind of shit are they cooking?"

"Is it as bad as that?" said Rosamund.

Then I lectured her on the decline of French cooking. "You used to be able to get good food in any *bistrot*. Maybe tourism has brought down the standards. Or isn't it possible that the disappearance of the peasantry is ruining French cookery?"

"One of the pleasures of living with you, Chick, is that you have so many thoughts on every subject. But you seem to have lost your appetite entirely. I have one theory myself: you've been so strained—overstrained, wrung out—that this peaceful place is too peaceful for you. You're just wound up too tight." She was evidently worried by the force and violence of my reactions.

"I have to get away from this awful food stink."

"Let's go out then."

"Yes, let's go. *You* need a meal, Rosamund—you should have a good dinner. I have no appetite, but I'd like you to eat."

My nights on this island had been restless—my heart misbehaving. I had increased the doses of quinine prescribed by Dr. Schley, the cardiologist. I swallowed tablets with glasses of quinine water. My head was clear enough but I complained of numbness in the soles of the feet. "Kind of an unpleasant thrill goes through my feet," I said.

"Perhaps it's the way you sit. Try to work standing. Maybe you're overdoing the quinine," said Rosamund.

"Dr. Schley said I could take any amount for the arrhythmia— the fibrillations—Good God! Everybody sounds like a doctor these days."

We walked on the beach to avoid the stink of the chicken and lobster stalls on the main street. At Le Forgeron the *patron,* lounging outside, pretended to be looking out to sea and didn't return my greeting. "Five thousand miles from France and he's been emancipated from *politesse,*" I said.

"We've stopped eating there. . . ."

"*Machts nicht.* He's a pig who was taught manners, but they didn't take. Terrible people everywhere. You can't make a silk purse out of a sow's asshole."

I didn't know how sick I was. All I knew was that I was fitfully irritable or somehow out of whack—a bit deranged. I was aware that I was repeating myself and that Rosamund was distressed. She was wondering what to do. Probably she blamed herself for bringing me here. One of my obsessions is perhaps worth describing. I often said to Rosamund that one of the problems of aging was the speeding up of time. The days flashed by "like subway stations passed by the express train." I often mentioned "The Death of Ivan Ilyich" to illustrate this for Rosamund. Child-days are very long but in old age they fly past "faster than the weaver's shuttle" as Job says.

And Ivan Ilyich also mentions the slow rise of a stone thrown into the air. "When it returns to earth it accelerates at thirty-two feet per second per second." You are controlled by gravitational magnetism and the whole universe is involved in this speeding up of your end. If only we could bring back the full days we knew as kids. But we became too familiar with the data of experience, I suggest. Our way of organizing the data which rush by in *gestalt* style—that is, in increasingly abstract forms—speeds up experiences into a dangerously topsy-turvy fast-forward comedy. Our need for rapid disposal eliminates the details that bewitch, hold, or delay the children. Art is one rescue from this chaotic acceleration. Meter in poetry, tempo in music, form and color in painting. But we do feel that we are speeding earthward, crashing into our graves. "If these were just words," I said to Rosamund. "But I feel it every day. Powerless thinking itself eats up what is left of life. . . ."

Poor Rosamund, she had to listen to such stuff night after night, at dinner—and this Caribbean holiday was to have been a romantic holiday, something of an additional honeymoon.

"Did you discuss this with Ravelstein?" she said.

"Well . . . yes, I did."

"What did he say to you?"

"He said that Ivan Ilyich had made a *marriage de convenance,* and that if he and his wife had loved each other things would have looked different."

"The poor things did hate each other," said Rosamund. "Reading that story is like crossing a mountain of broken glass. It's an ordeal." She was very intelligent, Rosamund. We could not only talk to each other but could also count on being understood.

We now turned to the volumes our friend Durkin had asked us

to look up, working together on the pages he had asked us to copy out for him. It was a short chore, really, and Rosamund did most of the work. There were no copying machines for volumes of this size. I read the extracts aloud, and Rosamund took them down on her word processor. I had started out with little interest in the material, but I was very quickly absorbed in it. Not the legal side of it, the copyright suit filed by Durkin's client. The author of the journal on which the book was based was an American physician who had spent years in the New Guinea rain forest under a research grant from the National Institute of Something-or-other, and spoke the pidgin or island lingo. That he wrote well made his report all the more effective—super-memorable at times. He described a cliffside covered with great flowers as a "crimson orchid waterfall." There were many near-purple passages, but you felt he was responding to the purple of nature. He had a firm scientific aim and the entire article was important—humanly binding. He started out by describing the shortage of protein in the diet of the tribes he had studied. He said that in the primitive wars, the natives couldn't afford to waste the bodies of their enemies.

Such scientific speculation was not my primary interest. I have several times mentioned that ordinary daily particulars were my specialty. Ravelstein also had several times pointed this out, not the noumena, or "things in themselves"—I left all that kind of thing to the Kants of this world. Black headless bodies in a jungle where crimson orchids stream downward for hundreds of feet *would* be phenomena, wouldn't they. The men were freshly killed and beheaded. The heads were set aside. The researcher who recorded all this said they were a currency used in wife-purchase. That's why headhunters hunt heads. But this American researcher had been attracted to the streamside ambush not by the struggling fighters but by the smell of roasting meat. "Just like a kitchen smell back home—a wholesome joint in the oven. Or a Thanksgiving turkey. Just as appetizing. Human flesh, too, can get you in the salivary glands . . . the warriors offered me some of their human shish-ke-bab. The victims were turned on their bellies. The ground was rich in red blood. The victors thought my facial expressions killingly funny. They said, 'Why, it's only meat, like any other meat.'" And indeed the writer went on more than was necessary about the appetizing fragrance. The hunters said that if they had been ambushed the other guys would have been cooking and eating them. With us, this might have been a rationalization. With them it was a fact of life. The jungles do not abound in game. Hunters often are exhausted and in critical need of a meal. The American goes on to speculate about Leningrad in the days when the Nazis besieged it, and to speak also of Japanese soldiers cut off in the Philippine jungles, eating their own dead, and mentions also the South American athletes whose plane crashed in the Andes. And surely our own nihilists who tell you that everything is permitted would have to agree that cannibalism is perfectly logical. "But what made the difficulty for me," writes the U.S. researcher, "was the savory smell of roast human thigh, cut from the corpse that still bled in this paradise of flowers. This was the hard thing for me. Not the heads which the fighters carry when they went a-courting, and swung them by the dusty hair."

Rosamund, now seeing that I really was sick—though I denied it—walked miles through the smoke and fire of curbside grills looking for a Thanksgiving turkey. None was to be found. The skinny local hens seemed to be growing hair, not feathers. At the bottom of a freezer in the market, she found packages of stony drumsticks and wings. She said they looked much worse when they were thawed. On this island of yams and coconuts there were no cooking greens. Nevertheless she managed after hours of effort to produce a chicken soup. Out of gratitude I tried to make a joke of my failure to get it down—remembering an immigrant mother of my childhood who cried out, "My Joey can't eat an ice-cream cone. He turns his head away from it. If he won't lick an ice cream, he's got to be dying!"

Perhaps because I felt the tropics as a death threat my instinct was to look for the comic angle in any question which had to be considered. For one thing I kept thinking that the ground was more porous here. It was not as solid as it was up north. It must be hard to bury somebody in this rotting coral soil. I was not going to take up this crazy topic with Rosamund. Rosamund was blaming herself for having sold me on this delightful holiday—but I knew I could trust her to do the right thing. I was feeling very odd, but I told myself that this was a malaise I had brought from the north—a kind of uneasiness or dislocation—something like the metaphysical miseries. Years ago when I had found myself stranded in Puerto Rico for a long stretch I had felt the same kind of noncomfort in the tropical surroundings—smells of trapped brine and decaying marine matter rising from the lagoons—the strange stinks of jungle plant-life and rotting animal matter. The mongoose in Puerto Rico was as common as street dogs elsewhere. You don't think of animals so large living along the roads and the village backstreets.

There were bursts of tribal music from the town at night. The roosters cut short your sleep. But I wasn't sleeping much, and could eat only corn flakes. I complained of the tap water and Rosamund, now very worried, went often to the shop to carry back heavy bottles of water.

I was obviously sick but I couldn't let it be said that I was. I felt that I was having abnormal thoughts, and by and by it became apparent that I was worrying away at the problem of evolution. Of course I believed in evolution—who could refuse to accept the thousands of proofs? What was not obvious was that it had happened through random changes as so many scientific true believers were convinced. "*Anything* can happen, given time enough, and billions of years give you time for all the mistakes and blind alleys." Watson, the geneticist, had laid down the law on this. But as I said to Rosamund, arguing still with Watson, if you took into account the subtle resources of the body, thousands of them, too subtle to be accidental, Watson was talking rough carpentry—boy's woodshop or manual training, not fine cabinet work.

In retrospect I'm sorry—I grieve for Rosamund, who now saw that I was sick. She tried to prepare remedies in her little kitchen. She cooked dinners that I would normally have eaten with pleasure. But the meat in the market was gross. When she made soups, I couldn't bear to swallow a spoonful. The French family below went on cooking shit dishes it maddened me to smell.

"How can nice, decent, agreeable, civil people bring themselves to cook—and eat!—such a stinking mess!"

Rosamund said, "It would upset them if I were to ask for the windows to be shut. But don't you think you should see a doctor? There's a French doctor down the road. We've seen his shingle dozens of times."

We were on the porch having a glass of wine before the dinner I would be unable to get down. I ate the stuffed olives Rosamund put

out. I like them stuffed with anchovies, Spanish-style. Here only
the pimiento ones were available. You couldn't study a Caribbean
evening sky without thinking of God, I was finding. Nor think of
God without your own dead coming into it. Then you renewed
your connection with your dead and ended by making as honest an
estimate as you could bear—reviewing a lifetime of activities, affec-
tions, attachments. In this I didn't do at all well.

And as I owed it to Rosamund to do everything possible to get to
the scientific bottom of things, I went next day to see the doctor.
Americans don't take much stock in foreign medicine. They're inclined to think that a French doctor will say you have a *crise de foie*
and must cut down your intake of red wine. The doctor down the
way had nothing to say about wine. He told me, however, that I had
a case of dengue. Well, that wasn't too bad. Dengue is a tropical disease carried by mosquitoes; you treat it with quinine. So I added local quinine to the Quinaglute the American doctor—Schley, the
very doctor who had scolded Ravelstein for smoking minutes after
he was released from intensive care—had prescribed to keep my
heart from running away with me.

Rosamund went once more to the pharmacy—a three-mile
round trip without protection from the sun. She seemed partly re-
assured by the French doctor's diagnosis. However serious dengue
might be it was treatable.

The neighbors, whose dinner stinks drove me up the wall offered
their help. They said they stood ready to drive me to the hospital at
the town of M. forty kilometers away. The road was scenic but
jammed, as I was well aware, with decayed farm vehicles and
guaguas (buses).

The doctor was mild, "understated," as we say, not inclined to

make melodramatic diagnoses. I decided therefore to accept my
dengue without fuss and drink the quinine mixture he prescribed.
Rosamund and I read *Antony and Cleopatra* together, recalling Ravelstein's dictum that without great politics the passions could not be
represented. Rosamund wept when Antony said, "I am dying
Egypt, dying," and when Cleopatra put the asp to her breast. After
this we got into bed and slept, but not for long.

On the cool tile of the bathroom I fainted. It was dark and I had
been groping myself out of the room when I fell. Rosamund
couldn't lift or roll me onto the bed. She ran down to wake the landlady, who immediately telephoned for an ambulance. When I was
told that the ambulance was on its way, I said I'd never agree to go
to the hospital. I had seen enough of such places. Colonial medicine,
especially in the tropics, was very chancy.

Rosamund said, "You *must*." But when she saw how obstinate I
was she went down again to call the doctor on the landlady's telephone. He was five minutes down the road. Very decent about being wakened, he shone his flashlight down my throat and into my
eyes. Two burly orderlies now filled up the doorway with a furled
stretcher. These black men in coveralls had already begun opening
the stretcher on the floor when I stopped them saying, "I ain't going
nowhere."

Rosamund asked the doctor for an opinion and he said, "Well, it
isn't absolutely *nécessaire* if he is so opposed." He sent the ambulance
away. It didn't make a great difference to the orderlies, who left in
silence. It was the engine of the ambulance that did the snarling.

We somehow got rid of the rest of the night, and in daylight,
without a mention of breakfast, I sat outside looking toward the
black reefs—atmosphere and water doing what they always do.
One of the attractions of the season were the clouds of pale moths, a

soft yellow variety. They were not big nor were they beautifully marked, hovering out to sea and back again to the vegetation.

Rosamund was below, using the landlady's telephone, which had never before been available to us. The landlady would take no messages for us. Guests were not allowed to make calls. But I was sick now, and she didn't want me to croak on the premises. I thought this must be apparent to Rosamund as well and oddly enough I had almost no feeling one way or another. The sun hadn't risen yet and there was just light enough to distinguish fluid from solid—a sea— a kind of flatness, and a corresponding inner emptiness. Only Rosamund, normally flexible, ladylike, deferential, and genteel now revealed (no question about it) an underlying hardness and the will that showed how well prepared she was to deal with the bad character of the landlady and the bureaucratic hard-heartedness of the airline's telephone staff. And when she climbed upstairs she said, smiling slightly, "We go back early tomorrow. There are plenty of seats out of San Juan because it's Thanksgiving Day. The flights to San Juan were the problem. But I said it was a medical emergency. They say they'll have a wheelchair waiting."

A wheelchair! I would never have guessed I was as sick as all that. It turned out that inexperienced Rosamund saw the facts more clearly than anyone. I never anticipated crises or emergencies.

Could we count on a taxi so early in the morning? Yes. For one thing, because the all-business, middle-aged, handsome, severe Afro-Caribbean landlady had taken note last night of the ambulance and the doctor. Probably she had had a word with the conscientious, not entirely truthful young Frenchman. But she didn't need his warning; one look at my wrinkled, bad-luck, pre-dawn face on the outdoor staircase would have been enough.

Rosamund, frightened by now, was only too glad to leave. Her

pale-dark face was now reset for Boston, with its thousands of doctors. She seemed to have gotten the message: It was certain death to
stay on the island. She asked me, "Which books and papers do we
dump?" This was easy enough. "Let's get rid of all the heavy volumes. And especially Browning's *Collected Poems.*" I had turned
against Browning. I classed him now with the cuisine and the
French neighbors.

What I wouldn't discard was my friend Durkin's magazine—the
cannibal number. I was hung up on the roasting human flesh, on the
cannibals and the severed heads looking upward from the blood-
sprinkled grass at the orchid-covered cliffs. The human flesh being
eaten crowded into my—I admit it—contaminated consciousness.
It was my sickness that made me peculiarly susceptible. I wouldn't
have left these pages behind for anything. I could plead sickness as
my cover. But they disappeared during the flight.

The relief registered by our sternly handsome landlady said it all.
How pleased, how proud she was of getting rid of me. Let him go
and die elsewhere—in a taxi or a plane. She got up before dawn to
see us off. The French neighbors also turned out. They must have
been awakened by the ambulance the night before with its sirens
and flashing lights. With kind hearts and sorrow they wished us
well and waved goodbye. Decent people, after all. The landlady's
goodbye signified "Get lost." In her place I might have agreed. In
the five-o'clock light she waved goodbye—well out of that!

Rosamund, speaking of our foiled holiday, said, "What a night-
mare." In the rattling speeding taxi, she said goodbye to the island
with a kind of wild relief. She was at least going to be rid of the
masked motorcyclist who once or twice a week took over the main
street. He was all gotten up in leather and a Buck Rogers helmet.

His big teeth were bared and set. The police disappeared when he made his sweep. People scattered when he came flying. He roared back and forth in storms of dust, and he'd surely kill the pedestrians. "The town crazy man," Rosamund called him. "I won't have him to worry about, coming and going to the pharmacy," she said.

At the vast green metal shed of the airport covering thousands of square feet, Rosamund helped me, the sick man, into the waiting wheelchair. I sat in it, feeling imbecilized, and signed traveler's checks in my lap, to pay the exit fees. I felt I didn't actually need a wheelchair. I was still able to walk, I said to Rosamund, and gave her a demonstration by climbing the many stairs into the aircraft. Then down again in San Juan, where I fell gratefully into the second waiting wheelchair. Most of the luggage was piled around my feet and on my knees. But then there was the passport inspection, for which I had to stand up. Worst of all was the customs examination. Rosamund had to get the large suitcases and garment bags from the carousel to the inspection tables—open them, answer questions, then lock them again and haul them down to be reloaded for the U.S. flight. She didn't have the male grip, the necessary muscle. And here I discovered that once and for all I was no longer the able-bodied passenger I once had been. Rosamund said to the inspectors that I was unwell, but they didn't particularly heed her.

It was Thanksgiving Day and the plane was more than half empty. The attendant said I might want to stretch out and led us to the rear, where she pushed back the arms of a row of seats. I asked for water and then more water. I had never been so thirsty. The chief steward, who had dengue in the South Pacific during the war, had many savvy things to say. He offered to give me oxygen. Rosamund urged me to take it but I asked only for more water.

She, meanwhile, was trying to reach my Boston doctors on the telephone. There were two of these—the "primary" one and the cardiologist. The cardiologist, on the golf course, couldn't be reached; the "primary" doctor had gone to New Hampshire for a family dinner.

I recall during the flight I began again to talk about the young friend of Grielescu who was murdered in a stall of the men's room.

"You've already told me about him."

"When was that?"

"Not very long ago."

"I don't seem to be able to rid my mind of him. I won't mention him again. But I think I've connected him to Ravelstein, somehow. You see, I didn't like Grielescu but I did find him a funny man, and to Ravelstein this was a cop-out, and it was also characteristic of me. To say he was amusing was to give him a pass. But he was suspect—thought to be in league with killers. I can't seem to get a tight grip on the meat-hook people."

Rosamund tried hard to be attentive. She encouraged me to talk. She was worried sick.

"He died in the middle of the act—easing himself. They shot him at close range. Ravelstein believed that it was one of my typical errors. . . ."

"Was he saying that Grielescu was tied in with murderers?"

"Exactly. He said that I should have known better."

"But this murder took place after Ravelstein died."

"He had made the right call, nevertheless. This famous bookish scholar Grielescu, he was saying, was after all a Nazi."

Trying to get me off the Grielescu merry-go-round, Rosamund said, "What common ground did you share?"

"He used to quote me to myself." He had dug up a statement I had made about modern disenchantment. Under the debris of modern ideas the world was still there to be rediscovered. And his way of putting it was that the gray net of abstraction covering the world in order to simplify and explain it in a way that served our cultural ends has *become* the world in our eyes. We needed to have alternate visions, a diversity of views—and he meant views not bossed by ideas. He saw it as a question of words: "values," "life-styles," "relativism." I agreed, up to a point. We need to know—our deep human need, however, can't be satisfied by these terms. We can't climb out of the pit of "culture" and the "ideas" that supposedly express it. The right words would be a great help. But even more, a gift for reading reality—the impulse to put your loving face to it and press your hands against it.

"But then, from left field, or do I mean right field, Ravelstein urges everyone to read Céline. Well, by all means. Céline was wildly gifted, but he was also a wild lunatic, and before the war he published his *Bagatelles pour un massacre.* In this pamphlet Céline cried out against and denounced the Jews who had occupied and raped France. To many in France, it was Jewry that was the enemy, not Germany. Hitler—this was in 1937—would liberate France from the Jewish occupation. The English, who were allied with Jewry, plotted with it to destroy *la France.* It had already become a Jewish house of prostitution. *Un lupanar Juif—Bordel de Dieu.* The Dreyfus Case was brought back again. The authorities received millions of poison-pen letters from anti-Dreyfusard Jew-haters. I agreed with Ravelstein that Céline wouldn't pretend that he took no part in Hitler's Final Solution. Nor would I trade the short-stop Grielescu for the right-fielder Céline. When you put it in baseball lingo you can see how insane it was."

Rosamund was humoring me. I had never been quite so sick as this. And it never occurred to me that I was sick. Unwell, yes; it was obvious that I was out of order. But I had lived long enough to be able to say that I was not dying but ailing. A reactionary secret society might determine that the time had come for you to die—a camarilla of your countrymen voted that you must be assassinated. And so a study was made of your program. This would be described as political but in fact it was the will to viciousness. An erratic playboy scholar who had regular habits sat down to attend to a natural necessity—the daily thing—and was shot by an assassin in the next cubicle and died in an instant.

Rosamund was all for going from the airport direct to the hospital.

But I insisted on heading for home. Once in bed I'd be okay. Of course, I couldn't see myself. I was past knowing how high my fever was—bent on showing how perfectly well I was. Rosamund gave in and stacked our bags and boxes into the trunk of the cab. At the other end of the ride it was obviously out of the question to haul the luggage upstairs after the fare was paid, and the driver, seeing trouble, took his money and rushed away. Our trouble was obvious to him, but not to me. I crept upstairs and got into bed.

"Glad to leave that vile isle," I said to Rosamund. "Can it still be the same day? Is it about twelve? We took off at dawn. 'The hand of time is on the prick of noon,' as Mercutio said—one of Ravelstein's favorite lines from Shakespeare."

Under my blankets feeling safe and well, I told Rosamund that a good sleep was all I needed. But it was early afternoon—not bedtime. Rosamund couldn't agree that sleep was the answer. By some faculty invisible to me she recognized that I was in desperate trouble. "You would have died in your sleep," she later said, and she went on trying to reach the doctors. "Thanksgiving is a family day—it's playtime, golf-time."

Rosamund kept herself in good shape. She meditated, she attended yoga classes. She could touch her temple with her toe. But she had overstrained herself with the luggage from Saint Martin. She managed somehow to drag it up the stairs to the apartment on the third floor. You'd never have thought that she had the muscle for it.

It was easier to do this, she said, than to get help from the hospital. None of her calls were answered. On holidays, when the doctors are off, the residents are supposed to cover for them. "Well, it isn't as urgent as you think," I said. "You can talk to the doctors tomorrow." But it was clear to Rosamund that I didn't know what I was saying. If I had stayed on in Saint Martin I should have died before morning. If I had missed the connecting flight from Puerto Rico I would have died in San Juan. And if I had had my way about a good night's sleep in my own bed I'd have been a goner. Rosamund said that without oxygen I couldn't have survived the night.

As the sun went down, the crows were sounding their klaxons. Here they have become city birds. Some French poet had called them *les corbeaux delicieux*—but who? I doubt that even Ravelstein would have known. My mind could no longer follow itself. But I was certain that my pillows and quilt would save me.

But Rosamund had reached her father in upstate New York by phone. "Think who is the most influential person you can reach," he told her. "Ask for his help."

In my address book Rosamund luckily found the home number of Dr. Starling, the man who had brought us to Boston. When she told him what was happening, he said, "Within ten minutes you

will hear from Andras, the hospital director. Keep your line clear."
Very soon Dr. Andras, a very old man, was questioning Rosamund
about my symptoms; then he said he was sending an ambulance to
bring me in. Rosamund told him that in the Caribbean I had refused to get into the ambulance. The old director asked if he could
talk to me about this? Well, yes, I told him I was comfortable where
I was, in my own bed, but to please my wife I would agree to be examined by the doctors. But I wouldn't be carried out on a stretcher.
Foolishly negotiating, I agreed to be a passenger.

"Done!" said Dr. Andras. "We need you here right away."

So sitting next to the driver I was taken by the ambulance with
lights twirling and throaty siren sobs to the emergency room. There
I was wheeled on a gurney into a corner where I was examined by
several doctors. I have no coherent knowledge of what followed. I
mainly remember that I was immediately put on oxygen. This was
followed by an extended delay. Some said I should go immediately
to cardiac intensive care. Others thought that breathing was the
problem. The nurse put an oxygen mask over my face, which I kept
pushing away. Rosamund was there to look after me. She said,
"You've got to have the oxygen, Chick, and I don't want them to tie
your hands."

"But I'm suffocating," I said.

I have my own version of what was happening. There was a doctor in charge who did not wear a white coat but was in shirt sleeves.
Talkative and technical, he had a high color and in a casual manner
he described my condition. In such circumstances men and women
arise, appear, they materialize. This talkative doctor seemed to be
talking about technicalities which had no bearing on my condition.
But I misunderstood entirely what was happening. I was sent to

cardiac intensive care and there, that same night, I had a heart failure. But I have no memory of this. Nor of the pulmonary intensive care unit to which I was moved. Rosamund tells me that both my lungs were, to use the clinical term, whited out by pneumonia. A machine did my breathing for me—tubes down my throat, up my nose.

I didn't know where I was, nor was I aware that Rosamund slept beside me in a reclining chair. She often spent her nights among the relatives camping in intensive care during the crises of sons or sisters. During the first ten days Rosamund didn't go home. She ate the scraps of food she found on trays. She refused to go to the cafeteria lest I should die while she was eating. When the nurses understood this they began to feed her.

All this I learned later. I was certainly not aware that I was fighting for life. During these weeks I was heavily dosed with Verset. One effect of this drug is to suspend all mental life. I didn't consider whether I was dead or alive. All appearances (the external world) were canceled. My late brothers, both of them, drew near, once. They wore their customary shirts, neckties, shoes, the suits their tailors made for them. My father was in the background. He didn't come forward. My brothers indicated that they were satisfied with their condition. I didn't call out to my father. *He* knew what the rules were. I didn't see the point in asking questions. Feeling myself more than halfway there, I was not urgently curious. I wanted information, but the answers could wait. Then my brothers withdrew, or were withdrawn. I did not think of myself as a dying man. My head was full of delusions, hallucinations, cockeyed causes and effects. Verset is said to deaden the memory. But my memory has always been tenacious. I can remember being turned often. Some nurse or orderly who knew what he was doing pounded me on the back and ordered me to cough.

I had visited Ravelstein and other friends and relatives in the intensive care units of various hospitals and with the natural stupidity of a sound, healthy man had sometimes considered that I might one day be the person strapped down, plugged into the life-supporting machines.

But I was now the dying man. My lungs had failed. A machine did my breathing for me. Unconscious, I had no more idea of death than the dead have. But my head (I assume that it was the head) was full of visions, delusions, hallucinations. These were not dreams or nightmares. Nightmares have an escape hatch. . . .

Mostly I recall that I was wandering about, having a heavy time of it. In one of my visions I am on a city street looking for the place where I am supposed to pass the night. At last I find it. I enter what was long ago, in the twenties, a movie palace. The ticket booth is boarded up. But just behind it, on a tile floor that slopes upward are folding army cots. There is no film being shown. The hundreds of seats are empty. But I understand that the air in here is specially treated and that it will be good for your lungs to breathe it in. You get medical points toward your recovery for spending the night here. So I join half a dozen others and lie down. My wife is supposed to pick me up in the morning. The car is in a parking lot nearby. Nobody here is sleepy. Nor are the men talkative. They get up. They mooch about the lobby or sit on the edge of a cot. The floor hasn't been mopped in fifty years or more. There is no heat. You sleep fully dressed in your buttoned overcoat. Hats, caps, and shoes are not removed.

Even before my release from the intensive care unit, I climbed out of bed thinking that I was in New Hampshire and that one of my granddaughters was skiing around the house. I was annoyed with her parents for not having brought her in to see her grandfather. It was a winter morning, or so I thought. Actually, it must have been the middle of the night, but the sun seemed to be shining on the snow. I climbed over the bedrail without noticing that I was attached by tubes and needles to hanging flasks containing all kinds of intravenous mixtures. I saw as if they were someone else's my bare feet on the sunny floor. They seemed unwilling to bear my weight but I forced them to obey my will. Then I fell, landing on my back. At first I felt no pain. What vexed me was that I couldn't get out of bed and walk to the window. As I lay helpless, an orderly ran up and said, "I heard you were a troublemaker."

One of the doctors said that my back was so inflamed that it looked like a forest fire seen from the air. The doctors put me through a CAT scan. It seemed to me that I was on a crowded trolley car and that I was being stifled and pushed from behind. I begged to be let out. But nobody was willing to oblige me.

I was then on very heavy doses of blood thinner and my fall was dangerous. I was bleeding internally. The nurses put me into a restraining vest. I asked my grown sons to call a taxi. I said I'd be better off at home, soaking in the bath. "In five minutes I could be there," I said. "It's just around the corner."

Often it seemed to me that I was just underneath Kenmore Square in Boston. The oddity of these hallucinatory surroundings was in a way liberating. I wonder sometimes whether at the threshold of death I may not have been entertaining myself lightheartedly, like any normal person, enjoying these preposterous delusions—fictions which did not have to be invented.

I found myself in a vast cellar. Its brick walls had been painted ages ago. In places they still were as white as cottage cheese. But the cheese had grown soiled. The place was lighted by fluorescent tubes—table after table after table of thrift-shop items, women's clothing, mainly, donated to the hospital for resale: underwear, stockings, sweaters, scarves, skirts. An infinity of tables. The place made me think of Filene's Basement, where customers would soon be pushing and quarreling over bargains. But no one was here to fight. In the far distance were young women who seemed to be volunteers doing charitable work. I was sitting, trapped, among hundreds of leather lounge chairs. Escape from this grimy-cheese corner was out of the question. Behind me, huge pipes came through the ceiling and sank into the ground.

I was painfully preoccupied with the restraining vest or pullover I was forced to wear. This hot khaki vest was constricting—it was killing me, binding me to death. I tried, and failed, to unravel it. I thought, If only I could get one of those Social Registry charity volunteers to bring a knife or a pair of shears! But they were several city blocks away, and they'd never hear me. I was in a far, far corner surrounded by BarcaLoungers.

Another memorable experience was this:

A male hospital attendant on a stepladder is hanging Christmas tinsel, mistletoe, and evergreen clippings on the wall fixtures. This attendant doesn't much care for me. He was the one who had called me a troublemaker. But that didn't stop me from taking note of him. Taking note is part of my job description. Existence is—or was—the job. So I watched him on the three-step ladder—his sloping shoulders and wide backside. Then he came down and carried his ladder to the next pillar. More tinsel and prickly evergreen.

Off to the side there was another old fellow, small, nervous, and fretful, going back and forth in carpet slippers. He was my neighbor. His living quarters opened at the end of my room, but he wouldn't acknowledge me. He had a thinnish beard, his nose was like a plastic pot-scraper, and he wore a beret. He would *have* to be an artist. But it seemed to me that his features were entirely lacking in interest.

After a time, I recalled that I had seen him on television. He *was* an artist, much respected. He lectured while drawing. His themes were fashionable—environmentalism, holistic flower essences, and so on. His sketches were vague, suggesting love of and responsibility for our natural surroundings. On a blackboard he first produced a hazy sea surface, and then with the side of his chalk he created the illusion of a lurking face—the wavy hair of a woman, like cooked rhubarb, glimpses of nature that hinted at a human presence—something mythic or, equally likely, a projection. Maybe an undine or a Rhine maiden. You couldn't actually accuse this fellow of mystification or superstition. All you could nail him for was self-importance and self-gratification—*suffisance,* in French. I like *suffisance* better than smugness, just as I prefer the English suffocating to the French *suffoquant—Tout suffoquant et blême.* (Verlaine?) If you're choking, why worry about being pale?

This Ananias, or false prophet (artist), was settled here—he had a narrow apartment along the side of the hospital building. His quarters were around the corner, so I couldn't see them from my bed. I had a glimpse of his bookcases and a green wall-to-wall carpet. The Christmas tinsel attendant was very deferential to the artist, who, for his part, took no notice of me. Nil! I wasn't allowed to register an impression. By which I mean only that I didn't fit into any of his concepts.

This TV *artiste,* anyway, had the air of being long settled here, but it soon was evident that he was leaving that day. Cardboard boxes were carried out of his flat—or wing. The movers were stacking items. The books were disappearing from the shelves, the shelves themselves were dismantled in a tremendous hurry. A van was backed in and swiftly loaded, and then in a long green-gold gown the artist's old wife came out, stooped, and was helped into the cab of the truck. She wore a silk hat. The TV artist stuck his carpet slippers into the pockets of his topcoat, he put on loafers and crawled in beside her.

The male attendant was there to see him off, and then he said to me, "You're next. We need the space, and my orders are to get you out this minute." Immediately a crew dismantled the shelves and took everything to pieces. The surroundings were knocked down like theater flats. Nothing was left. A moving van meanwhile backed in, and my street clothes, my Borsalino, electric razor, toilet articles, CDs, et cetera, were stuffed into supermarket shopping bags. I was helped into a wheelchair and lifted into a trailer truck. There I found an office—no, a nurse's station, small but complete, with electric lights. The tailgate came up; the upper doors were not shut and the van roared directly underground, down into a tunnel. It continued for a time at top speed. Then we stopped, the giant engine idling. It went on idling.

There was only one nurse in attendance. She saw that I was agitated and offered to shave me. I admitted I could use a shave. She therefore lathered me and did the job with a disposable Schick or Gillette. Few nurses understand how to shave a man. They lay on the foam without softening the beard first as old-time barbers used to do with hot towels. When you haven't been soaped and soaked the scraping blade pulls the stubble and your face stings.

I said to the nurse that I was expecting my wife Rosamund at four o'clock, and it was already well past four on the big circular clock. "Where do you think we are?" The nurse couldn't say. My guess was that we were underneath Kenmore Square in Boston, and if they had stopped the engine idling we would have been able to hear the Green Line subway trains. It was now going on six o'clock, whether A.M. or P.M. who could say? We were now docking slowly beside a pedestrian passageway where people—not too many—went up into the street or came down from it.

"You look a little like an Indian brave," the nurse said. "Also you've lost so much weight that you're more wrinkled, and the beard grows inside the furrows. It's hard to get at. Were you stout once?"

"No, but my build has changed many times. I always looked better sitting than standing," I said, and despite my sad heart I laughed.

She wasn't able to make anything of these remarks.

And there had been no van. I had had to vacate my room—it was urgently needed—and I was moved in the night to another part of the hospital. "Where have you been?" I said to Rosamund when she arrived. I was annoyed with her. But she explained that she had suddenly sat up in bed wide awake and uneasy about me. She telephoned the intensive care unit, learned that I had been transferred, jumped into a cab and rushed over.

"It's evening," I said.

"No, it's dawn."

"And where am I?"

The attending nurse was remarkably quick and sympathetic. She pulled the curtain around my bed and said to my wife, "Take off your shoes and get in with him. A few hours of sleep are what you need. Both of you."

213

⌒

One more brief vision, for purposes of orientation.

Vela figures in this one.

So here are the two of us on exhibit for all the world to judge. Her open, elegant hand directs attention to my uneasy posture.

She and I find ourselves in this scenario standing before the polished stone wall of a bank interior—an investment bank. On this occasion we were again on the outs. But I had come to the bank to meet at her request. She was escorted by a Spanish-looking and very elegant man in his mid- to late-twenties. A third man was present as well, a banker who spoke in French. Before us, set into the glamourous marble wall, were two coins. One a U.S. dime, the other a silver dollar with a diameter of ten or twelve feet.

Vela introduced me to the Spanish companion. It wasn't much of an introduction, since he did not acknowledge me. She then said, explaining simply, "Until now I never had any experience of glamourous sex before, and I figured, in what you always call the sexual revolution, I should have a sample of it—to find out for once what I was deprived of with you."

I said, "It's like a huge rabbit hutch, millions of rabbits, with the does sampling all the buck rabbits."

But this first phase of the meeting was quickly behind us. Its purpose, evidently, was to fill me with guilt and inject me with a mental solvent or softener.

"Can you tell me where we are?" I asked. "And why we are meeting here in front of these coins? They signify—what?"

Then the banker came forward and said that over a period of years the dime on the right would turn into the dollar with the ten-foot diameter.

⌒

"How long will it take?"

"A century or a little more."

"Well, I don't doubt the arithmetic is right—but for whom would this be done?"

"For yourself," said Vela.

"Me? And how do you figure?"

"Through cryonics," she said. "A person lets himself be frozen and stored. A century later they thaw him or her back to life. Don't you remember that we read in a tabloid how Howard Hughes had himself frozen and would be thawed and revived when they found a cure for the disease which was killing him? This is called cryonics."

"Let's hear what you want me to do. Guesswork is no use. What have you got in mind—when would you like me frozen?"

"You'd do it now. I'd go later. Then we'd wake up together in the twenty-second century."

The gray glow and the high polish of the marble slabs were calculated to persuade anybody of eternal dollar stability. But it was also the facade of a cold-storage plant—or crypt. This was foolish, perhaps. Your body would be stacked with other investors behind the marble facade. You would lie in a lab with technician-priests who tended you generation after generation, regulating the temperature, the moisture, and keeping tabs on your condition.

"You'd live again," Vela said. "Figure the compound interest per million. We would both live."

"Companions of old age? . . ."

The bank man, actually wearing a cutaway coat, said in a practiced voice, "By then the life span will be upward of two hundred years."

"It's the only chance for our marriage," Vela told me.

There was a certain Serbian grace note (B-flat A, B-flat C) at the great word "marriage."

"Oh, for Christ's sake, Vela! This is no way to approach the subject of death. To postpone it for a century solves nothing."

I must remind you that I had already died and risen again, and there was a curious distance in my mind between the old way of seeing (false) and the new way (strange but liberating).

English was not Vela's first language, and she couldn't reformulate anything because so much effort had gone into composing the formulations she put forward. All she could do was repeat what had been said. She again stated the facts as she understood them, which didn't advance the discussion.

I told her, "I can't do this."

"Why can't you do this?"

"You're asking me to commit suicide. Suicide is forbidden."

"By who is suicide forbidden?"

"It's against my religion. Jews don't commit suicide unless they lose the siege as they did at Masada, or are about to be hacked to pieces, as in the Crusades. Then they put their children to death before they kill themselves."

"You never fall back on religion except to win an argument," said Vela.

"Suppose you turn around and sue the bank, as soon as I'm frozen," I said. "And then you claim my estate because I'm dead. They can't prove that I might be thawed out and restored to life. Or do you think they'd bring me back just to win the lawsuit? The whole case argued before some judge who couldn't find his ass with both hands?"

When lawsuits were mentioned the bank's representative went

pale and in a way I sympathized with him, although I wasn't well, myself, my heart having sunk so low.

"You *owe* me this," said Vela.

What did she mean? But it is a principle with me not to argue with irrational people. I simply shook my head and repeated, "It can't be done, it can't be, and I won't do it."

"No?"

"You don't understand what you're asking," I said.

"No?"

"You mean by the way you say it that *I* don't know what *I'm* doing. Fair enough." I was never more out of line than when we stood together in the judge's chambers to be married. An old school friend I had invited to the wedding was greatly taken with Vela. He whispered in my ear, as the judge was looking for the marriage service in his book, "Even if this doesn't last six months, even if it's only a month, it's still worth it—with a bosom and hips and a face like hers."

Resuming the dialogue in the bank with Vela, I could hear myself saying, with the conviction of ultimate seriousness, "I adjusted myself long ago to dying a natural death, like everybody else. I've seen plenty of dying in my time, and I'm prepared for it. Maybe I've been a little too imaginative about the grave—the dampness and the cold. I've pictured it in too much detail and maybe feel a little too much—feel abnormally—for the dead. But there's not a chance in the world of convincing me to put myself in the hands of experimental science. I feel insulted by your proposition. But if you could induce me to marry you, perhaps you feel that I can also be talked into being frozen for a century."

"Yes, I do think you owe me something," said Vela, on top of what I was saying.

One of our difficulties, and a source of much misunderstanding, was that my outlook was incomprehensible to her. Dogs can understand a joke. Cats never, but never, have occasion to laugh. Vela, when others were laughing, would join in. But if cues were lacking ("This is funny"), she didn't smile. And I, when I amused a dinner table, was suspected by her of making her the butt of my jokes.

I may not have been aware, when I believed myself to be in a bank, with a small dime and a huge dollar set in polished marble, that in the real world my life was being saved. Doctors by drugs, nurses by tending me, technicians with their skills, were working to assist me. When or if I was saved, I would go on with my life.

And if it hadn't been for the article about Howard Hughes, Vela would not have suggested that being frozen for a century was a wonderful idea—that she would do lewd things with the Spanish boyfriend (by the way, he never had said so much as good morning to me) while I lay frozen, a block of ice, awaiting resuscitation or resurrection.

And I did not doubt the reality of this bank, these coins, those companions—Vela, her Spanish stud, the investment counselor, and Vela's remarks about the sexual revolution.

"That meeting in the bank you believe in," my wife, Rosamund, the real wife, later said, after I had described the moment to her. "Why would it be always the *worst* things which appear to you so real? Sometimes I wonder if I'll ever be able to talk you out of being sadistic to yourself."

"Yes," I agreed. "It has a specific kind of satisfaction, the bad of it guarantees it as real experience. This is what we go through, and it's what existence is like. The brain is a mirror and reflects the world. Of course we see pictures, not the real thing, but the pictures are dear to us, we come to love them even though we are aware how distorting an organ the mirror-brain is. But this is not the moment to turn metaphysical."

I was the sort of intensive care patient the staff would have made book on, if they had been the gambling sort. But these were people too serious to lay bets on whether you would survive. I'd run into some of them later in other departments of the hospital, and they'd say, "Ah, so you made it—wonderful! I wouldn't have guessed you would. Well . . . that was quite a fight you put up. I wouldn't have given two cents for your life."

And so . . . *hasta la vista.* We'll see each other in the life to come.

If these encounters had been longer (although I preferred them to be as short as possible) I should have mentioned my wife, given her due credit. Here and there a specialist materialized who had noted her: "What a pretty woman." "How devoted she was." Often the relatives of the dying are like dazzled birds confused by the lights over center field, flying blind. But that was not the case with Rosamund. To save me she would have done whatever it was necessary to do. That was why, for her, the intensive care staff stretched the rules. They had a wide and complex knowledge of brothers, sisters, mothers, husbands, and wives. In my case survival was not a likely option, and she seemed to be backing a loser. To some others, mainly women, it would have seemed that Rosamund was keeping me on this side of the death-line.

Was love credited among these women with saving lives? If they were answering the questions of a pollster they'd have denied it. As Ravelstein had famously said, American nihilism was nihilism without the abyss. Love should by rights—or by modern lights—be seen today as a discredited passion, but the nurses in intensive care on the front line of death were more open to pure feelings than those who worked in the quieter corridors. And Rosamund, this slender, dark-haired, straight-nosed beauty was paradoxically recognizable as a natural. Although highly educated—a Ph.D., too smart to be taken in—she loved her husband. Love found secret support among these nurses in the end zone, eighty percent of whose cases ended in the morgue. The staff stretched the rules for her—for us. She was allowed to sleep beside the bed, in my cubicle.

When I graduated from the ICU they let Rosamund give a little supper. Dr. Bertolucci brought the pasta marinara from home. I sat up and ate a few forkfuls and lectured on cannibalism in New Guinea, where butchered enemies were roasted beside cliffs where they had tropical flowers dropping hundreds of feet, like waterfalls.

When I was sent down from intensive care, Rosamund was still allowed to come and go, free from all restrictions. After dinner she drove home in the Crown Vic. To reassure me she said, "It's stable, it's dependable. It's the cop car of choice, and I feel safe in it at a stoplight. For all the bad actors know, I'm a plainclothes police officer, and I carry a gun."

Even so, the side window was shattered one night in the parking lot behind our building. Nor did she like nightly to see the rats sitting in rows where they could see and smell the odors of the restaurant on Beacon Street. "They're in rows like the jury in the jury box," she'd say, "and their eyes pick up all the light there is."

When she had limped up to the third floor the cat was there to greet her, or to accuse her of neglect. He was a country cat and had lived on mice and chipmunks and on birds. He now spent his days watching the grackles, blue jays, and giant crows. These look much bigger than crows in the woods—perhaps because of the smaller scale of domesticated city plants. Late in the afternoon they sound off from our rooftop like metal-saws.

I suppose it served some biological purpose but I was not interested. I was deaf to theory just then—just as I refused to think of what I was doing as a struggle for existence. If I had stopped to consider it, I would have been aware that I was underground digging myself out with bare hands. Some would have thought well of my tenacity or loyalty to life. To me it was no such thing—it was as dull as potatoes.

Rosamund after looking into the bare fridge (there was no time to shop) chewed some cheese rinds and then with her hair protected by a tall cone of turkish towels she stood under a hot shower. In bed, she telephoned her parents and chatted with them. Her alarm was set for seven, and she was at the hospital very early in the morning. She could name all the drugs prescribed for me, and the doctors found that she could tell them how I had reacted to each one, what I was allergic to, or what my blood-pressure readings had been the day before yesterday. There was an extended sorting apparatus in the pretty woman's head. She told me, confidently, that we would live to be very old, well into the coming century. She said I was a prodigy. I saw myself rather as a sort of freak.

There was no subject raised which she didn't immediately understand. Ravelstein would have been well pleased with her. Of course he'd never had my advantage, the access to her that I had. And after the crisis Rosamund said she never doubted that I would survive. And I seemed to believe that I wouldn't die because I had things to do. Ravelstein expected me to make good on my promise to write the memoir he had commissioned. To keep my word I'd have to live. Of course there was an obvious corollary: Once the memoir was written, I lost my protection, and I became as expendable as anybody else.

"But that couldn't apply to you," said Rosamund. "Once you had felt your way *up* to it, nothing could have held you back. Besides, you'd survive for my sake."

I often recalled asking Ravelstein which of his friends were likely to follow him soon. "To keep you company," was the way I put it. And after he had thoroughly examined my color, my wrinkles, my looks, he said that I was the likeliest to follow. He was like that. If you asked him to be direct he wouldn't spare you. His clarity was like a fast-freezing fluid. Did he mean that I would be the first of his friends to join him in the afterlife? This was what the tone of our exchange suggested. But then he didn't believe in an afterlife. Plato, by whom he was guided in such matters, often spoke of a life-to-come but it was difficult to say how seriously he took this. I was not about to get into the rink with this Sumo champion representing Platonic metaphysics. One bump of his powerful belly and I'd be out of the brilliant ring and back again in the noisy dark.

He had, however, asked me what I imagined death would be like—and when I said that the pictures would stop he reflected seriously on my answer, came to a full stop, and considered what I might mean by this. No one can give up on the pictures—the pictures might, yes they *might* continue. I wonder if anyone believes that the grave is all there is. No one can give up on the pictures. The pictures must and will continue. If Ravelstein the atheist-materialist had implicitly told me that he would see me sooner or later, he meant that he did not accept the grave to be *the* end. Nobody can and nobody does accept this. We just *talk* tough.

So when I made my remark about the pictures, Ravelstein had given me his explosive laugh-stammer: "Har har." But he had some regard—some respect for the answer.

But then he let himself go so far as to say, "You look as if you might by and by be joining me."

This is the involuntary and normal, the secret, esoteric confidence of the man of flesh and blood. The flesh would shrink and go, the blood would dry, but no one believes in his mind of minds or heart of hearts that the pictures *do* stop.

Roughly forty percent of intensive care patients die in the intensive care unit. Of the remainder some twenty percent are permanently disabled. These invalids are sent to what the health industry calls "chronic care facilities." They can never be expected to lead normal lives. The rest, the lucky ones, are said to be "on the floor."

On the floor, I was no longer attended by the ICU team of physicians. Worn out by hundreds of hours in the unit, two of them now stopped by to say that they were going on holiday. Because I was one of their great successes they looked me up on the floor to say good-bye. Dr. Alba brought chicken soup from her own kitchen. Dr. Bertolucci's gift was a homemade lasagna dish and a supplement of meatballs in tomato sauce, like the one I had eaten in intensive care. I was still unable to feed myself. The spoon shook in my hand and rattled the dish; I couldn't bring it to my mouth. Dr. Bertolucci came to dine with Rosamund and me. Far from normal, I kept bringing the conversation back to the subject of cannibalism. But

Dr. Bertolucci was very pleased with me saying, "You're just about out of the woods." He had saved my life. I was sitting up, eating a dinner the doctor himself had cooked, and chatting, nattering away. Rosamund too was pleased and excited. This was my first night on the floor, and I wouldn't be going to a chronic care institution to begin a cripple's life.

When I was transferred to the floor the neurology resident gave me a preliminary examination. My medical history in a thick binder was available at the nurse's station. Rosamund had kept a journal of her own during the weeks of crisis and the resident questioned her too.

That same night, Dr. Bakst, the chief neurologist, appeared at midnight and he too questioned her. She had been asleep in the armchair beside the bed.

I had been treated for pneumonia and heart failure. And though I was on the floor, I was not out of the woods. Not yet. Not quite. What my problems were is only partly relevant here. Let me say quite simply that things were far from normal, and that my future was still uncertain.

Dr. Bakst came with his packet of pins. Examining me—sticking pins into my face—he discovered that my upper lip was (to put it in my own way) lame. Even when I spoke or laughed it was strangely immobile or partially paralyzed. He put me through some simple tests—I failed them. At various times he asked me to draw clock-faces. I was unable at first to draw anything. My hands were useless. I had no control of them at all. It was impossible for me to eat my soup or to sign my name. I couldn't manage a pen. When he said, "Do me a clock," a crabbed zero was all I could draw. My symptoms seemed to Dr. Bakst to be due to poisoning. Bédier in Saint Martin had served me a toxic fish. The neurologist said that I was a victim of cigua toxin. I was now willing to believe the worst about the Caribbean. The French doctor I saw there had diagnosed my trouble as dengue. He might, just possibly, have known better. An Australian cigua-toxin expert described the symptoms of that disease on the telephone to Dr. Bakst in Boston. Some of Bakst's Boston colleagues did not accept the diagnosis. I was partial to Bakst, however, for reasons which had little to do with medicine, strictly speaking.

To put matters plainly, I had to decide whether I should or should not make efforts to recover. I had for long weeks been unconscious, my body was wasted—unrecognizable. My sphincters were confused and I wasn't so much walking as stumbling—hanging on to a metal frame. I had once been the youngest of a large family. I now had adult children of my own. When they came to visit, those that had inherited my features gave me the feeling that I was being looked at by my own eyes—still germane but soon to be replaced by a later model. Ravelstein would have advised me to keep my head. I felt very nearly done for but I was, however damaged, sick of it all, not yet discharged from the service.

Rosamund was determined that I should go on living. It was she, of course, who had saved me—flew me back from the Caribbean just in time, saw me through intensive care, sleeping in a chair beside my bed. When I struggled to breathe she would raise the oxygen mask to swab the inside of my mouth. It was not until the respirator was brought in that she went home for an hour to change into clean clothing.

The one physician who came regularly to visit me was Dr. Bakst. He came irregularly, too—at odd hours. He would say, "Draw me a clock at 10:47." Or, "What is today's date? Now, don't tell me you live on a superior plane and don't have to know exact dates. I want specific answers from you." Or, "Multiply seventy-two by ninety-three—and now . . . divide five thousand three hundred and twenty-two by forty-six."

Thank God I had kept my multiplication tables in good order.

He had no wish to discuss "deeper" questions with me—or questions relating to the extent of my recovery.

At the age of eight I had had to recover from peritonitis complicated by pneumonia. Returning from the hospital what I needed to decide was whether I was going to be a lifelong invalid with two older brothers hating me for monopolizing the affection and concern of our parents. How such decisions are made in childhood is beyond comprehension. I see now, however, that I chose not to be a weakling. In some junk shop I turned up a book on physical fitness by Walter P. Camp, and I did as the famous football coach had done—I carried full coal-scuttles at arm's length up from the cellar. I chinned myself, I worked out with a punching bag and Turnverein Indian clubs. I studied an inspirational tract called *How to Get Strong and How to Stay So*. I told everyone I was in training. This was no exaggeration. And the fact was that I had no gift for sports. Still the choice I had made at the age of eight remained effective. Some seventy years later I was preparing to do it again.

By a rare coincidence, Dr. Bakst had another patient upstairs with cigua toxin. She had been infected on a trip to Florida. The toxin ravages the nervous system but is soon excreted, so that in a few days there is no sign of it. Luckily in her case the disease was caught in an early stage, and after the fish-carried poison was filtered out of her bloodstream she was well enough to go home.

I was still pushing the walking frame through winding corridors, determined to recover the use of my legs. I was held upright in the shower and felt humiliated as I was soaped and rinsed by kindly nurses who had seen everything and were not shocked by my body.

I assumed that my senior neurologist and good angel was familiar with cases like mine and knew exactly "where I was at." My damaged hands and legs would wither and my sense of balance would be lost if the small muscles were allowed to atrophy. If I were inclined that way, I could decide not to make the effort. You do get tired of performing the tricks, kneading the ball of putty and fitting jigsaw puzzles together only to see, when you examined yourself, the long wrinkles of your desiccated inner arms.

It's only now that I come to understand how much tact there was in the doctor's conduct and to see that he knew perfectly well I would disintegrate if I didn't do the drill he prescribed. I loathed the drill but I couldn't allow myself to fall apart. Moreover, I owed it to Rosamund to work at recovery. Yes, I was tempted to drop out, but she had concentrated her soul entirely on my survival. My quitting would be an insult to her. And, lastly, to live necessarily meant to do what I had always done, and I had to be strong enough to perform independently the jobs of which my life consisted.

Dr. Bakst was a crack diagnostician, I considered, but in my case his diagnosis had been challenged. Ciguatera toxin is a tropical disease. The toxin is carried by reef-feeding fish—"piscavores" the doctor called them. No amount of broiling or boiling could destroy the poison carried by the red snapper set before me by Bédier, a tough guy playing the Frenchiest of French hosts. He had come to the tropics to make money to educate his little daughters—they no longer get a *dot,* they get an education. (Ravelstein, who haunts these personalities and occasions, would have preferred to have me say *dot,* not dowry.) Beyond playing the role Bédier owed his clients nothing. They took their chances with the piscavores of the coral reef, as he did with his investments. Neither Bédier nor the doctor who had told me that I had dengue answered the inquiries from Boston.

At my age one has had a considerable experience of the ins and outs, the dodges that accompany self-interest. All such considerations are wildly mixed.

Dr. Bakst's cigua-toxin diagnosis had been challenged by other doctors. So he had an additional interest in proving himself right. He sent me to every corner of the hospital for CAT SCANs, MRIs and dozens of other esoteric examinations, in which the forces of the entire planet are upon you. I was able, but only up to a point, to separate his professional concerns from his other motives. The fact was that he knew I needed his "personal" visits, his daily presence—that I depended upon him.

It occurred to me during one fragmented and hopeless day that I might be one of those cunning patients whose master plan is to drink up the doctor's attention. The sick man sees that the physician must portion it out, and he also recognizes a special need to get ahead of his sick and dying rivals. The doctor naturally has to protect himself against these monopolizing impulses—perhaps I should say instincts—of people who are blindly recovery-bent, who have the deep and special greed of the sick when they have decided not to die.

Dr. Bakst was solidly built but with an odd tendency about the head, which he carried like a boxer. It was of course out of the question to guess what he was thinking. He came and went as he saw fit. His glasses might turn toward you when his eyes did not. This led me to realize that it would be a mistake to try to communicate the many odd things I was experiencing. The problems he was setting me in arithmetic were much like the challenges thrown at David Copperfield by his wicked, tyrannical stepfather—"Nine dozen cheeses at two pounds, eight shillings, four pence. This reckoning should take you no more than three minutes." I had been good at sums in my schooldays, and it carried me back to childhood to work at them. For my fingers, too, they were good therapy, and I was soon able to sign checks and pay my bills.

The doctor now adopted a rougher style with me.

"What day of the week is it?"

"Tuesday."

"It's not Tuesday. Every adult knows what day it is."

"It must be Wednesday, then."

"Yes. And what's the date?"

"I have no idea."

"Well, you're preparing to make a stab at it—a gamble. But from now on you're going to know the date like any normal person. You'll check it out every morning, and you'll be ready from now on to tell the day of the week and the exact calendar date." Then he pinned a calendar on the wall for me. The doctor had seen that my days were a morass of self-neglect and that I was demoralized, drifting and losing heart through slackness and disorder.

It is possible that Dr. Bakst saved me. I believe I owe my life to him and of course to Rosamund. Bakst didn't think that it had been a mistake to put me "on the floor" or that I was bound for a chronic care facility. He believed that I could—and therefore *should*—make the grade. Somehow he sized me up as capable of coming back. I wonder what medical practice would be if doctors were to dismiss such intuitions. Dr. Bakst, like a skillful Indian scout of the last century, pressed his ear to the rail and heard the locomotive coming. Life would soon be back, and I would occupy my seat in the life-train. Death would shrink into its former place at the margin of the landscape. The patient's desire is to crawl or limp or maneuver himself back to the life that preceded the illness, and to entrench and fortify himself in the old position.

If I had died I would naturally have been released from the promise I had made years ago to write a short description of Ravelstein and to give an account of his life. Having come near death myself, I don't need to fear the guilt the living often feel about those others—parents, wives, husbands, brothers, and friends—in their graves.

Just out of college in the late thirties I was a research assistant helping to compile a geographical guide, and I learned that there was an Athens in almost every state of the union. It was also a fact that A. N. Whitehead had prophesied during a sojourn in Chicago that it was destined to lead the modern world. Intelligence was here for everybody's free use, and so it was highly possible that this city might serve to be a new Athens.

When I told this to Ravelstein I remember that he laughed exorbitantly and said, "If this happens here it won't be because of Whitehead. There wasn't enough philosophy in him to fill a birthday balloon. Not that Russell was much better."

I was interested in such opinions not because I had philosophical ambitions but because without much knowledge of political philosophy, I was preparing to write, had agreed to write, a memoir of

Ravelstein, a political philosopher. And I couldn't say whether Whitehead and Russell had or had not developed ideas worth examining. Ravelstein sharply told me not to bother my mind with their studies, essays, and opinions. But I had already read five or six of their books. We should be grateful for good advice in these matters since life is too short to risk a waste of time—an entire month, say, on Russell's *History of Philosophy,* an obviously deformed and even cranky book, very modern in that it tries to spare you the study of several German and French philosophers.

In his own way Ravelstein tried to protect me from poring over the works of the thinkers he most admired. He ordered me to write this memoir, yes, but he didn't think it was necessary for me to grind away at the classics of Western thought. But for the purposes of a short biography I understood him well enough, and I agreed that it should be done by someone like me. Furthermore, I am a great believer in the power of unfinished work to keep you alive. But your survival can't be explained by this simple one-to-one abstract equivalence. Rosamund kept me from dying. I can't represent this without taking it on frontally and I can't take it on frontally while my interests remain centered on Ravelstein. Rosamund had studied love—Rousseauan romantic love and the Platonic Eros as well, with Ravelstein—but she knew far more about it than either her teacher or her husband.

But I would rather see Ravelstein again than to explain matters it doesn't help to explain.

Ravelstein, dressing to go out, is talking to me, and I go back and forth with him while trying to hear what he is saying. The music is pouring from his hi-fi—the many planes of his bare, bald head go before me in the corridor between his living room and his monumental master bedroom. He stops before his pier-glass—no wall mirrors here—and puts in the heavy gold cufflinks, buttons up the Jermyn Street Kisser & Asser striped shirt—American Trustworthy laundry-and-cleaners deliver his shirts puffed out with tissue paper. He winds up his tie lifting the collar that crackles with starch. He makes a luxurious knot. The unsteady fingers, long, ill-coordinated, nervous to the point of decadence, make a double lap. Ravelstein likes a big tie-knot—after all, he is a large man. Then he sits down on the beautifully cured fleeces of his bed and puts on the Poulsen and Skone tan Wellington boots. His left foot is several sizes smaller than the right but there is no limp. He smokes, of course, he is always smoking, and tilts the head away from the smoke while he knots and pulls the knot into place. The cast and orchestra are pouring out the *Italian Maiden in Algiers*. This is dressing music, accessory or mood music, but Ravelstein takes a Nietzschean view, favorable to comedy and bandstands. Better Bizet and *Carmen* than Wagner and the *Ring*. He likes the volume of his powerful set turned up to the maximum. The ringing phone is left to the answering machine. He puts on his $5,000 suit, an Italian wool mixed with silk. He pulls down the coat cuff with his fingertips and polishes the top of his head. And perhaps he relishes having so many instruments serenading him, so many musicians in attendance. He corresponds with compact disc companies behind the Iron Curtain. He has helpers going to the post office to pay customs duties for him.

"What do you think of this recording, Chick?" he says. "They're playing the original ancient seventeenth-century instruments."

He loses himself in sublime music, a music in which ideas are dissolved, reflecting these ideas in the form of feeling. He carries them down into the street with him. There's an early snow on the tall shrubs, the same shrubs filled with a huge flock of parrots—the ones that escaped from cages and now build their long nest sacks in the back alleys. They are feeding on the red berries. Ravelstein looks at me, laughing with pleasure and astonishment, gesturing because he can't be heard in all this bird-noise.

You don't easily give up a creature like Ravelstein to death.